**Jane Lane** was born Elaine
was published when she was
the pen-name of Jane Lane to
of her books, Lane being t
grandmother, a descendant of ti                    ...ich of
Lanes who sheltered King Chai            ... nis defeat at
Worcester. A versatile and dynam.. author, Jane Lane has
written over forty works of fiction, biography and history
as well as children's books.

# JANE LANE

# Ember in the Ashes

HOUSE OF
STRATUS

This edition published in 2002 by House of Stratus, an imprint of
Stratus Books Ltd., Lisandra Hosue, Fore Street, Looe,
Cornwall, PL13 1AD, UK.

www.houseofstratus.com

Typeset, printed and bound by House of Stratus.

A catalogue record for this book is available from the British Library
and the Library of Congress.

ISBN 0-7551-0851-5

*To my good friends*
*Robbie and Paddy*

# PART ONE

# Chapter One

Sir Hubert Thorne, baronet, slept badly on his last night at school. For one thing, there was a bright moon; for another, he had been celebrating in the Rhetoricians' Study; and last but not least his tiny box of a bedroom was separated from that of his younger brother Robin only by a very thin wooden partition. And Robin, having played 'Over the Water to Charlie' on the bagpipes in the President's garden, had climbed to his bedroom by means of the convenient bullet-holes left by the great siege of Douai in 1710, and had kicked and muttered and banged about for the remainder of the night. It was like trying to sleep next to a restive carthorse.

The moon, shining brightly through his dormer window, turned Hubert's room into a stage-set, each object significant. Melancholy upon a hook hung the familiar uniform, a black cassock and surtout with plain collar-bands worn since that day, five years previously, when he had been hurried surreptitiously over the sea from the home he had never seen since. Laid over a chair were breeches and coat, black also, for he was in mourning for his mother, but of a secular cut, the garments of emancipation; and most suggestive of all was the tie-wig on its block.

3

On the dresser was a pile of ink-stained volumes, Horace and Virgil, Cicero and Sallust, which he must hand in this morning to the Prefect of Studies. His trunk stood ready locked; an open valise awaited his nightclothes; a riding-whip was propped against a chair; and carefully swathed in sacking were the altar panels, carved during his spare time with the Emblems of the Passion, and designed for his domestic chapel at home.

He drew a long trembling breath as he regarded these things, but his excitement was not untinged with sadness. He loved Douai with that deep, restrained affection which was an essential trait in his character, and since he was eleven he had known no other life but school.

Every day for ten months of the year he had risen at 5 a.m., knelt before his crucifix and placed himself in the Presence of God as he had been taught, gone to the Chapel (on tiptoe, because the *magnum silentium* must be most strictly observed), endeavoured to fix his drowsy mind on the preludes, considerations, and resolutions of formal meditation, assisted at the Community Mass always offered for the conversion of England, eaten his breakfast of milk pottage and bread and butter in the Refectory, made his bed, and sat down to his studies at eight o'clock.

He was neither brilliant nor dull, and he had spent the normal year in each of the five Schools of the Humanities, thereby acquiring a sound knowledge of Latin, Greek and French, and of very little else besides. At noon he had partaken of half a pound of meat, which was doubled on Sundays. From two till four he had worked at his books again; from four till supper he had played at handball or football or gossiped with his friends. At half-past eight he had assisted at Night Prayers, which included the Litany of the Saints for the conversion of his native land; and immediately afterwards, at the beginning of the Great Silence, he had retired to bed.

A staid, monotonous routine, broken by feast days, ordinations, the coming of distinguished visitors, the brief holidays of Christmas and Easter spent here at Douai, and the whole glorious month, beginning on Corpus Christi, when the school went to their country house, La Croix, at Coutiche. He had grumbled at the hard work and the plain food and the dullness, but only in a conventional way. From the first he had settled easily and happily into the soothing rhythm of this English school in a foreign land, getting on well with everyone, making a few close friends and no enemies, and knowing at the back of his mind that Old Park was waiting for him over the sea on that remote day when his school life should be over.

And now that day was here.

He turned over on his back, stretched his long legs to the limit of his bed, clasped his hands behind his neck, and tried to assimilate the astonishing fact that in about a fortnight's time he would be in England, the master of Old Park.

Yesterday, in the course of his customary parting 'bleat', Dr Thornburgh, the President of Douai, had spoken very seriously of Sir Hubert's responsibilities. There had been a great deal about 'the noble sacrifices made by your dear parents (God rest their souls) to give you and your brothers a Catholic education'. The continued existence of the Faith in England depended, under God, on those ancient families – now, alas, decreasing in numbers – who were ready to suffer any kind of penalty rather than violate their consciences; and as the heir of one of those families who had never lapsed, from whose house the Blessed Sacrament had never been removed even in the hottest times of persecution, Sir Hubert, said Dr Thornburgh, had the solemn duty and privilege of carrying on this proud tradition. In due time, it was to be hoped, he would marry a lady of his own religion, and beget heirs who in their turn would maintain that small fortress of truth in the midst of a heretic wilderness.

Hubert had listened seriously, for he was a serious boy. But lying here in the moonlight he was unable to fix his mind on so solemn a programme, because it was full of a vision of Old Park.

So vivid was that vision in the bright colours of a childhood memory, that the little room faded, and he saw the myrtle tree on the lawn at home, the rose garden with its sundial, the lilies floating on the lake, the Thorne motto carved on the gateposts, that motto he had learnt when very young to translate from the old French as *Thorne guards the Flower of Honour,* the arbour, resembling a small Greek temple, erected by his grandfather after that gentleman had made the Grand Tour, and which in those remote days before Hubert had come to Douai had served so often as a besieged fortress, or as 'home' in a game of hide-and-seek.

He could hear the summer sounds, the tinkle of the fountain in the hot solarium, the swish of a scythe through grass, the drowsy cawing of rooks in the 'cathedral trees', the faint whisper of the sea beyond the cliff. The dampness of wet woods was in his nostrils, and the aromatic scent of pines and the strange foreign odour of the eucalyptus tree by the lake. Figures moved through these cherished scenes – his father who had died when he was eight, his mother whose death had occurred at the beginning of this his last term; but they were only kindly ghosts whom he would not miss because he scarcely remembered them as they had been in life.

Then he had a slight qualm of conscience, said a prayer for the souls of his parents, added a rather vague one for the welfare of his sister Magdalene, Robin's twin, and two minutes later was fast asleep.

(ii)

"You will find, I think," said the Procurator of the College, pushing a paper covered with neat rows of figures across the table, "that these accounts of the monies you brought with you when you came to us are correct. This morning I have been obliged to deduct three francs for breakages. You broke a number of glasses at the Rhetoricians' Feast."

"But *of course* I had to smash them after drinking to the King and the Prince of Wales, sir," protested Robin Thorne. "It would be *hideous* to charge me for such a loyal gesture. Why, it would be almost lèse-majesté!"

"They were College property, for which I am responsible," remarked the Procurator primly. "Sign here, if you please; and with your real name, not your alias."

"Mr President enjoyed my loyal serenade last night," observed Robin, dashing off 'Robert Thorne' in an untidy hand which was full of character. "I knew he would. Some ninnies wagered I'd get flogged for it, but I knew better."

The Procurator regarded him in silence.

Like everyone else at Douai, this grave, middle-aged priest long ago had succumbed to Robin Thorne's vivid charm. The boy's career had been a series of pranks and punishments. The poor had benefited greatly from the number of halfpennies he had been fined for unpunctuality; the Prefect of the Wardrobe had birched him repeatedly for wearing his best suit because his uniform was buttonless; the General Prefect had doomed him to study in his recreation time for the carelessness of his Greek construing; the Prefect of Studies had waxed eloquent on the subject of a boy with brains who had stuck for eighteen months in Grammar simply because he would not work; the President himself had remonstrated when, in the minute garden in which each boy was supposed to raise salads, Robin had planted a white rose bush instead.

But the President's staunchly Jacobite heart had melted when a white rose, emblem of the exiled Stuarts, had been laid on his desk by a reverent though grubby hand. The floggings and the forfeits had been suffered with the greatest good-will; the lack of discipline so obviously had its origin in a vitality and a romantic chivalry which not even the General Perfect could resist; and, despite lack of application, Robin had taken Syntax in his stride, had positively cantered through Poetry and Rhetoric, and now, at only fifteen, was ready to leave school with his elder brother.

The Procurator put his hand before his mouth to conceal a smile as he imagined the interview between Dr Thornburgh and Robin this morning. He knew precisely how it must have gone.

The President would have started off very solemn and severe. Your exhibition of last night was quite intolerable; bagpipes, and in my garden, too!...disturbed the whole College...every rule broken...bad example...cause of scandal to your very young brother just beginning his school life...your dear mother so lately dead...most heartless...time you settled down; and so on.

And Robin would have stood there, as he was standing here, looking as fresh and bright-eyed as though he had never tasted wine; and he would say: Yes, sir; I'm sorry, sir; I really thought you wouldn't mind, sir; I only wanted to please you, sir; I learnt the pipes on purpose, sir; my dear mother was such a staunch Jacobite too, sir. And Dr Thornburgh would find his righteous indignation giving way to a genuine regret at having to say goodbye to a boy who had caused everyone at Douai a great deal of trouble.

For somehow or other you could not help liking the headstrong, irresponsible, charming Robin Thorne.

(iii)

The Quadrangle of the College was in a tremendous bustle this morning, for it was the start of the summer holidays. Trunks were being carried down, wagons loaded; the younger boys indulged in horse-play, while their elders pretended a superb indifference to the fact that the great day had come at last. There was a group clustered round the statue of Cardinal Allen, Founder of the College, saying goodbye to Hubert and Robin Thorne, those familiar companions who already, in their new clothes, actually with swords at their sides, looked strange and remote. The Thornes were going to England, to that strange land for whose conversion one prayed every day, to which this school formed an outpost in a foreign country, but of which one had only such very vague memories.

Hubert shouldered his way out of the group presently, and went in search of his youngest brother, Michael, who had arrived only this term, just before their mother's death. Michael had been a mere baby when Hubert had left England, and during the term they had seen little of each other, for Michael was down among the infants in Figures and under the care of the Housekeeper.

After some difficulty, Hubert found the child all by himself in the cloisters, engaged in the favourite pastime of the small boys of Douai, known as 'drawing the cart about'. He looked solemn and lonely, and Hubert's heart smote him. He ought to have got to know this small brother of his before leaving him here among strangers; but Robin seemed to have taken him under his wing, and Hubert took it for granted that the child, like everyone else, would prefer the company of the lively Robin.

" 'Lo, sir," said Michael politely, pausing in his admonitions to an imaginary steed to 'Git up'.

9

"You'll like it at La Croix," said Hubert. "Let's sit down on this trunk for a minute or two. There are no lessons, and you can fish and play at ninepins and have double-dinner every day."

"Yes, I know," said Michael placidly. "And next term I shall be able to have lots of bon-na fights." (He had picked up the school slang very quickly, it seemed.) "Now Robin's going; he would interfere and make me look a baby, I was having a bon-na fight the week after I came, and then he came and thrashed the other boy 'cause he was bigger, the boy, I mean, and spoilt it all. So I'm glad Robin's going."

Hubert gave him a blank look.

"I don't like him, and I've had to mention not liking him in confession," the child continued with a certain relish. "But I 'splained to Mr Grafton that I don't like not liking him, and if you haven't any 'tachment to sin, it isn't sin. Mr Marrowbones told me so."

"Mr who?"

"Mr Maribon; you know, our chaplain at home. You 'member you always called him Marrowbones. I had to mention to him my First Confession that I didn't like my sister Magda, and then he told me about 'tachment."

"Don't you like any of your family?" demanded Hubert, taken aback.

"O, I like you, sir, very much indeed; though you shouldn't have 'tachment to people, only to God," said Michael smugly. "And I liked my mother, only she was always so busy that I didn't get to know her very well; and she and my father are both in Heaven, so I can't like them now, can I? And you can't *rely* on Robin, and Magda *would* make me be a heretic."

"Michael!"

"In our games, I mean. We used to play at martyrs and heretics, and just 'cause she was older than me she always made me be the heretic, and sometimes I had to be the 'cutioner as well. And it was *hijus* to make me, 'sidering I'm called after our Martyr, Blessed Michael Thorne, and I'm going to be a priest, and everything."

"Oh, are you?" murmured Hubert, bewildered by this stranger of a youngest brother.

"Yes, so you won't see me for about ten years, and when you do you'll have to ask my blessing." Michael replied complacently. "When I've finished with the Humans – "

"The Humanities."

" – I'll go on to Flossophy and Thology, and I'll be called a 'divine', and I'll make a 'clamation in Latin to 'stinguished visitors, and I'll sit in the choir in Chapel and wear a sur-plus, and I'll have figs and raisins with my dinner, and I'll not go to bed till nine o'clock."

"Oh well, that's splendid," said Hubert. "I was afraid you might be – they're calling me, Michael; I must go."

"Goodbye, sir," said Michael, becoming formal. "I've made a novena to St Christopher for a safe journey for you, so you'll be all right."

"Thank you very much," said Hubert gravely.

He had turned away when the child's voice recalled him.

"Please don't tell Robin where I am; I was hiding from him 'cause he'd want to kiss me in front of everyone." Two small arms suddenly clutched Hubert round the waist. "Goodbye, dear, *dear* Hubert! I love you very much, and I don't care about not having 'tachment, and please look after my dog Roger and don't let that Stephen tease him, and don't be sad at home."

The shrill voice echoed in his mind amid the bustle of mounting, the chorus of farewells, the grasping of hands, the rather forced jokes, the last long look at familiar things. How odd a thing for a child to say to one whom to Michael was quite grown-up! Sadness at leaving Douai was, of course, inevitable; the battle-scarred buildings, the pepperpot towers, the apse of the newly rebuilt Chapel, the voice of Cracked Tom, the bell that had received some injury in the siege, the pitch on which so many games had been played, the garden sacred to the Rhetoricians where Life had been so solemnly discussed with his friends, the statue of the saintly Founder, so often irreverently dressed up on feast days, these things this morning were most poignantly dear.

But to be sad at home, at Old Park! What a very strange admonition. But then Michael, it seemed, was rather a strange little boy.

# Chapter Two

With her skirts tucked up in an unladylike fashion and her chin on her fists, Magdalene Thorne sat on a rock in the cove she had christened 'My Little Bay', and contemplated death by drowning.

She had always lived largely in a world of dreams, which tended to be morbid. When she was very young they had centred round certain pagan deities with which her late father (to the scandal of his chaplain) had adorned his gardens. In the centre of the lily-lake Aphrodite rode upon a shell drawn by dolphins, and at the side of a particularly dark path in the woods sat Pan, his shaggy legs crossed, a sly smile playing round the corners of his bearded lips to which he held his pipes.

And at dusk in the gardens, returning from some long, lonely ramble, Magdalene had fancied that she heard the patter of hooves in pursuit of her, the faint, enticing bubble of pipe music. Dreaming here on the rocks of her little bay, she had terrified and delighted herself by imagining that she saw Neptune's trident, dripping with seaweed, beckoning her to his watery domain. The companionship and affection of humans might be denied her, but she was beloved of the immortals; she had invented a dozen different versions of the exquisitely poignant occasion when she succumbed to the wooing of a god and her family sought for her in vain.

The pagan period had passed, and she was honestly ashamed of it. But the dream of an untimely death remained. With the unwilling assistance of her youngest brother, Michael, she had been pressed to death at Newgate for refusing to plead, she had been beheaded on Tower Hill, burnt at Smithfield, and hanged, drawn and quartered at Tyburn. (She had treated with contempt the assertion of the practical Michael that this latter form of execution was reserved for men.)

She was not, in the strict sense of the word, a neglected child. Nana, here mother's old nurse, a hideous crone with a birthmark empurpling one cheek, had taught her to brew, to bake, to sew, and certain other arts not so healthy; Clare, Lady Thorne, had instructed her only daughter in embroidery and playing upon the harpsichord; the domestic chaplain had grounded her in the three Rs, besides teaching her the doctrines of her religion. At fifteen, therefore, Magdalene was as accomplished a young lady as most country girls of gentle birth. But for recreation she had to make her own.

Since her father's early death, her mother had been perpetually preoccupied with the management of the estate; her two elder brothers had disappeared overseas when she was ten, and Michael, who would follow them in due course, had been too young to be a satisfactory companion. And though there were young folk of her own social class in the neighbourhood, she had learnt very early that between herself and them there was the unbridgeable gulf of religion. She was never invited to hunt or dance; there was no interchange of visits.

As she grew older, she had overheard snatches of talk between Lady Thorne and Nana on the subject of her future. Quite a big girl now, Miss Magdalene, Nana had

14

muttered; time to think of a husband. But not a Catholic gentleman of rank in the whole county. What would become of poor Miss Magdalene? A convent perhaps? But no, Mr Maribon says she shows no signs of a vocation to religion. Why, then, she must just stay at home and make herself useful about the house.

Make myself useful about the house, repeated Magdalene, seeing reflected in her mirror the short upper lip, the clear complexion, the glossy dark curls of the handsome Thornes. To grow older and older and never see anybody or go anywhere, never have a husband or new clothes or a home of my own.

And so she had taken refuge in unhealthy day-dreams. She would die young, preferably (when she was in a pious mood) for the Faith. Only a few generations separated her from the days when those of her religion, women as well as men, had made the supreme sacrifice for their beliefs; and here at Old Park there were many reminders of those stirring times. There was the Hiding Oak, which could be found to be hollow only by tapping it, and in which her grandfather had hidden during the madness of the Oates' Plot in Charles II's reign; there was the huge dovecote where a Jesuit had lain concealed in his vestments while the pursuivants searched the yard beneath him; there were cunning hiding-holes contrived behind panelling and in chimneys in the days of Elizabeth; and above all, there was the portrait of the Thorne Martyr, Magdalene's great-great-uncle.

It hung at the head of the staircase, in full view of anyone entering the hall; a prie-dieu stood beneath it, and every night, as the family ascended to bed, the head of the house would kneel there and ceremoniously invoke the Martyr's intercession. On the anniversary of his execution at York his portrait was always decked with flowers, while the light of two wax candles illumined his sad face with its expression of faint surprise as though he wondered to find a knife embedded in his breast – an artistic touch added to his portrait after his martyrdom.

The waves of the incoming tide were slapping at Magdalene's rock. In a few moments more the rock would be surrounded, and then the water would creep up and up until it washed her away, away from all her problems, away from the two daunting strangers, her brothers, who were coming home tomorrow, away from the horrible, humiliating future of becoming an old maid and making herself useful about the house.

A little wave creamed over her feet. She whispered a hasty act of contrition for playing with thoughts of mortal sin, slithered down from the rock and ran stumbling up the stony beach, trying not to think of all the ghost stories Nana had told her as she hurried home through the dusk.

(ii)

"The park wall needs a lot of repair," remarked Hubert, frowning.

"This horse is past repair," replied Robin. "They seem to have sent us the worst beasts in the stables."

The brothers had been met at the inn where the stagecoach called and, sending their baggage on by the cart, were riding home alone. Emotion had mounted in Hubert ever since landing in England, and he was trying to conceal it by appearing the practical young landowner concerned only with the material appearance of his estates. But as he rode on through scenes which grew more and more familiar, the beginnings of a sick bewilderment blighted the joy of his homecoming; surely Old Park had never looked as neglected at this.

"There are the 'cathedral trees'!" exclaimed Robin, who was in his usual spirits. "D'you remember how we used to call that fungus stuff 'bug-whiskers'? And there's Carpenter's cottage, where they carried me when I sprained my ankle out hawking that time. Lord, it's good to be home!"

He chattered on in his vivacious way, but Hubert was silent; more and more silent as they came to the main entrance to the park, and saw one of the great iron gates lying flat on the grass, and the drive full of ruts and pot-holes, and the parkland overgrown with thistles, and nettles thick on the verges. He drew in his breath sharply as they skirted the lily-lake and he saw how a great tree had crashed into it, breaking one of Aphrodite's dolphins and lying there bleached and drowned. And when he reached a turn in the drive and listened and could not hear that for which he listened, he cried out at last, boyishly:

"The fountain! We always heard it from here."

But then they had topped the last rise, and his bewildered disappointment was swallowed up in the emotion of the returning exile as he had his first full view of Old Park.

It was a house which had that knack peculiar to certain old buildings – of absorbing all forms of architecture into one harmonious whole. From the days when it had been a Norman keep, successive Thornes had tinkered with it, added to it, pulled down and rebuilt; but the sea mists had softened glaring white stone and new red brick into a uniform mellowness; and even the monstrosity of a porch with Corinthian pillars, erected by Hubert's own father on his return from his youthful travels, did not seem out of place. The personality of Old Park was so strong that, like a truly elegant woman, it could wear the most outrageous fashions and yet remain itself.

He had one sharp, sudden stab of grief at not seeing his mother standing there on the terrace; but there were other familiar figures waiting to greet him. He knelt for the chaplain's blessing, kissed the tall girl, his sister, whom he remembered only as a little child, and with a new unconscious dignity went from one to other of the servants, saying a word to each. He noticed how, after her formal greeting to him, Magdalene turned eagerly to Robin, but that was natural. She was Robin's twin sister, and in any case Robin was everybody's favourite. He had never felt the slightest twinge of jealousy of his brother, for he too was susceptible to the boy's charm.

But perhaps because he was tired, he felt depressed at supper. Nothing in his memory had warned him of the decayed aspect of Old Park, an aspect as conspicuous within-doors as without. There was a pervading smell of damp and mice, and everything looked shabby. His glance encountered the portrait of his mother over the hearth, and his sudden realisation of her loss was tinged with a new understanding. She had always seemed rather preoccupied, he remembered, and she must have had a heavy time of it, left a widow so early. No wonder the estate looked decayed; it needed a man to attend to it. Well, that was his job now.

"I could not hear the fountain as we rode up," he remarked suddenly to Magdalene.

"Oh, it got broken long ago," his sister said indifferently. "Everything's broken here."

A hound which had been lying on the shabby hearthskin came and put its head upon his knee, its great eyes wistfully questioning him. This must be Michael's dog, he thought; he asked me to see that somebody called Stephen (I don't remember him) doesn't tease it. And as he stroked the silky head, there recurred to him his brother's strange admonition at parting – 'Don't be sad at home.'

"But everything will be mentioned soon," Robin's voice said confidently. "Even the fountain, of which old Hubert thinks so much."

And then he smiled a secret sort of smile.

(iii)

Hubert spent the next few days visiting his tenants and riding round his estates, accompanied by Mr Filton, his bailiff; and the bewilderment he had felt at his homecoming was immeasurably deepened. Lying in his box of a bedroom at Douai, he had seen with the eyes of a boy a vision of his beloved home; now he began to see it with the eyes of a man, and he was appalled by what he saw.

The grey-green furry growth on the trees was no longer the pretty 'bug-whiskers' of childhood, but an evil parasite. The ivy was not fanciful chain-mail, but strangling ropes. The white trumpets of the convolvulus proclaimed the triumph of weeds throughout the gardens; in the woods dead trees leaned against each other because they had no room to fall. The shrubberies had encroached like an invading army; the gate into the lane, that gate on which he had swung so often or had used as a horse before he had learned to ride, was just a bit of wood rotten from lack of paint, broken from its hinges, and tied up with a piece of rope. Cottages and farmhouses which had been part of his fairyland became tumbledown dwellings in need of thatch or tile, the homes of tenants who struggled desperately to scratch a living from land which cried out for more labour and for the replenishing of everything from livestock to new implements.

"I know, Sir Hubert, I know!" cried Mr Filton, waving his hands. "I do assure you I have done my best; and as for your late mother, never was a lady a more careful steward.

But we cannot afford repairs, and when the old servants are past their work we have the utmost difficulty in hiring new ones. The tenants' sons tend to migrate to the towns, where they can get higher wages, for I'm afraid they're infected with the spirit of the age. And then there's Whiteman, one of your principal tenants; he conformed a year or so ago, and now refuses to pay his rents, and is within his rights too, for Catholics are prevented by law from suing for debt. And it has set a very ill example to others," he added with a sigh.

It made little sense to Hubert; only when he came to examine his estate accounts with his bailiff did he begin to understand.

It seemed that all recusants, as the Catholics who refused to go to the Protestant service were called, were required to pay double land-tax. Over and above this, after the failure of the Jacobite rising in '15 the late King George I had appointed a commission to 'enquire into the estates of Popish traitors and recusants, and of estates given to superstitious uses'. This had resulted in a statute authorising the sum of one hundred thousand pounds to be assessed on Catholics above the age of eighteen, whether or not they had taken part in the rising.

Quite apart from such crippling taxes, the Thornes' religion cost them dear. The estate was charged with a considerable sum for the maintenance of a chaplain who served the Catholics of the entire county, and for everything pertaining to the mission of which they were the patrons. Moreover, there were orphans to be provided for, boys to be assisted to study for the priesthood, temporal wants to be relieved. Dr Challoner, Coadjutor to the Vicar Apostolic of the London District (which covered ten counties), had been Lady Thorne's almoner; and the sums set aside for these charitable purposes must be sent to him in London regularly and in full, no matter how pressing were the needs of the estate.

Hubert listened gravely, and his dismay began to be mingled with pride. His character, naturally one of courage and integrity, had been formed by his school; and though he was beginning to wonder whether a classical education was going to be of much use to him, he had been taught to accept responsibility and to rule his conduct by fixed principles. His religious devotion, though unostentatious, was very real; and not only did the situation put him on his mettle, but it began to assume the aspect of a sacred trust. His talks with Mr Maribon, his chaplain, drove home the lesson of his responsibility as the head of this ancient Catholic house.

The chaplain was a little grey man with a leathery complexion, the result of being out in all weathers. He had the privilege of saying three Masses on Sundays, and after celebrating the first in the chapel at Old Park at dawn, he would ride off fasting to different parts of the country where, maintained by the Thornes, were two other concealed Mass-centres for those who lived too far away to come to Old Park itself. He was for ever at the beck and call of the scattered Catholics within a radius of fifty miles, riding his old nag through roadless wastes to administer the Last Sacraments to the dying, to visit the sick, to hear confessions, to baptise children.

Hubert found him rather reserved at first, but the priest melted under his young patron's friendliness, and it transpired that Mr Maribon's manner was due very largely to the anomalous position he occupied in the household. He was the son of a local carpenter, and as was customary had been taken into the service of the late Sir Hubert, without reference to the Vicar Apostolic, much as a steward or a butler might be hired. He sat below the salt at table; he was never invited into the withdrawing-room; and

21

Hubert's father, a haughty gentleman, had gone so far as to compel his chaplain to wait at the altar until the patron had been pleased to say:

"Mr Maribon, you may begin Prayers."

"Prayers?" repeated Hubert wonderingly, when the chaplain had confided this story to him. "Do you mean Mass, Father?"

Mr Maribon's reaction to this innocent question amazed him.

"Sir Hubert, please!" the old man cried in great agitation, glancing nervously round as though they were in a public place instead of in the priest's little room in this isolated house. "We never use these terms in England. We speak of 'Prayers' when we refer to the Holy Sacrifice; and I do beg you never to address me as 'Father', or to mention the word 'priest'. You will excuse me, Sir Hubert, if I warn you that you must accustom yourself to the most exact discretion, lest such terms might slip out when you are in company."

"But surely the penal laws are rarely enforced nowadays," objected Hubert, privately deeming the old man very timid.

"You can never tell when they might be," persisted Mr Maribon. "I do not think they would hang, draw, and quarter us as they did our fathers, even though that law remains upon the Statute Book; for publicity inflicted martyrdom has always been shown to stiffen resistance, and moreover, our age has no need of that kind of persecution when it has such a much more effective one at hand."

"I don't understand, sir."

The old man's look grew tender.

"I am afraid you will understand all too soon, Sir Hubert. We exist on sufferance; we are persecuted by a public ignoring of our existence; they are trying to bury us alive."

Hubert smiled to himself. The poor old man had grown fanciful, he thought, by being as it were buried alive himself. He never met his fellow clergy; he was completely cut off from the vigorous mainstream of Catholic life abroad; his mind had rusted, and his outlook had grown so narrow that he even disliked, Hubert found, the attempts of the industrious Dr Challoner to provide English Catholics with new translations of old spiritual classics, the language of which had become archaic.

But, on the other hand, he performed his sacred duties with the most heroic strictness; and the manner in which he had succeeded in keeping his scattered flock together was brought home to Hubert, soon after his homecoming, in a way he was never to forget.

(iv)

It was the Feast of the Assumption, one of the 'Eight Indulgences' of the year, when devout Catholics approached the Sacraments after a lengthy preparation, to be followed by a thanksgiving equally prolonged.

Hubert did not get to bed at all on the eve of the feast. As soon as dusk fell there began to be stir and movement in the woods which encompassed the old house; singly or in groups the faithful of the county came to the tryst, on horse- or donkey-back, by boat to the deserted coves below the cliff, many more trudging on foot, carrying little baskets of food with them that they might break their long fast after receiving Holy Communion, and old cloaks and sacks for improvised bedding. The women and children, and the old, were accommodated in barns and stables; the men encamped cheerfully in the open, though it was pouring with rain; and all through the night there was a long queue to the room where the priest was hearing confessions.

In the park, meanwhile, Mr Filton was setting sentinels to warn of the approach of strangers; and for the first time Hubert really understood that the English Catholics practised their religion at their peril.

"We have been lucky so far," Mr Filton said to him, "because of the remoteness of the house and the number of bolt-holes its woods afford. But you never know when some officious magistrate might decide to make a raid, and then, apart from the penalties we all should suffer, I tremble for what would happen to poor Mr Maribon."

"But he himself told me that they would never enforce nowadays the savage Statutes of Elizabeth."

"There are other Statutes," Mr Filton replied darkly. "Particularly that of William III by which a priest convicted of saying Mass may be sentenced to life imprisonment."

Hubert had asked to serve the Mass, and just before dawn he went to see that all was ready for the Holy Sacrifice. He was a little light-headed with fatigue, and as he stood here he had a most vivid mental picture of the splendidly rebuilt chapel at Douai, filled with rich carving and statuary, with the great beam carrying the rood and the figures of St Mary and St John, and the fresco behind the high altar depicting the one hundred and sixty martyrs who had gone forth from this school to suffer for their faith.

How different was this poor little chapel at Old Park!

Once it, too, had been splendid, enriched by successive Thornes. At the Reformation it had concealed itself under the guise of a store-room except during Mass; during the brief reign of James II it had been put into thorough repair and reopened with great solemnity. Then at the Revolution it had suffered at the hands of a gang of roughs, who had stolen the jewelled reliquaries and the gold monstrance and other treasures, and dressing up a dummy in vestments had burnt the effigy on a bonfire in the gardens.

The fury had died down, and Old Park was left in peace again; and the little steady spark in the lamp under the hanging pyx had continued to proclaim the Presence of the Lord in the Blessed Sacrament. But for over fifty years now, Mass had had to be said behind locked doors and with sentries posted in case of a raid; the vestments and altar-cloths were darned and patched; the images were chipped from the assault of the roughs at the Revolution; and the only material treasures left were a monstrance and crucifix of Corinthian brass and a silver-gilt chalice.

As he went about his duties in the Sanctuary half an hour later, the contrast between this Mass and those at which he had assisted at Douai was still more moving to Hubert. He heard in memory the boom of the great organ, the solemn strokes of the bell in the tower, a sound echoed by all the churches in the town, proclaiming to the sick and the dying and the captive that once again the Creator had obeyed the summons of His creature, and had come down upon the altar under the veil of bread and wine. But here in his own chapel he must ring a hand-bell very, very softly, just in case there might be some informer lurking; he must celebrate the feast of God's Mother furtively, behind locked doors, just in case some magistrate decided to make a raid, always just in case...

But as he watched the humble congregation press up to the altar rails at the Communion, an enormous pride thrilled him. Some two hundred souls depended for the reception of the Bread of Life on him, the patron of the only Catholic mission in an entire county. He remembered what the President of Douai had said to him at parting – that he had the duty and the privilege of maintaining one small fortress of truth in a waste of heresy. And he looked through blurred eyes at the spark in the lamp which, throughout the centuries, had proclaimed that here in this shabby chapel was the Presence of God who had promised to be with His faithful all days, even unto the end of the world.

To maintain that tiny light of faith, to ensure that it was never put out, was his vocation. To that all else must be sacrificed, for that all penalties must be braved, all hardships cheerfully borne. This Thorne, like all his ancestors, must guard well the flower of honour, at whatever cost. And with profound humility and pride he vowed he would be worthy of so great a trust.

# Chapter Three

Hubert had not been long at home before he began to learn for himself some very bitter lessons connected with his position as a Catholic landowner.

There was first what Mr Maribon had termed 'public ignoring'. Sir Hubert's ancient lineage and the fact that there had been Thornes at Old Park since the days of the Conqueror, ought to have entitled him to a foremost part in all county activities. He knew, of course, that the penal laws forbade his being appointed to any civil or military office, but he had expected that he would be consulted unofficially by the local dignitaries. He found instead that he was not even asked to join the local Hunt; and that his neighbours among the gentry, though few went to the length of cutting him in public, consistently refrained from visiting him or sending him invitations. Except for the barest courtesy, they studiously ignored him.

He felt it keenly. He was young and full of energy; he was fresh from the camaraderie of school. He had enjoyed an infinitely superior education to that of the neighbours who ostracised him, and at Douai he had learned the courtly manners which they lacked. At sixteen it was hard to be forced to live as a recluse.

27

But there were handicaps more serious than this social ostracism. He discovered the first of them when he went over to Newtown one day to enquire for a mason to mend a part of the roof which was so decayed that it had caused great patches of damp on the inside walls. At first the man put him off with excuses; he had not the kind of stone Sir Hubert needed; he had no workmen available; and so on. At last, however, the mason agreed to come over to Old Park and inspect the damage; and when he had done so, Hubert asked for an estimate of the cost.

"A hundred pounds, sir," said the mason promptly.

Hubert stared at him a moment, then burst out laughing.

"A hundred pounds? Come, man, be reasonable. I'm not asking you to rebuild the entire roof."

"That's my price, sir," said the mason in an insolent tone. "But if you don't like it, you can leave it."

"I certainly shall," snapped Hubert, his temper rising. "And hope to find another of your trade to give me a fair price."

"Why, perhaps you will, sir, of your own religion," the mason said with an obvious sneer. "I wish you luck."

So that was it, thought Hubert furiously. But if tradesmen thought they were going to blackmail him in this way, they were very much mistaken. He tried two other masons, with the same result; and was driven to the conclusion that it was he who had been mistaken. They did not want to work for a Papist, and if they did they would force him to pay through the nose. All right, he thought, setting his teeth; I'll learn to do such tasks myself with the help of my tenants.

The next lesson he learnt came as a far greater shock. Ever since they had come home, his brother Robin had been plaguing him about buying a decent riding-horse; and one day Robin burst in upon him, all smiles.

"I've got a bargain!" he cried. "I've discovered a horse-dealer who'll let me have the keenest little bay mare you ever saw for only twenty-five pounds. There's no sharp practice; I've looked her well over and tried her out. She's seven years old and just my weight, and I can have her right away."

Hubert regarded him thoughtfully. Among the elder boy's many problems, Robin loomed large. Their financial position would make it necessary for Robin to earn a living, but in what capacity? The penal laws closed to a Catholic the Army, the Navy, Parliament, medicine, the Bar, and the teaching profession. There remained the possibility of taking up Law as a conveyancer, or of getting a post as bailiff to some Catholic of substance in another county. Or, of course, there was trade; but Hubert could not bring himself to the point of suggesting this to a Thorne. Robin himself, whenever the subject was mentioned between them, became reproachful.

"Give me time, Hubert!" he would cry. "I've slaved at my books for five years and have earned a few months' leisure."

Besides, there was plenty to occupy them both at Old Park. The place was overrun with vermin, and he would undertake to clear it, *if* he had a good horse.

"Well, it does sound a bargain if the mare is all you say," said Hubert presently. "Though twenty-five pounds is hard to find. However, I'll give you the money, and then you really must set to work on getting the foxes and conies down."

Robin was extravagant with promises and thanks, and the next morning rode proudly home on the bay mare. Hubert, called down by his brother to the stableyard, was watching her being put through her paces, when he saw two strangers enter the yard. He was about to ask them what they wanted, when Robin, passing them at a hand-canter, called out gaily:

"Why, here's Mr Woodcock who sold me this beauty. Come to see whether I'm fit to ride the pick of your stables, eh?"

The man he addressed exchanged a glance with his companion, and replied gruffly:

"I've come to take her back, Mr Thorne."

Robin, intent on his riding, apparently did not hear. But Hubert, who had heard very clearly, stepped up to the man and demanded:

"What the devil do you mean? Were you not paid?"

"Ay, I was paid, sir," said the horse-dealer, pulling some coins from his pocket. "And so shall you be. Five pounds, sir; that's what I'm bound by law to pay you for taking back my horse."

As Hubert stared at him blankly, Robin leapt out of the saddle and came up to them, a high colour in his face.

"I don't know whether you're mad or think we are," he barked. "I gave you twenty-five pounds for this mare, the price you asked. And if you're not out of the yard in two minutes, I'll – "

"No use to talk that way, young gentleman," interposed the other man. "I'm a lawyer, and I can tell you that what Mr Woodcock says is true. He can take back for five pounds any horse he sells to you, under the Act of William III which forbids any Papist to possess a horse above that value. It would be as well for you young gentlemen to make yourselves acquainted with that Act – "

"I'll make the pair of you acquainted with the horse-pond," snarled Robin, advancing on them with whip upraised.

Hubert stepped quickly forward and caught his brother by the arm.

"Take a hold on yourself, Robin," he said abruptly. "If that's the law, we're helpless, and I'll have no violence here."

"If you lay a finger on me," bleated the lawyer, as Robin wrestled to free himself from his brother's hold, "you'll find other laws set in motion against you. You want to watch your step, you do, you Papists – "

"Stand off, Hubert! Let me get at the dog!" shouted Robin, struggling furiously.

But then, as Hubert turned to call the grooms to his assistance, Robin suddenly tore himself away from his brother and stalked towards the house. He paused once and looked back over his shoulder; his face was white and his lips drawn back in a snarl.

"You're a tame one, brother, I must say!" he sneered.

But as Hubert turned back to the two intruders, there was a look about him which made them slightly uncomfortable. He might be only sixteen, but he had the self-control of a man.

"Take your horse," he said quietly, "and kindly get off my land. Unless of course you have any other little sharp practices by which you can enrich yourselves under colour of the law."

"Now, you don't want to talk that way, Sir Hubert," blustered the lawyer. "You don't want to provoke me, sir. If I had a mind to stand by the letter of the law, I could confiscate that shot-gun you're carrying. Ay, I know it's only a sporting-gun, but the Act of King William says no Papist is to possess arms of any kind. If you don't believe me, you've only to go to a justice and ask to see a copy, and that's the best thing you can do, otherwise you may find yourself in further trouble. There's the 25 and 30 of Charles II, which says – "

"There is also, or there was, the law of trespass," interrupted Hubert, still coldly calm, "which you appear to be

31

breaking. Or cannot Papists claim protection even under that?"

"No, they can't," said the lawyer flatly. "They can't claim protection under any law. No more than can any other enemy of the realm."

With which parting shot he took himself off, accompanied by his friend leading the mare. As soon as they had gone a buzz of angry talk broke out among the grooms, but Hubert said nothing. He walked steadily out of the yard and into the house. Only when he had entered the chapel, had shut the door, and knelt down, did he give way. He cried aloud from the depths of his humiliation:

"Oh God, God, God!"

(ii)

Among those who had witnessed the little scene in the yard was the gardener's boy, Stephen Vickery.

His father, Thomas Vickery, head gardener at Old Park, had been already middle-aged when he had taken a wife, who had died at the birth of her first child. This Stephen henceforth had been the apple of his old father's eye; and as the years passed, his doting parent really had found some excuse for believing that he had begotten a prodigy. It was true that little Stephen was not attractive; he was undersized, with a pair of very close-set, calculating eyes, and legs afflicted with the distressing distortion known as 'cheese-cutter'. But in the big barn on the estate where, in defiance of the law, a Catholic schoolmaster taught the tenants' children, Stephen was always top of his form in every subject, displaying in particular a positive passion for arithmetic, a science quite beyond the ken of his old father.

Fourteen now, he was an aloof, silent boy, never playing with the other lads, observing the world with a cold superciliousness, and keeping his own counsel. His sole amusement, apart from working out complicated sums and reading newspapers, consisted in prowling about the woods after dark. He would crouch for hours where the undergrowth was thickest, or tiptoe softly along a walk roofed and walled by the invading trees, always watching and listening, as though on the track of some quarry.

"Ain't you afeared of the dark, Stevie?" his admiring father would ask him. "Ain't you afeared you'll see ghosties in they woods?"

"*I* ain't afeared of anything," Stephen would answer, slightly stressing the personal pronoun.

For there was someone he knew who was afraid of the dark, and it was she he was shadowing – the long-legged, dark-haired, lonely young daughter of the house, Magdalene Thorne.

He hated her and he wanted to frighten her. He had the stirrings of an adolescent lust for her, and he wanted to kiss her. But his hate was uppermost, not so much against Magdalene as an individual as against her family. He was clever and they were dull. He could do really intricate sums in his head, while they could only read Latin and Greek and play on the harpsichord. Yet he was the gardener's boy, slaving away with a broken dinner-knife digging weeds out of the drive or trundling a heavy barrow, while they lived in a fine house and amused themselves and patronised him. He had to pull his forelock when he encountered them, and address them as 'sir' or 'madam'.

But in the great world beyond the park they were outcasts. He hugged that knowledge to himself, and he had relished greatly the little scene in the yard. He knew nothing of the great world except what he gleaned from the newspapers, yet he had gathered enough to be sure that he could make his fortune there if he could penetrate to it. He had brains and tenacity, and already, at fourteen, no scruples of conscience. He despised the religion in which he had been bred; he was a natural agnostic.

One day, somehow or other, he would find the means of getting out of this stagnant backwater into the current of real life. Meantime there was Miss Magdalene, so demure when he saw her at Mass, so wild and solitary and vulnerable a creature when he spied her from his hiding-places, running with her skirts held high, talking to herself, mooning on a rock in a lonely cove, or attitudinising and playing the heroine to an imaginary audience in woodland glades.

(iii)

Magdalene was hurrying home to supper from her bay. She had lingered this evening until the tide had crept right round her rock, and she had had to wade ashore. Things had been worse since her brothers had come home, and she had persuaded herself they would be better. She had imagined them needing her, asking her advice, telling her how pretty she was; but Hubert was as preoccupied with the estate as their mother had been, and Robin was out all day and would not tell her where he went. He, her own twin, had some mysterious secret he refused to share with her, saying that such matters were not for girls.

Her hands clutched her damp skirts, her heart hammered against her chest, as she sped across the cliff where adders lurked and saw the lowering front of the woods before her. This was always the worst bit, especially on so still an autumn night, when an owl would hoot suddenly or an animal rustle in the undergrowth. Holy Mary, Mother of God, pray for me; oh, my good angel, whom God has appointed to be my guardian, watch over me; Blessed Michael Thorne, protect me…

How dared she pray, when she was in mortal sin! But she had not given full consent to the thought of suicide, and she had told the cards with Nana only for fun. Thus she argued nervously with the Douai Catechism on which she had been reared. To distract her thoughts, she tried to picture the little book lying beside her bed, the holy pictures between the leaves, the alphabet printed in four different types on the back of the title-page, with a cross at the beginning of each row.

Something touched her shoulder and she froze with fright. Silly, it's only a branch! Oh, my God, I am sorry and beg pardon for all my sins and detest them above all things, because... What was that? The sigh of the trees in the wind? But there was no wind. The creak of the little gate into the gardens? But she had shut it behind her. Or a footstep, a stealthy footstep that paused when she paused, that was now behind her, now in front of her?

...Because they have deserved Thy dreadful punishments, because they have crucified my loving Saviour, Jesus Christ, and most of all because they have offended Thy... Surely there had been a presence, an evil presence, looking down upon her from the top of the cliff when she had been playing with temptation this evening. The sweat tasted acid on her lips and her teeth began to chatter as she plunged into the gloom of the last and thickest of the shrubberies which separated her from the safe wide spaces of the lawn.

She had reached the middle of that dank path when her heart seemed to stop beating altogether and a scream was petrified in her throat. For like some demon barring the way a figure had risen up from the ground immediately in front of her, a figure surely too small to be a human being. Then the sweat broke out all over her body, and she turned sick with relief, as she heard the squeaky voice of Stephen Vickery, the gardener's boy.

"Evening, Miss Magdalene," said Stephen softly.

She stepped up to him and slapped him hard across the cheek.

"Oh, you wicked imp, how you startled me! What are you doing here at this time of night?"

"I've been a-follering you," whispered Stephen, rubbing his cheek as though he rather relished the sting of her slap, and sidling up to her in a sly fashion. "I've been a-follering you for ages. I seen you go off by yourself, I have, into the woods and down to the shore."

"How dare you!" shrilled Magdalene, tears of humiliation and anger trickling down her face. "How *dare* you follow me! I'll tell my brother Sir Hubert, and he'll have you whipped."

"No, you won't," chuckled Stephen, weaving in front of her as she made to brush past him, " 'cause if you do, Sir Hubert won't let you go a-prowling. And you do like prowling, don't you now? And I won't say nothing if you'll give me a kiss. You're pretty, and I like pretty maids." And a thin arm seized her round the waist, a hot, sour breath fanned her cheek.

Then indeed did Magdalene scream. Revulsion, fear, and a sort of dawning excitement were mingled in that scream; and it was answered immediately by a crashing in the undergrowth. The next moment, with a hooded hawk wildly 'baiting' on its jesses and his riding-whip brandished in the other hand, Robin came bursting through the shrubberies.

"Magda! What's wrong? Who's this? Oh no, you don't!" He made a long arm and caught the intruder who had been in the act of sidling away.

"He – he tried to – kiss me," blubbered Magdalene.

"Hold my hawk," her brother commanded, "while I deal with this young cur in a way he won't be likely to forget."

Grasping by one ear the kicking and howling Stephen, he marshalled the culprit through the shrubberies and across the lawns to the terrace, where the lights from the house made a pale radiance. And here, in a cheerful and business-like fashion, just as he had done at school to impertinent small boys, did Robin bestow upon the puny rear portions of Stephen a sound but perfectly humane beating. Holding the ruffled hawk, Magdalene looked on, half frightened and half gratified, feeling like a heroine of a romance whose champion had appeared in the nick of time.

Next morning a troubled old Thomas Vickery begged the favour of a few words with Sir Hubert. From a tangle of apologies and laments, Hubert gathered that, though Stephen's father heartily acknowledged the justice of the beating, he had an excuse for his boy.

"He's too clever, Sir Hubert," moaned the old man. "His heart's not in gardening, and that makes him restless-like. Always at his books and a fair wonder at ciphering; 'tis like magic, what he does with they figures. Schoolmaster says to me, Thomas, he says, your boy could get a place at Grammar School in Newtown, and there he ought to go, he says, for I can't teach him no more, he says. But that do cost money, sir, and I'd forgo my wages for the rest of my life if so be your honour would be so kind as to make up the sum."

So the precocious Stephen disappeared to the Grammar, School at Newtown, largely financed by Sir Hubert; and the incident was forgotten.

Or rather, it was forgotten by Hubert, by Stephen's father, and by Robin, who had taken so many beatings himself as a matter of course at school. Magdalene remembered it sometimes, though she tried not to think of the part before the appearance of Robin, because the memory of that thin arm squeezing her waist and of that squeaky voice telling her she was pretty gave her an odd, not wholly unpleasant disturbance.

But Stephen remembered it very vividly indeed; it had set the seal upon his old envious hatred of the Thornes. He had been thrashed, in full view of the house and in front of a girl, by a lad not much older and much less clever than himself. He tucked the memory into the back of his warped mind, deliberately encouraging it to fester.

# Chapter Four

Among the many weighty problems that had pressed on Hubert since his homecoming, that of his brother was the most perplexing.

Apart from his distaste for the idea of earning a livelihood, Robin could not, as Hubert was forcing himself to do, accept the hard conditions of life at home; continually he beat his head against the frustrations he met with on every side, and raged against a state of things which made young gentlemen of energy and intelligence outcasts in their own county. At school he had been popular with everyone, and therefore found ostracism doubly hard. Ordinarily sweet-tempered, he often now would sneer at his brother for turning the other cheek and swallowing insults.

When Robin was not raging against the conditions of life at Old Park, he was harping on a theme familiar to Hubert from their schooldays: the chances of a Stuart restoration. His obsession with this was natural enough; ever since the Revolution the hopes of the English Catholics had been centred upon the return of the rightful King or his heir; and the whole tone of the English College at Douai, from the President downwards, was one of staunch loyalty to the House of Stuart. King James III and

39

his two sons, Charles Edward, Prince of Wales, and Henry, Duke of York, were prayed for publicly in the chapel; their respective birthdays were kept as holidays; and new appointments at the College invariably were referred to King James for his approval.

But Hubert, though both his head and his heart concurred in allegiance to the King *de jure*, had too broad an outlook ever to let such allegiance become an *idée fixe*. Robin, on the other hand, impulsive and romantic by nature, was a born partisan and unable to enter into the minds of those who were not. During his last year at school his tendency to hero-worship had found a most satisfying object in Prince Charles Edward, a young man obviously destined for romantic deeds. From visitors who called at the College, Robin had collected a hundred little anecdotes relating to the Prince; Robin had had his Royal Highness' portrait hanging in his box of a bedroom, had grown white roses in his tiny garden, had learnt to play the bagpipes (because it appeared that the Prince was inclined to fix his hopes upon the loyal clans of Scotland), and had dreamed of fighting under Charles Edward's banner and marching in triumph to St James's.

There was plenty of excuse for his optimism, for early in 1744 the hopes of Jacobites everywhere had run high. The War of the Austrian Succession had thrown all Europe into the melting-pot; and in order to divert the English forces from the struggle, Cardinal Tencin, the director of French policy, a prelate who owed his Hat to the House of Stuart, had proposed a direct attack upon England under colour of another attempt to restore the rightful King. At Douai, Robin had talked of nothing but the huge invasion force said to be preparing under the joint command of Prince Charles Edward and Marshal de Saxe; he had been still at the highest pitch of excitement when, in March, the devastating news had arrived of the great storm which had scattered the French transports and ruined the expedition. Marshal Saxe was appointed to command in the Low Countries; even the Cardinal had talked no more of French aid to the Stuarts, and Jacobite hopes had sunk to zero.

But Prince Charles Edward, it seemed, was not a young man to accept defeat. He had returned safely from the abortive invasion, and there were rumours that if he could not have French aid he had vowed he would cross to Scotland alone in a fishing-boat and rely on his adherents there to rise for him. Robin, of course, lapped up such stories; a young prince taking his hazard alone, crossing the seas in a fishing-boat, appealing to the loyalty of picturesque Highland chiefs – it was a story straight from the pages of some old romance.

Hubert, listening to his brother's excited chatter, paid little attention. It seemed highly unlikely that such rumours could be true, and in any case he himself was too much occupied with sordid, day-to-day problems to think very much about public affairs. It was not until the brothers had been home a full year, in the summer of 1745, that Prince Charles Edward suddenly loomed large on Hubert's horizon, and he sensed danger in his junior's hero-worship.

(ii)

Hubert came in to dinner one day in a cheerful mood. It was fine weather; he had been cutting hay with his men, and though his hands were blistered, the rhythm of the scythe and the peaceful country talk had soothed him. Moreover, as he rode back to the house he had heard the horn of the post-boy in the lane, and found there was a letter for him. Cut off as he was from the outside world, a letter was a great event, and he was happier than ever when he recognised the round schoolboy hand of his youngest brother. The image of the boy had lain at the back of his mind throughout this past troublesome year, arousing his affectionate compassion; poor little Michael must have found Old Park melancholy, or he would not have begged his elder not to feel sad at home.

'Dear Sir Hubert,' wrote Michael, 'I've had strodinary 'creation twice for being diligent at my books, and I had a fight with a boy and licked him, and I have my hair powdered every Sunday by the housemaid, and I walk with my toes turned out, and I say a Hail Mary for you every night. I hope Roger is well, and that Stephen doesn't tease him, and please see that his nails are cut, otherwise he breaks them.'

Here, it seemed, Michael's subject-matter had run out, and there had been a pause for inspiration. One or two attempts to draw a face had been made before, signing himself by his Douai alias, he had concluded formally:

'Pray present my frat'nal greetings to my brother Robert and my sister Magdalene and give my love to yourself. Your humble servant, Mr Michael Clare.'

It was impossible for the present to convey Michael's fraternal greetings to his brother Robert, for Robin's place at the dinner-table was empty. It was often empty of late, and Hubert, though he thought it unmannerly of his brother to absent himself without notice, had refrained from saying so because Robin had seemed so much happier these last few weeks. He was out all day on mysterious excursions from which he returned looking flushed and excited; there were none of those jibes and grumblings which had made the atmosphere so unpleasant.

The chaplain had said Grace and the meal had begun, when Hubert heard the garden door bang shut and quick footsteps come down the passage. So vivid was the exultation that radiated from Robin as he burst into the room, that the dogs began barking and leaping about him, and Braithwayte, the old butler, forgot to quiet them. Robin said a silent Grace, sketched a perfunctory sign of the Cross, flung himself down in his seat, and exclaimed:

"Prince Charles has landed in Scotland!"

Mr Maribon dropped his knife, which clattered on his plate.

"With seven men," gabbled Robin, waving away a dish the butler was offering him. "I'm too excited to eat. Think of it! Seven men to conquer three kingdoms! He's been planning it for months, but kept it secret because of the spies. They say that even the King his father didn't know where he was or what he was doing before he sailed. But he was right! The clans have risen for him and the heather's afire. God bless him, oh, God bless him!" shouted Robin, snatched up his wine-glass, tossed off its contents, and flung it over his shoulder, where it splintered on the hearth.

"There is nothing in the newspapers," began Hubert slowly; but his brother interrupted with a fiercely contemptuous laugh.

"The newspapers! We never get them till they're weeks old. And there's nothing in them, anyway, because the Government is still hoping against hope that the whole thing's a rumour."

"But you know better?" asked Magdalene, leaning across the table towards her brother. She had idolised Robin since the Stephen Vickery incident.

He tilted back his chair, shook the bright hair out of his eyes, and surveyed his family with a grin.

"Yes, I know better. I've made it my business, ever since I came home, to get the real news. There's a Jacobite club in Newtown of which I'm a member, and we're in touch with other such clubs throughout the kingdom. And today we had word that his Royal Highness landed in Scotland three weeks ago, that practically all the chiefs have raised

43

their clans for him, and that he has called on all loyal Englishmen to fight for their rightful King."

"Oh, how I wish I were a man!" cried Magdalene.

Hubert, mechanically eating pondered the astonishing news; but Mr Maribon shook his head and murmured something about hoping that it was only a rumour. Robin flung round on him.

"You hope it is only a rumour, sir?" he barked. "I don't understand."

The priest glanced up and down again, his hand playing nervously with his napkin.

"Of course, I wish his Royal Highness well, Mr Robin," he said timidly, "and pray for him always, as I'm sure we all do. But such a very rash attempt can only make our state worse, as did his father's failure in '15. You would scarcely believe how many ancient Catholic families apostatised after that disaster – "

"You seem to take it for granted that the Prince will fail," Robin interrupted in high indignation.

"I must confess," sighed Mr Maribon, "that the consequences of his failure concern me more than the very slight chance of his success – for I do think it slight, Mr Robin. The House of Hanover is so firmly seated."

"Charlie and his Highlandmen will kick 'em out!" exulted Robin, bending a rabbit-bone until it snapped.

"The old pernicious calumnies would be revived that all Catholics are traitors," the priest went on, as if talking to himself. "Even the Embassy chapels in London might be closed, and here in the country those who are always awaiting a chance to harry us would seize the excuse to destroy our little missions. And there would be new fines," he went on, glancing at the silent Hubert, "perhaps new legislation against us poor Catholics. Yes, I must confess, Mr Robin, I hope the report of his Royal Highness' landing in such an exceedingly rash manner, without an army, proves unfounded."

Robin snorted, turned his shoulder on the chaplain, and began to pour into the eager ears of his sister the wonderful things he had heard at his club.

(iii)

For some while after this Hubert searched the newspapers, but as they continued to be silent about the 'Young Pretender' as they called him, he concluded that it was a false alarm. He did not know whether to be glad or sorry; undoubtedly a Stuart restoration would bring back the Faith, but, on the other hand, he had been impressed by Mr Maribon's warnings of the result of failure, and agreed with him that an attempt such as Robin had described would be extremely rash.

He heard no more news of the North from Robin himself, who, it seemed, was displeased by his lack of enthusiasm. But that Robin was still obsessed with the matter was plain. He disappeared at all hours to some unspecified appointment, and spent the rest of his time in the company of his sister. They had appropriated to themselves the garden-house, and as Hubert passed he would hear the weird sounds of the bagpipes or two voices chattering excitely; at meals they exchanged looks and secret smiles. It was a kind of game, thought Hubert, and at least it had made Magdalene look less discontented and sullen. As for possible danger, he gave Robin the credit of being sensible enough not to engage in treasonable talk among strangers.

Hubert himself was happier nowadays. Life at Old Park continued to be hard and lonely and frustrating; but he had ceased to kick against it and had accepted it as his vocation. Here as at Douai religion was the framework, giving everything a meaning. And forced into a premature maturity, he was forced also into a deep, sober interior life which was both his refuge and his inspiration.

The outward observances of his religion became precious because he practised them at his peril. Like the early Christians, he had been driven into the catacombs; and whereas at school each small devotional act had been automatic, at Old Park such acts were charged with a deep significance, and he performed them now, not out of obligation but because he wanted to. Each morning he served his chaplain's Mass; each Friday he abstained from meat; on Saturdays, and throughout Lent and Advent, he fasted, eating neither eggs nor cheese. Each evening he knelt in the chapel at the head of his household, making the responses to Night Prayers and the Little Office of Our Lady. Each night on his way to bed he paused at the head of the stair to beg the intercession of Blessed Michael Thorne for those who, while they were not asked to give their lives for the Faith, were called upon to endure with patience a persecution which by its very pettiness and lack of drama tried to the uttermost a man's constancy. Within this framework even his burden of responsibility and his sense of frustration lost their first sting. In his loneliness he had discovered the meaning of the Communion of Saints; from his narrow life he had turned to infinity.

And, above all, he began to understand the privilege handed down to him of having the Blessed Sacrament beneath his roof. Often when he was in the fields, tired with the labours he shared with his men, or when he heard the note of a hunting-horn and the cheerful shouts of the neighbours who shunned him, or when he sat over his accounts with Mr Filton and wondered how he was going to pay his way, there would come to him the thought of that Prisoner of love hanging captive in the pyx above the altar.

And when he slipped into the chapel and knelt there, not praying vocally, not even trying to meditate, but simply looking at the little steady spark in the lamp, and remembered how, through all the centuries, under every form of persecution, his family had kept that spark alight, he felt one with the handful of faithful who had stood at the foot of the Cross.

November had come, the harvest was safely garnered, the autumn brewing was in full swing, the sea mists wrapped the old house in kindly blankets for its winter sleep – when this new fragile peace of his was rudely shattered.

He had been far afield, that dull, damp day, seeing a distant tenant, and riding home under the dripping trees he felt tired and slightly unwell. As he dismounted stiffly in the stable-yard, the butler came hurrying towards him, as though he had been on the watch for his master's return.

"Sir Frederick Lessing has called, sir," said the old man, rather agitated. "When he heard you were out, he said he would wait for you, and since he did not wish anyone else to know he was here, I have put him in the steward's room."

With a faint feeling of apprehension, Hubert hurried into the house; and as soon as he saw his visitor's face he knew that something was very much amiss.

In days gone by, the Thornes and the Lessings had been close friends; both were of ancient lineage, and both had adhered to the old religion through all the years of active persecution. But after the failure of the Jacobite rising in '15 the present Sir Frederick's father, along with numerous other old Catholic families, had conformed to the Establishment in order to save his heirs and estates from ruin, and the former visiting between Old Park and the Hall, the Lessings' country seat, had ceased. The Lessings had flourished as a result of their apostasy; offices had come their way, the sons had found careers open to them, and the daughters had married well.

But the present head of the house of Lessing, a man many years older than Hubert, retained in his heart an affection for the faith of his fathers, and as the principal magistrate of the county made a point of not noticing the absence of the Thornes and their tenants from the parish church on Sundays. Soon after Hubert's homecoming the boy had made the acquaintance of Sir Frederick in the latter's official capacity, for by an Act of George I all Catholics were obliged to register themselves and their estates under pain of forfeiture, in order that a check might be kept upon them and their property. And Hubert had found Sir Frederick kindly and sympathetic; as long as he was discreet, Lessing had told him, and saw that his tenants were equally so, he would have nothing to fear. More than once since then, Sir Frederick had given the boy a friendly hint if he heard that one or other of Hubert's people had been guilty of some trifling indiscretion such as some justice of the peace, less sympathetic than himself, might seize on as an excuse for taking action.

But it was, it transpired, a far graver matter than that of some yokel forgetting himself and getting into an argument about religion over his ale-can which had brought Sir Frederick to Old Park today.

"My dear lad," said Lessing, as soon as the door of the; steward's room was shut, "I am afraid your brother has been behaving unwisely – very unwisely indeed."

"Tell me, sir," said Hubert, sitting down beside him.

"I have heard rumours of this sort of thing before, but would not credit them. Today I have seen for myself what he has been at in Newtown, and rode straight here to warn you. It seems he had been drinking at the White Hart with some friends, and got foxed, I suppose, for what must he do but go into the public street (and on a market-day, too!) and force passers-by to drink a health to – er – the Young Pretender."

"He's but a boy and means no harm," said Hubert quickly.

"He will bring harm upon his family. Feeling runs high in Newtown because of the rumours from the North. Rumours, I call them; but some of them are true, Hubert."

His companion glanced at him sharply, but said nothing.

"The Government is doing its best to stifle the news in order to avoid public panic, but my brother writes me from Court that there is no doubt now that the Young Pretender has beaten Sir John Cope. It is even said he is marching to the Border at the head of his Highland barbarians. Upon my soul, I know not what to believe or to think; only this I know, that if ever you and all those of your religion had need to be discreet, it is now. Give the Government the least provocation and the penal laws will be enforced most rigorously. On the other hand, you have my solemn word that if you stay peaceable and keep your brother and your tenants so, I will do my utmost to protect you."

"I am greatly in your debt, sir, both for the warning and the promise," said Hubert, his voice rather deep. "I shall see that Robin behaves himself in future."

The older man looked at him a moment with compassion and a faint shame. Then he took the boy's hand, pressed it hard, and was gone without another word.

Hubert sat on for a while, staring with steady grey eyes into the fire. Then he rose with a squaring of his shoulders, went straight to the stables, and rode bareback up the drive to the gate on to the lane which led to Newtown. Here he awaited Robin's return, framing little sentences which would sound firm without being smug. He was furiously angry with Robin, and strangely more fond of Robin than ever before in his life.

The gate, repaired and repainted now, creaked as he leaned against it with his rein over his arm. He thought of all the times when they had swung upon it, he and Robin, in their childhood, talking of what they would do when they were men. They had been such close friends; Robin was wild, but Robin was intelligent and good at heart. Surely they could talk as equals now, instead of Hubert having to be the heavy elder brother...

Far down the lane someone was singing at the top of his voice:

> *"The auld Stuarts back again,*
> *The auld Stuarts back again –*
> *Let traitor Whigs do what they will,*
> *The Stuarts will come back again!"*

"Shut your fool mouth!" bawled Hubert, and was appalled by the panic in his own voice.

The singing ceased; only the thud of a horse's hooves and the melancholy dripping of the 'cathedral trees' broke the silence. Hubert's heavy heart sank lower as through the dusk he noticed his brother stumble as he slipped out of the saddle. Robin's voice was slurred as he exclaimed:

"This is an honour! The master of the house comes to the verge of his estates to welcome me."

"Listen, Robin," said his brother, determined not to quarrel. "I've heard what you've been at in Newtown, and had to have a word with you in private. Sir Frederick Lessing – "

"That renegade! So he's been spying on me, has he?"

"There was scarcely need to spy, considering that you advertised your principles to the whole of Newtown on a market-day."

"*I'm* not ashamed of my principles. *I've* always understood that we Thornes subscribed to the motto, 'God and the King'."

Hubert put a friendly hand on his arm.

"Robin, let's talk like men, not children. I too subscribe to the motto, 'God and the King', but in that order. My sympathies are all with the Prince, but religion must come first. By keeping an exact discretion, Catholic life can go on here at Old Park; one act of folly would deprive the whole county of Mass and the Sacraments. As the patron of a struggling mission, whatever my private sympathies I can do no more than pray for the Prince's success."

"You ought to have been a 'divine', you know, like our pious little Michael," sneered Robin. "Pray! Oh yes, that's what half the so-called Jacobites of England are doing, praying, and drinking to the King Over the Water, and that's why he's remained over the water for so long. Prayers and sympathy are cheap – "

"You're drunk," interrupted Hubert, his voice hardening. "I shall talk to you in the morning. Kindly go to your room as soon as we get home, and I'll tell Magda and the servants that you are unwell."

"Untruthfulness? Tut, tut! You'll have to mention that in confession, my saintly brother. But ash matter o'fact I think I'm going to be sick," added Robin, dropping his bitter sarcasm.

He suited the action to the word, and afterwards rode home in a sullen silence which Hubert did not attempt to break.

(iv)

It became clear from their talk on the following morning that Robin was entirely unrepentant and in a state of mind in which it was impossible to make him see reason.

Therefore was Hubert compelled to assert his authority as head of the house, absolutely forbidding his brother to go near Newtown, and extracting a promise to that effect. He had won his point at the cost of his private feelings, and at the price, it seemed, of alienating his family. Robin and Magdalene spoke to him only when common courtesy demanded it, but spoke *at* him continually, making it clear that they regarded him as a disgrace to the name of Thorne and as a hypocrite who used religion as an excuse for sitting still.

He bore it as well as he could, thankful that Robin's drunken folly in Newtown appeared to have been ignored. The authorities, indeed, had something far more serious to occupy them than boys in their cups drinking treasonable healths; the newspapers suddenly became full of the 'Young Pretender', their contemptuous tone ill concealing a general consternation. For the bombshell of Prestonpans, when he and his Highland 'barbarians' had made Sir John Cope and his dragoons take to their heels in ignominious flight, was followed in quick succession by the Prince's neat capture of Edinburgh, his march to the Border, and his summons to Carlisle, which surrendered without a blow.

Of course he would be halted, the newspapers somewhat hysterically impressed upon their readers; the Duke of Cumberland had been recalled from Flanders with his Dutch and Hessian troops, and His Royal Highness could be relied on to deal with this insolent Perkin as he deserved. Robin and his sister devoured these papers in the privacy of the garden-house, through the closed door of which Hubert could hear their gleeful laughter as he passed.

They did not notice, it seemed, the ominous incitement of the old fear of Popery deliberately worked up by the news-writers. But Hubert did; and though every natural instinct in him made him long to share his family's enthusiasm, he realised more than ever that a strict neutrality was his duty. There were caricatures of the Prince leading 'Papal bulls' from whose nostrils issued curses and the fires of Purgatory; or he was depicted as drawn in a coach by horses variously labelled Superstition, Rebellion, and Arbitrary Power, with the Pope as coachman, the Devil as footman, the King of France as postilion, and Liberty being crushed beneath the wheels. The *Penny London Post* appeared with 'No Popery! No Wooden Shoes!' printed in conspicuous characters round its margins. An outbreak of cattle disease solemnly was affirmed to be the work of Papists who had poisoned the pools round the capital, and men were warned against eating 'Popish' beef or butter. A proclamation was issued ordering all Catholics to withdraw ten miles from London, and the City petitioned Parliament to enforce the penal laws.

Hubert was riding past a farmhouse one evening towards the end of November when he heard his brother's voice up-raised in a tone of authority. He checked his horse and listened, an appalling suspicion leaping up in his mind. He remembered now that sometimes lately he had thought he had noticed a new secrecy among his tenants in their man-ner towards himself; more than once a conversation had been broken off abruptly when he came upon them at their work. Yet surely Robin could not be so mad...

On a sudden impulse he dismounted, hitched his rein to a post, and walking forward on tiptoe, peered into the farmyard round an angle of the wall.

The light of a lanthorn, held by a woman, showed him a scene which would have been ludicrous had not its implications been so alarming. A row of sacks stuffed with straw had been suspended from nails on the walls of a byre, and a dozen or so rustics in smocks and clogs, armed with an assortment of scythes, pitch-forks, and sharpened sticks were solemnly attacking these dummies; while Robin, his legs straddled, his young face earnest, presided over the primitive drill.

"You're better than you were a week ago, lads," he encouraged them, "but you *must* advance together. You must rush in a body on the foe, as the Highlanders did at Prestonpans. Pretend these dummies are Johnnie Cope and his dragoons, and *give* it 'em – *give* it 'em! Now, try it again. Present your arms – "

"What's the meaning of this?" demanded Hubert briskly, stepping round the angle of the wall.

Someone gave a sort of yelp of dismay; hands tried to secrete weapons, voices mumbled, cheeks reddened, forelocks were pulled. Only Robin seemed inclined to face it out, but Hubert was not going to have an argument in public.

"Have you finished the milking, Jake?" he asked, forcing himself to appear natural. "That heifer's coughing again; you'll have to bring her in tonight. Tom, I expected that fence mended by this evening, and find it only half done. Please get back to your work, all of you; and you, brother, pray give me your company on our way home."

Without waiting to see his orders obeyed; he turned and walked calmly out of the yard. Fear, anger, pity, all inextricably mixed together, made such havoc in his heart that he dared not trust himself to speak to Robin until he had got control of himself. He waited till he heard Robin ride out of the yard, then cantered ahead down the lane between the glimmering grey trunks of the 'cathedral trees'. Only when the green gate into the park was reached did he rein-in, and when his brother came up with him said evenly:

"Kindly explain."

He had braced himself for defiance, for heavy sarcasm, for plausible excuses. What he found himself faced with was something far harder to bear. It was Robin at his most endearing, the Robin whom not the sternest of schoolmasters had ever been able to resist.

"You can't have heard the news, Hubert, you simply can't! A drummer and his doxy summoned Manchester for the Prince – and took it! His Royal Highness has given Wade the slip; he's marching straight for Derby – but ninety miles from London! – and they're wagering he'll spend Christmas at St James's. Men everywhere are putting on the white cockade, and even those old women of the White Rose Cycle have given orders for their members to rise for him. The miracle has happened, Hubert!" cried the boy, the tears running unashamedly down his face. "The miracle our fathers dreamed of, a Stuart restoration. We can't sit still, we Thornes; religion itself is at stake – "

"I know." There was such controlled agony in those two words that Robin was silenced for a moment. They faced each other, each still in the saddle, through the dusk. "You may call me a poltroon, jeer at me for a pious hypocrite, but I swear to you, Robin, that that is the only thing that concerns me, that I must *allow* to concern me – our religion."

A hand shot out and gripped his arm so fiercely that he winced.

"But don't you *see*? Only a Stuart restoration can bring back the Faith. It's been our only hope for the past fifty years and more, and that hope seemed dead. We've had to depend on the indulgence of renegades like Lessing not to prosecute if they don't see us at church, to put up with the sort of injustice that happened over that mare I bought, to ruin ourselves paying fines and double land-tax, to think ourselves lucky to be left alone to rot. And you can't get it into your thick noddle that the miracle's happened after all, that the Stuarts and the Faith are coming back. Oh, Hubert, don't you *see*?"

"The miracle has not happened – yet."

"I won't believe you are so cold and cautious."

"I'm not cold. I sympathise with all you say, but – "

"No buts." The hand that gripped him shook with passion. "Ride with me, Hubert, ride with me to the Prince! Tonight! Magda, God bless her, has sold the jewels Mama left her for our expenses, and we have enough to reach the Midlands with our following. Oh, we shall be a brave troop! Every able-bodied man on the estate is mad to go – "

"They would be mad to go. But they are not going. I shall ride round my estates tomorrow and forbid any man in my service, or who holds his lands of me, to stir."

"Hubert, listen! Hubert, you must listen! Suppose the Prince fails after all. You heard what old Marrowbones said when I brought the news of his Royal Highness' landing. Catholics will be punished anyway, even those who haven't risen."

"There's a chance that we shan't be if we stay quiet. Lessing has given his word to protect us on that condition."

"You'd accept protection from that apostate, that – "

"I'd accept protection from anyone to keep open our chapel. You might do me the favour of believing that I'm not thinking of my own skin, not even of the ruin of my family, but of my responsibility as the patron of the only mission in the whole county."

The hand dropped from his arm.

"You force me to speak like this, Robin; you force me to sound a prig. You have kept on asking me to listen, but you won't listen to me, you won't even try to see my point of view. So I am compelled to give you orders. I forbid you to meddle with my tenants. Is that clear?"

Silence except for the nostalgic complaining of the green gate.

"Robin, I demand – "

"You *demand*. You have said the word, sir. You are at pains to remind me that you are now the head of the house of Thorne (hitherto noted for its loyalty), and that I am dependent on you for my daily bread. Very well. I give you my oath that I will not 'meddle with your tenants', as you term it. And now, unless you please to make me your prisoner as well as your pensioner, I would be obliged if you would allow me to ride home without further sermons, and eat my supper and go to bed like a good little boy – while our lawful Prince cuts his way through England with his sword, and cares not whether he has a supper to eat or a bed to sleep in."

The melodrama was so pitiful, the voice so tell-tale shrill, the disappointment so deep, the misunderstanding so real, that Hubert could have wept for him like a girl. He said never a word for he could not, as he rode doggedly through the overgrown parkland behind Robin, who provokingly sang the latest Jacobite song.

# Chapter Five

Hubert had invited some of his larger tenants to a hawking party next day. As he mounted in the stableyard he noticed Magdalene, who was not accompanying them, taking what seemed an unnecessarily long farewell of her twin, but he thought little of it, for Magdalene was a sentimental girl and seemed to worship Robin of late. Robin appeared his usual self, though perhaps a trifle heavy-eyed as though he had slept ill. His manner towards Hubert was coldly polite.

The sport was good, and in the exhilaration of it Hubert shook off his cares and became just a boy of seventeen with a fiery little goshawk on his fist and friends about him. When the time came to go home, there was no sign of Robin, but Hubert was not in the least disturbed; doubtless the lad was gossiping with a tenant or had accepted an invitation to supper with some yeoman. It was only when he was sitting down to his own supper at Old Park that Hubert began to feel uneasy. For he noticed that his sister ate nothing and that her eyes were red and swollen.

"Are you not well?" he asked gently. "Is anything the matter?"

"Yes – no – what should be the matter?" mumbled Magdalene. She rose so clumsily that she knocked over a chair; and without so much as an apology ran from the room.

He thought about her as he ate. He had never got to know her very well, and often she irritated him when they were together; she seemed to have absolutely no self-control. Manlike, it did not occur to him that his sister could feel as frustrated by the conditions here as he did himself. And, after all, she had Robin as a companion... Robin. Come to think of it, he did not remember to have seen Robin once during the sport today.

Night prayers were said, and still there was no sign of Robin. Hubert took his chamber candlestick at the foot of the stair, and knelt as usual on the landing to say a prayer before the picture of Blessed Michael Thorne. But as he passed his sister's door he paused, and on an impulse tapped softly, for he had noticed a thread of light beneath it. There was a distinct pause before she called:

"Who is it?"

"It is I, Magda. May I speak to you a moment?"

He heard a bolt withdrawn, and a moment later was confronted with his sister, still fully dressed.

"What is it, Hubert? It is very late," she said, carefully avoiding his eyes.

"It is about Robin," he replied, watching her closely.

He saw her glance quickly over his shoulder as though fearful of being overheard. Then she motioned him to come in, and shut the door behind them. It was plain from the look of the room that she had been indulging in a very emotional time with herself. On her pillow lay an old flannel donkey which he recognised as a childhood treasure of Robin's; a wreath of clumsily fashioned white cockades bedecked a crude likeness of Prince Charles Edward, bought by Robin at Douai; and Robin's own portrait, a miniature in wax of him as a child, had been taken down from the wall and was propped on the ledge of the prie-dieu. It gleamed in the candlelight as though wet with tears.

"Robin has not come home," said Hubert, sounding abrupt because he was touched and at the same time faintly nauseated.

"I know."

He rounded on her.

"What do you mean – you know?"

"I mean that my Robin has gone to join the Prince," she cried, as pitifully defiant now as Robin himself. "Oh, you needn't think you can catch him; he has a whole day's start, for he never was at the hawking. He's done what Papa would have done had he been old enough in '15, what all the Thornes would have done – except you."

He felt suddenly very cold, and scarce knowing what he did walked to the fire and held his hands towards the glowing logs.

"He's gone alone," continued Magdalene dramatically. "You forbade him to take any of *your* tenants or *your* servants, though there was not a man among them but would have followed him to the ends of the earth. And the money I gave him was my own; I have not robbed you, Sir Hubert Thorne."

Words rose in him, and he pressed his fists against his mouth to keep them back. He wanted to remind her that he was her brother and that he as well as Robin had a claim on her affection. He wanted to upbraid her as an equal; he wanted to slap her for her silly dramatising; he wanted to take her in his arms and comfort her as a poor, doting, ignorant girl of sixteen. But he could do none of these things, because he had the reserve of youth and the premature wisdom of a man, because he knew that she and Robin had defeated him, and that whatever happened he must always be alone.

"I see," he said tonelessly at last. "Good night, Magdalene; try to sleep well."

(ii)

A week went by and then even the Whig newspapers lost their contemptuous tone.

For the rumours of that astonishing march from the North had proved sober fact; Prince Charles had passed through Macclesfield unhindered, had neatly evaded ponderous old Marshal Wade, and was on the direct road to Derby and London. A panic-stricken beating for recruits was going on throughout England; special prayers were ordered to be read in all the churches. In London there was a run on the Bank, which saved itself from breaking only by refusing to pay out in any coin but sixpences; the press-gang combed the streets, the shops were shut, the wealthy had fled to their country fastnesses, the Guards were encamped at Finchley, King George had his yachts, laden with his treasures, moored at Tower-quay, preparatory to a flight to his native Hanover. Ministers shut themselves up in their houses, waiting to discover the exact moment for an open transferring of their allegiance from George to James; the *London Courant* actually published a set of verses welcoming the young hero, whose health was drunk openly now in every tavern.

This trimming of sails to the prevailing wind was reflected in a sudden change of front on the part of Hubert's neighbours. The County, who either had looked carefully the other way or had given the stiffest of bows to this young Papist, became friendly overnight. The post-boy's horn sounded often in the lane of the 'cathedral trees', announcing elegant little billets full of compliments. Footmen rode up the weed-grown drive bearing invitations to dine or sup; hats were swept right off and gloved hands waved when Hubert rode into Newtown. He was genuinely puzzled, and applied to Sir Frederick Lessing for an explanation.

"You are too young to be cynical, thank God," grunted Sir Frederick. 'It means, my dear lad, that a Stuart restoration has become a distinct possibility, and that it will be useful to claim friendship with a family whose loyalty to the old religion and régime has never wavered."

At Old Park, even the cautious Mr Maribon became infected with optimism, and asked permission of his patron to pray in the presence of the household for the Prince's success.

"I am sorry, sir, but I cannot allow it. Someone might talk," Hubert replied with an effort.

His chaplain looked hurt. Sir Hubert would scarcely believe, he said, how already there were signs that a Stuart restoration would bring back the Faith. He himself had been summoned by several of the neighbouring gentry (secretly, indeed, and by night, but that was only natural), to reconcile them to the religion they had always, they assured him, cherished in their hearts.

"Why, that is very well, sir," said Hubert. "But we, who have practised it openly, must hold aloof from politics, and trust that his Majesty will understand why, if by the blessing of God he is restored."

He winced inwardly even while he spoke; his warm heart told him he was being a prig and a poltroon, that what he really cared about was keeping Old Park. And from without the pressure was appalling; his sister exulted that at least there would be one Thorne present when his Royal Highness rode into London at the head of his gallant troops. Over the tea-table she hummed Jacobite songs, and in the withdrawing-room she stitched at a gown she was making in readiness for that great day when, for the first time for nearly sixty years, the Thornes would be invited to

Court. The tenants and even the servants looked askance at the young master who had prevented them from taking part in this glorious enterprise. Old Nana went so far as to mumble under her breath some rustic maledictions against the 'enemy in the house'.

He said nothing. His silence and his stubborn look concealed the struggle he knew he must wage alone. He was steeped in traditional loyalty to the Stuarts; he was itching for action, sick and tired of the uphill fight to maintain a decayed estate; he had natural pride and spirit, and he was at war with his own heart. When in his private prayers he begged for the Prince's success, he felt a hypocrite; the portraits of armed ancestors seemed to reproach him; even common sense whispered that he was being merely self-willed, that it was worth a risk, that nothing could be worse than the passive persecution to which Catholics had been subjected for so long.

But when he knelt before the hanging pyx in the chapel, he knew again beyond all doubting where the hard path of duty lay. Had he been a man without dependents it would have been otherwise; as the patron of some two hundred souls, he must preserve discretion till it looked like cowardice. To fight for his rightful King might be, yes, still might be, to deprive the faithful of a whole county of the Presence signified by the little steady spark in the lamp.

On a night in mid-December he was awakened by the sound of bells, and for a moment imagined that he was back at Douai listening to the voice of Cracked Tom. But these bells were distant and mellow, and they seemed to be ringing a peal of joy. He sprang out of bed and flung himself down before his crucifix.

"Oh God," he prayed, "grant it may be the news of our Prince's entering London! And if it is, show me how I must behave myself towards my family and my servants.

63

Because I shall never be able to make them understand how I had to choose between my King and You… "

He started violently as a dull thud sounded against the window-pane. It was a still night, with the snow lying frozen on the ground, but it was not the cold that made him shiver as he paddad barefoot to the casement, opened it, and looked out. A figure was visible beneath, in the act of scooping up another handful of snow, and in the strange white light he recognised his bailiff.

"I will come down," he called softly. "Go to the back door."

At first he was so certain what the news must be that he did not notice the note of panic in the voice of the ordinarily stolid Mr Filton, as the bailiff gabbled broken sentences. He had been to see his sister in Newtown, it seemed, and had got caught in the crowd; he scarcely knew how he had managed to get clear of the town, so thick was the press. They were lighting bonfires and dancing and brawling and forcing everyone to drink and…

"Then the Prince has reached London?" interrupted Hubert; and suddenly his heart seemed to sing like a bird.

The bailiff stared at him a moment, stricken; then he gulped noisily and echoed:

"Reached London, Sir Hubert? No, no! He has turned back from Derby; he and his Highlanders are in full retreat."

There was a kind of high humming note inside Hubert's head and a mist before his eyes. Filton's voice seemed to come from a long way off.

"But they say he will never reach the Border. The Duke of Cumberland is at Lichfield and Wade at Doncaster; there's fifty thousand pounds reward offered for his capture – dead or alive." The man's voice broke grotesquely. "God have mercy on him, and on Mr Robin," he choked, and buried his face in his hands.

64

(iii)

I *tell onlie the sunnie houres*, ran the motto on the sundial in the tangled rose-garden at Old Park.

But there were no sunny hours to tell that winter and spring of 1746; the skies were as heavy as was Hubert's heart. The newspapers screamed denunciation of the 'rebels' now that the Prince's cause was lost, now that it was really safe to come down squarely on one side of the fence and vilify someone who so nearly had attained his goal and become a fêted victor. Whig and Tory news-writers gloated over his coming capture and death, carefully omitted to inform their readers of any trifling successes he achieved on his bitter, fighting retreat, and went into details of the vengeance which would overtake all who had joined him or were suspected of being in his interest.

And of Robin there was no news.

There could not be, Hubert tried to persuade his frantic sister. He was a soldier on active service; he could not write, and he was not important enough for there to be any public report of his fate. She turned on him in savage reproach; with superb feminine unreason, she now blamed Hubert for letting Robin go.

"You sent him to his death," she raged. "You could have stopped him, or at least you could have let him take the tenants. Too cowardly to fight yourself, you prevented my brother from having an escort on his gallant enterprise."

Though such injustice cut him to the heart, he bore with it because she was like a wounded animal that attacks all who try to succour it. It was useless to tell her that he was as much in anguish for news of Robin as she was herself.

Late in April came the final blow; Prince Charles had been utterly defeated on Culloden Moor, and was either dead or a fugitive. Hubert tried to hide from his sister the newspapers with their ghastly details of the vengeance of the man jocularly nicknamed 'Butcher Billy Cumberland', and himself endeavoured not to think of Robin lying, perhaps, among those wounded who had been murdered in cold blood on a bleak Scottish moor.

But Magdalene insisted that Robin would come home, and tormented herself and Hubert by elaborate preparations for the wanderer's return. Robin's clothes were often to be seen airing by the fire; when the chaplain was out of the way, she and Nana would read the cards or the tea-cups, and always there was good news there. Robin's favourite falcon must be exercised every day, ready for its master; a certain kind of sweetmeat, sacred to Robin, was concocted each week in the stillroom, kept till it was stale, thrown away, and a new batch made.

All night long a light must be left burning to guide her dear one home; at the hour when the post-boy rode by in the lane, Magdalene was always at the gate; and when there was no letter, why surely there would be one tomorrow. Perpetually she had an air of listening; she would break off a conversation and sharply turn her head as though certain she had heard the sound she longed to hear; often she would be seen poring over recipes for glisters and balms, for her dear Robin, she was sure, must have received some wounds of honour. Either it was all an instinctive escapism to save her reason, or else it was Magdalene's innate love of dramatising a situation, a sort of hideous game.

In May, on his eighteenth birthday, Hubert received a bitter gift in the shape of a justification of his own fruitless efforts to prevent a provoking of the authorities by taking sides in the late rising.

Mr Maribon was called away from the dinner-table, and did not return. Hubert supposed it was a sick-call, and was going to the stables afterwards to ride out on some business connected with the estate, when to his surprise the chaplain met him in the yard, holding a paper in a hand which trembled violently.

"I have been waiting for you, Sir Hubert," quavered the old man. "I must see you in private, sir, and immediately, if you please."

They went in silence to the priest's room, and there, without a word, Mr Maribon gave him the paper, which proved to be a letter written in a clerkly hand.

'To Mr Joseph Maribon. In pursuance of an Order and Resolution of the Parishioners of the Parish of St Cuthbert's in the County of Southshire, made and taken at a Vestry held in and for the said Parish on Friday, the fourteenth day of this present May, 1746, I hereby give you notice that unless you do remove and depart from the said Parish of St Cuthbert's and the neighbourhood thereof within one Calendar Month from the date hereof, and if you afterwards return there again, the Parishioners will prosecute, and put the laws concerning Popery in execution against you without further notice. Miles Manning, Solicitor for the Parish of St Cuthbert's.'

"I know who is at the bottom of this," whimpered the old priest. "That fanatic joiner, Saunders. Ever since he was elected to the parish council he has sworn he will get the laws enforced against us, and now, because the whole neighbourhood knows that Mr Robin went to join the Prince, he has seen his chance."

Mr Maribon sank on to a chair, rocking himself to and fro. He looked like a lost child.

"And what is to become of me if I am turned out? I have lived here all my life; and I have no kith and kin. I shall starve, Sir Hubert; I shall be forced to beg."

Hubert comforted him as well as he could; and rode straight over to the Hall, where he asked to see Sir Frederick Lessing.

"Ay, I was afraid of this," said the magistrate, when he had read the letter. "Saunders has been bragging everywhere of late how he would burn out that wasps' nest of Popery and treason, as he is pleased to call Old Park. And, my dear boy, I can do nothing; he has won over the parish council and is within his rights. And I must warn you, Hubert, that not content with this he is endeavouring to get an order served on you to close the chapel."

"And if I ignore it, sir?"

Lessing lifted his shoulders.

"You know the penalty. They would fling you into jail. In the present state of affairs, they might even proceed to extremities and confiscate your estates. Feeling is running very high against Catholics since the rebellion; I hear from London that even the Embassy chapels are closed (though they will have to allow them to open again presently because of diplomatic rights), and that the prisons are full of those of your faith."

"They may do what they please," said Hubert, staring into an untasted glass of Sir Frederick's fine sherry, "but I shall not close my chapel."

The older man clapped a hand on his shoulder.

"You shall not, if I can prevent it. I gave you my word I would protect you, and so I will, though there's little enough I can do. Your brother's folly was no fault of yours, and I'll not stomach your being persecuted by a fanatical rogue on such an excuse. But the priest must go, Hubert;

you cannot, I think, expose him to the risk of life imprisonment."

"No, I cannot," said the boy drearily. "He must go."

"And Saunders must rest content with that. After all, no priest, no Mass."

(iv)

No priest, no Mass.

Those words repeated themselves in Hubert's mind as he served Mr Maribon on the chaplain's last morning at Old Park. That was the price of Robin's romantic gesture; for the first time in all the long history of this house, the Sanctuary lamp must be extinguished. He knew that from the Reformation onwards it had been the policy to deprive the faithful of their central act of worship, the Mass; if that were taken away from them, only the most heroic would stand fast. His chapel would not be closed; the exertions of Sir Frederick on his behalf had been successful; but the priest must go, and with him must go also the sacramental Presence in the hanging pyx·

Hubert had found a refuge for his chaplain with some of his late mother's relations, the Darells of Kent, and when he had taken his farewell to the old man and seen him start on his long journey, he rode round his tenants, explaining the situation and begging their co-operation.

"I ask you to continue to come to Old Park on Sundays and holy-days," he said earnestly, "and say your prayers with the family. We have this blessing at least, that we may keep our chapel open, and it will be easier for us all to pray together in a consecrated place."

They promised readily enough. They were indignant at losing their priest; one or two expressed gratitude to Hubert for his wisdom in keeping them at home during the late rising, for if he had not done so the chapel might have been closed and the images confiscated. For a little while they kept their promise. But then he began to notice a thinning of the congregation, a lessening of the voices that answered the Rosaries and the other ancient prayers he led.

"It's a fairish long walk, Sir Hubert, specially in foul weather," the delinquents excused themselves, "when there's no Mass at the end of it."

He could not blame them, but his heart was sick. The old were dying without the Last Sacraments, the newly born could not be baptised, the young men and women were marrying Protestants without requiring the promise of the Protestant partner that their sons should be brought up in the Faith; some began to go to the parish church on Sundays, others gave up any practice of religion. In another generation what had happened in so many districts would happen here – the Faith would die out altogether. And he, who had seen his *raison d'être* as the tending of that flower of honour here in his own county, was helpless.

He began to feel desperate. The interior peace he had found was shattered; it was not yet of so hardy a growth that it could sustain him when all else was gone. Horrible thoughts haunted him. After all, was he not being as romantic a fool as Robin? was he not clinging to an impossible ideal? He had done his best; he had prayed, but the heavens were as brass. He was young and his life was still before him; older and wiser men than he, men like Sir Frederick Lessing, went to their parish church on Sundays and believed in the same God and lived decent, upright lives. What was the use of enduring the penalties of being a Catholic when he could not live as a Catholic? Surely God would understand...

But he could not overcome his own integrity, and he was too fundamentally honest to deceive himself. His will resisted all the specious arguments, though it was beginning to be at the cost of his health. Lines appeared on the young forehead; there was a look in the eyes which ought not to have been there at eighteen; and for the first time in his life he experienced the tortures of insomnia.

One night in July, after hearing the clock strike one, he put on his bedgown and went downstairs to fetch a book. He was not a great reader, but he was desperate now for contact with another mind. Some impulse made him turn to the shelf where his mother had kept her favourite volumes, and his interest was caught by the fact that nearly all were by the same author, who, for discretion's sake, appeared only under his initials, 'R C'. There was *Think Well On't,* a little collection of meditations; *The Garden of the Soul,* which combined the devotions in the old Manual and Primer with a miniature treatise on the spiritual life; *Memoirs of Missionary Priests,* a complete account of the English martyrs; various controversial tracts; and a large volume, new and with the pages still uncut, *Britannia Sancta*, containing short biographies of nearly four hundred English saints.

'R C', Richard Challoner, the spiritual father to whom the Catholics of ten counties automatically turned in trouble of soul and in material difficulties, the man who, since his return to England as a missionary priest sixteen years previously, had dedicated himself to the multifarious needs of his flock, and who, since the Vicar Apostolic was old and past his work, was the real head of the London District.

At Douai, Hubert had heard much of Dr Challoner. There were some who had found him rather dull and cold when he had been Professor of Theology and later Vice-President there; but even these had spoken of him with reverence, and others had regarded him as a saint. In Hubert's first year there had been almost a quarrel between

71

the College and Bishop Petre, because the former had nominated Challoner as President on the death of Dr Witham, and the latter had threatened to lay down his post of Vicar Apostolic unless he could have Dr Challoner as his Coadjutor. The Bishop had won, and henceforth had lived quietly at his ancestral seat in Essex, leaving all the administrative work to the younger man.

One of Dr Challoner's first cares had been to make a Visitation of his enormous district; and when Hubert had come home from Douai his tenants were still talking of that great event. A bishop had visited them (for Dr Challoner had been consecrated Bishop of Debra), coming all the way from London, riding along the miry ways with but one servant behind him, calling on cottagers and treating them not only kindly but with a sort of respect. Real English, they had found him (a high compliment), and so clever; he'd written a book about the martyrs, and Blessed Michael Thorne was in it. He had given Confirmation in the chapel at Old Park, and then put on his secular clothes again and ridden off to the next county; but not before he had had an encounter with the Vicar.

"Vicar knew who he was, it seems," one farmer had told Hubert, chuckling at the memory. "Met by chance one day when Vicar was out a-hunting, and he pulls in his horse on purpose to say some hard things against the Faith. You wouldn't believe the change in my Lord Bishop! So mild, he seemed ordinarily, and so humble, but now his eyes light up, and he says a thing or two which made Vicar feel he'd caught a tartar."

This, then, was Dr Challoner, the son of a Dissenting wine-cooper, a man whose whole life was dedicated to steering the storm-tossed remnant of the faithful in England through these miserable waters. At Douai, both as schoolboy and professor, he had subscribed sincerely to the Jacobite sympathies of the College; but during the late rising he had used all his exertions, according to Mr Maribon, to prevent the English Catholics from joining the Prince; while at present, at his post in London, he was the universal refuge of those who had fallen under suspicion. Surely, then, he was the very man to advise a troubled boy of eighteen who was at the end of his tether and who had no one in whom to confide?

On the following morning Hubert announced to his sister that he was going to London to see Dr Challoner who, if news of Robin was to be had, was the one to obtain it, since he was in touch with the Vicars Apostolic of Scotland and the Northern District. So after an exhaustive conference with his bailiff, who must be in charge of the estate during his absence, Hubert took the stagecoach to London, that huge, unknown place, to consult Dr Richard Challoner.

And, though he did not know it, to meet his future wife, Miss Barbara Masson.

# Chapter Six

## (i)

Hubert arrived in London on a Saturday towards the end of July, and engaged a room at the Six Cans and Punchbowl in Holborn. Here he would be within a few minutes' walk of Dr Challoner's abode; since his appointment as Coadjutor, Challoner had lodged with a Mrs Hanne, first in Devonshire Street and now in Lamb's Conduit Street, for by being a mere lodger he avoided a summons to sit on a jury or to fill some parochial office.

In reply to Hubert's letter requesting a consultation with him, the Bishop had sent the most detailed instructions as to how the young man was to behave himself in this dangerous town. He was never on any account to leave his room or display in public a rosary, a holy medal, or a Catholic book. If in conversation with other Catholics he wished to speak of the Pope he must refer to His Holiness as 'Mr Abraham', and if he mentioned Rome it must be as 'Mother Hilton'. He was to adopt his Douai alias of Clare; he must ask for the Bishop as 'Mr Fisher'; he must avoid as far as possible all converse with strangers, since the town was infested with spies and informers waiting to trap the unwary into indiscreet speech.

On Sundays he might assist at Mass at any of the Embassy chapels save the French, which was closed on account of the war; and here he might appear openly. But since the Embassy chapels theoretically were only for foreigners and sermons in English prohibited there, if he wished to hear a sermon he must go to a small tavern called the Ship in Little Turnstile and give a certain password to the man at the door.

Since his homecoming Hubert had grown used to the elaborate precautions necessary for the practice of his religion; but even so it was rather a shock, when he was admitted to the Ship's garret, to find everyone seated with a beer-mug before him. This, he rightly supposed, was to give the appearance of a convivial gathering in case of a raid. A powerful Irishman armed with a cudgel stood sentinel at the door, allowing no one to enter without the password; and as soon as the Bishop arrived the door was locked on the inside.

Though he had heard so much of Bishop Challoner, this was the first time Hubert had seen him, and he was surprised by what he saw. He had expected someone austere and formal; but the word that came instantly to his mind as he looked at the man who sat at the head of the table, with a Bible and a beer-mug in incongruous association on the board before him, was 'sweetness'. An irregular nose, rising slightly at the tip, gave humour to a face which was a veritable map of fine wrinkles, and there was something faintly puckish about the whole expression. It was not the face of a fighter, and yet there was strength there; it might well be, thought Hubert, observing the tranquillity and gentleness which underlay the keenness of the eyes, the face of a saint.

It was Dr Challoner's habit to preach for an hour, and although he said nothing new or startling and used no fine phrases, he infused the warmth of his devotion into every word. Yet Hubert was at an age and in a state of mind when not even the most inspired sermon could have kept his thoughts from wandering. First he began surreptitiously to observe the congregation, and then found his attention concentrated upon a young girl who sat facing him across the table.

Loneliness has this great quality: it makes the sufferer sensitive to those similarly afflicted. And as soon as ever Hubert Thorne became aware of this girl, he knew, without knowing how he knew, that she was as desperately lonely as he was himself. Yet there was nothing, except perhaps an unconscious sadness in her eyes, to tell him this. He judged her to be about his own age; she was very neatly but unmodishly dressed, with an undefinable air of good breeding about her, and that kind of attractiveness which so often is more pleasing that classical beauty. Her expression was serious, yet he knew instantly it would be easy to make her laugh. She had brown curls under a little gypsy hat that was tied under a firm chin, and her eyes were set unusually wide apart.

There was something else he observed about her, and that was when, the sermon over, the congregation was stealing out of the garret in the usual furtive manner of such illegal gatherings. He saw her glance shyly at the faces round her, and a tentative smile lift her lips. But there was no answering smile on any of those faces; instead, there was a quite obvious appearance of wanting to avoid her. So she went away; and Hubert, who had been meaning to approach Dr Challoner and introduce himself, followed her, simply and unashamedly followed her, down Gate Street, past a low archway which gave on to the Sardinian Embassy, and through a wicket gate into the public garden which had been laid out some years previously in Lincoln's Inn Fields.

The girl with the brown hair walked purposefully as to some appointment; but when she reached the centre of the garden, where there was a fountain, she appeared to have reached her goal, and sat down on an empty bench. Hubert, who had been following a few yards behind, was left with the alternative of walking on or of boldly and unconventionally accosting her. To his infinite astonishment he unhesitatingly chose the latter. He lifted his hat, blushed violently, and said:

"I beg your pardon, madam. I saw you at the preaching."

She half rose, gave him a blank look, and murmured:

"Oh?"

"It is most unmannerly of me to accost you," hurriedly went on Hubert. "But the fact is, I'm a stranger in London, and you being of my own religion, I – I mean, well, I hope you won't take it amiss," he ended feebly.

To his dismay the girl fished out a handkerchief and began to scrub at her eyes with a sort of anger.

"I'm so sorry," she mumbled. "I hate self-pity, I hate it like the – like the devil. There!" She glanced at him, and grinned at him, and screwed the handkerchief into a ball. "If only they would stop suspecting me of being a spy!"

"A spy?" He was so bewildered that, without asking her permission, he sat down plump on the bench beside her.

"Because I'm a convert. It's natural, of course, that they should be wary of me; it's a closed society, isn't it? A sort of club. They all know each other and they don't know me, and it's only two months since I was received; and they've been persecuted for so long that they keep together and suspect every stranger. Oh, I do understand how natural it is," she added doggedly, as if trying to convince herself.

He said nothing, trying to assimilate the fact that this obviously intelligent, well-bred girl was a convert to his religion. He did not know there were such people nowadays, except very rarely from among the lower orders. One heard constantly of apostasies and lapsings; occasionally of a man who, having conformed in order to avoid ruin or to get some office, was reconciled on his death-bed. He knew that since the beginning of the century the number of Catholics had dwindled, gradually but steadily, until there were now no more than sixty thousand in the whole of England. And here was this young girl...

"How blue the sky is!" she exclaimed, with a complete change of tone. "So blue it makes you thirsty. Oh lord! that sounds like a hint for you to offer me some refreshment. But it isn't, really it isn't." And she went off into the most infectious of giggles.

"I do beg your pardon again," said Hubert, feeling slightly unreal. "I ought to have introduced myself after forcing my company on you. The name I go by in London is Clare, but it's really Thorne, Sir Hubert Thorne, and I live near Newtown in Southshire. I've come up to see Dr – I mean Mr Fisher, and to try to get news of my brother who is – lost."

She said, with quick, genuine sympathy, that she was sorry he was here on so sad an errand, refrained from asking for details, and very simply and naturally told him that her name was Barbara Masson, that her father kept livery-stables in Southwark, and that she was a governess.

"It's my free day, and I always spend it here if it's fine, because this garden reminds me of home. And I always sit on this particular bench if it's empty, so that I can watch the fountain and listen to its lovely cool sound. My parents live on the Kent Road, just on the boundary of Southwark and Camberwell, and a little stream runs across the turnpike there, called Thomas-a-Watering. I love running water."

'But don't you ever go home?" asked Hubert, curiosity again overcoming his good manners.

She seemed surprised.

"Well, I can't, not since I was received. My father's a Methodist and he thinks I'm damned, and in any case what I've done is illegal. But sometimes, my mother meets me at a coffee-house, though that's rather awkward for her. You see she's told all her friends that I've gone to stay with one of my married sisters at Weymouth, so she's always afraid of being seen with me in town. Poor mother! She thinks of me as though I'm suffering from some low disease, like – like ringworm, and to her it's vital that her genteel friends shouldn't find out."

He was silent again, trying to imagine her astonishing situation. It was an astonishing conversation too; here was he, so strictly schooled in the correct deportment of a gentleman, first of all following an unknown girl to a secluded spot, then forcing his acquaintance on her, and lastly prying into her most personal secrets. But although she, too, was obviously well-bred (for all her father kept livery-stables), she did not appear in the least embarrassed or displeased.

"And you are a governess," he murmured at length.

"Well, that's a polite name for servant really," said Barbara, with that schoolgirl giggle of hers. "This Mrs Humphreys, my employer, needed someone to teach her children their hornbook, and to supervise the domestic staff – that's what she said, only when I came I found there wasn't any domestic staff. But please don't think I'm complaining; I find it all rather diverting really, and I don't in the least mind hard work, and I have to earn my living. Only I *do* wish," added Barbara with a sudden sharp sigh, "that she wouldn't keep hinting that I may have insinuated myself into her household only to be able to inform against her for practising her religion."

He felt he hated the unknown Mrs Humphreys. He said, blushing at the stilted words and at his own boldness:

"You must have been very strongly attracted to the Faith, Miss Masson, to have sacrificed so much to embrace it."

He received a shock. Barbara said, immediately and simply:

"I wasn't at all attracted to it, and I still rather dislike it."

"You – you *dislike* it?"

" 'Prayers' are so strange, so unlike Morning Prayer at St George the Martyr's, where I used to go with Mama. And I can't understand the Latin, and people are always making the sign of the Cross and bobbing down at unexpected moments and jingling beads and kissing holy medals, and they all look so hang-dog, which is natural, of course, because they're doing something illegal. But I expect I shall get used to it, and, anyway, Mr Fisher has explained to me that the feelings don't matter, only the will."

"'Tachment," murmured Hubert.

"I beg your pardon?"

He laughed.

"I'm sorry. What you said then reminded me of my youngest brother, Michael, who's still at school. He was great on what he called 'tachment. But why did you – I mean, if you really dislike it... ?"

"Oh, it's so obviously, so rather dreadfully, true, isn't it?" said Barbara impassively.

Hubert's silence this time was very profound indeed. He was roused by the bells of St Clement Dane's playing the pretty nursery tune of 'Oranges and Lemons', and became shy and boyish again.

"It's dinner-time in the country," said he, "though here in town they seem to eat at a much later hour. But I'm hungry."

"Then you must go home, sir, and dine."

"Home? A strange inn where everyone stares at you unless you can afford a private room, which I can't. And you, Miss Masson? May I be permitted to ask where you dine on your – your free day?"

"Here," she answered, smiling delightfully and looking about fourteen. "See the sparrows! I declare they know it's noon. We have dinner together, the sparrows and I." And she laid her hand on a small covered basket on the bench at her side.

Suddenly their eyes met, honest, lonely, young eyes.

"But they are heretic sparrows;" said Barbara, wrinkling up her nose at them, "and for you and me it's Sunday and a feast day. So if you don't mind just bread and cheese and milk, they shall fast for once."

(ii)

But it was not just for the once. The sparrows went on short rations many times after that first meeting.

For the past two years Hubert had had no intimate friend; in all his problems and troubles he had been starkly alone. Nor had he ever known feminine sympathy. And now, in the most unconventional circumstances, he had met this girl who not only was of his own faith but had suffered bitterly for her courage in embracing it. This alone would have made him eager to pursue the acquaintance, but there was much more to it than that. For as he got to know Barbara Masson, he discovered that she was a very exceptional person.

She was a fascinating mixture. She had an independent mind, a strong sense of justice, and a conception of honour such as he had always believed to be exclusive to his own sex. On the other hand, she was intensely feminine in her compassion and quick sympathy, while possessing the gift of regarding with detachment those she loved or disliked, and she could always laugh at herself. One moment she was giggling like a schoolgirl, the next she was displaying the shrewdness of maturity. Above all, she was absolutely natural and candid.

As he began to fill in the picture of her background, he was shamed by her cheerful acceptance of the sacrifices she had made, and amazed by her large tolerance and understanding of her parents' treatment of her. She described it as 'natural' – her favourite word. For some while he hesitated to ask her, though he was burning to do so, what had made her become a Catholic; but when at last he did, she answered with perfect frankness and composure.

"I was poking round the book-shops near St Paul's one day when I went into the City for my music-lesson, and I happened to begin reading a little book. It was called *The Grounds of the Old Religion –* "

"Why, that's by Mr Fisher."

"Yes; I know that now, but it was published anonymously and I'd never heard of him then. It sort of hit me between the eyes. The wrangles about religion at home had given me a distaste for all set forms, and I'm afraid I felt dreadfully superior to my parents. I believed in God as much as I believed in the sun; but He was just a comfortable Presence who didn't make any demands."

She grinned ruefully.

"This little book suddenly made Him appear as Somebody who had to be searched for, who had revealed the way He wished to be worshipped, and who was very demanding indeed. And the arguments in the book seemed unanswerable. Of course I knew there must be counter-arguments and I found plenty of books which gave them, but though I wanted to be convinced, because I didn't want impossible demands made on me and to have to leave home, as I knew I would have to do if I became a you-know-what, I found them singularly unconvincing. So at last I felt I couldn't live myself until I'd investigated the forbidden thing at first-hand."

"What did you do?" asked Hubert, deeply interested.

"Oh, I remembered hearing Papa raging against the existence of the Embassy chapels where what he called the 'Popish abominations' were practised openly; so one day I went to the Sardinian chapel over there in Duke Street and asked to see one of the chaplains. He spoke hardly any English, and he looked exactly like a woodcut in a Protestant tract. And he was *most* suspicious of me. But, anyway, in the end he consented to instruct me, and one day I was received into the Church in that little garret at the Ship where Mr Fisher preaches."

"And what did your parents say?"

"My mother blamed my father first. My mother married beneath her, and she's never forgiven Papa for it, and then he went and joined the Methodists and became a lay-preacher, and he used to make me go with him on Sunday evenings to a rather nasty little meeting-house in the Borough High Street. So she said he'd infected me with that vulgar thing, enthusiasm, which according to the Church of England is either dangerously fanatical or distressingly ungenteel. And then she told me she thought a change of scene and some sea-air might help; and would I go to my sister's at Weymouth."

"But why – "

"I told you she seemed to think I was suffering from some unmentionable disease, and she was terrified in case the neighbours got to hear of it. But of course my father didn't talk about Weymouth; he talked about the Beast and the Whore of Babylon and cunning Jesuits and Bloody Mary, and in the end he told me not to darken his doors again."

"How – how absolutely cruel of him!" Hubert exclaimed indignantly.

"It wasn't really. You don't understand. Apart from the fact that I was breaking the law, he truly believes that all Papists are damned. He's a very sincere man. He got converted by Mr Wesley at a field-preaching at nine minutes past noon on Tuesday, August 10th, 1743, and ever since then he's believed that only the Methodists are the Elect. I've always been fond of him, but I can't help remembering how much nicer he was before it happened; and it was so embarrassing having to listen to him at that meeting-house, telling the congregation about his lurid past, which I'm sure didn't exist, and everyone crying and groaning and going off into faints."

Hubert tried to picture the scene, but his imagination boggled at it.

"I don't mean to be uncharitable," went on Barbara, "and I do see that Methodism happened because the Church of England has completely lost touch with the people. When my father met Mr Wesley, I think it was the first time he ever felt that someone really cared whether he saved his soul, and told him, in language he could understand, how to do it. Mr Wesley's an autocrat, but ordinary people like despots provided they're sincere and benevolent. And Papa got that wonderful feeling of belonging; at the Class Meetings he could exchange accounts of his spiritual progress with folk who had the same experiences, and at the services at Moorfields he learnt the comfort of bawling out catchy hymns to a marching tune, with the whole congregation roaring them out around him. The Church of England doesn't approve of hymns; they're ungenteel."

"It's just emotionalism," objected Hubert. "A kind of drug."

"Of course it is," tranquilly agreed Barbara. "But unless you have the good fortune to be given the grace of – well, you know what I mean – you need a drug, especially if you live here in London. You've no conception how rotten the whole structure of society has become. I know that sounds priggish, but it's true. The upper classes are a mixture of womanishness and brutality, and the common people ape their manners, especially their resort to violence on the slightest provocation. Every newspaper you read is full of poisonous scandal; at the playhouse everyone in the public eye is ridiculed, cruelly and grossly, under fancy names which are perfectly understood by the audience. Even the King is lampooned. There isn't any self-respect or respect for others; it's *démodé* to believe in anyone or anything. And so honest men like my father turn to Methodism and the common folk forget their wretchedness in gin."

Her face was flushed and her talk had become rapid and indignant. Then suddenly she turned into the schoolgirl again, giggled, and touched his sleeve.

"Oh, do look at that beau! Oh no, I forgot, they call them fribbles now. It's as good as going to the playhouse to sit here."

The gentleman she indicated was mincing slowly along a walk nearby, tipped forward by the height of his scarlet heels. His coat-skirts were so stiffened out with whale-bone that they resembled a hoop, and even from this distance they could smell the little cloud of eau-de-luce in which he was enveloped. He was playing with the pantin, a puppet of pasteboard strung together so that by each touch of his finger it was thrown into some grotesque or indecent attitude.

"You oughtn't to come here alone, Miss Masson," Hubert exclaimed, alarmed, disgusted, and experiencing for the first time a prick of something he did not recognise as jealousy.

"Oh, I'm quite safe, I assure you," laughed Barbara. "These fribbles are far too busy admiring themselves to molest a dull girl like me. But he can be dangerous. A passer-by happened inadvertently to jog his elbow the other afternoon so that his precious toy's antics were interrupted, and our fribble had his sword out in a trice. I tell you, they're women half the time and savages t'other half."

"I don't believe you're afraid of anyone," said Hubert slowly.

She said nothing for a moment, and glancing at her he saw that her face had grown serious.

"Not of *anyone*, perhaps," said Barbara "but of individuals when they become a mob. When I was a child, my father's stables were burnt down by a mob (thank God all the horses were saved), and the frightening thing was there wasn't any reason for it. It was just wanton destruction by a gang of roughs who had been spending the evening in a Geneva-shop. Gin makes men mad; and yet because so many people in London live in such squalor and insecurity, and haven't anything or anyone to believe in, they pawn everything they possess for gin."

(iii)

There was another person besides Barbara who made Hubert glad he had come to London: Dr Richard Challoner.

It was not that the Bishop was able to give him much practical help. In regard to Robin, he could but send a description of the missing boy to his colleagues in Scotland and the Northern District, begging them to make enquiries. And as for the taking away of Hubert's chaplain, while he grieved deeply that a whole countryside had been deprived of Mass and the Sacraments, he could not, he said, supply a priest to take Mr Maribon's place.

"It would not be safe, for one thing, Sir Hubert," said the Bishop, "at least until this wave of persecution, consequent upon the late unforeseen rising, has died down. And for another, there are less than sixty priests to serve the whole of the London District. Nowadays there is a lamentable reluctance among the young men in our Colleges abroad to go upon the English Mission, and some who are sent to us quickly become infected with the spirit of moral depravity they find here. There is more than one I have known who, rebuked for his loose living, has turned informer, and of that miserable breed of men your apostate priest is the most to be feared; for he knows all our secrets."

Such talk might have been calculated to deepen Hubert's depression to the point of despair had it not been for the effect upon him of the Bishop's character. Though his queer apathy about worldly affairs gave a first impression of coldness, his absolute dedication, his devotion to his people, and his quiet reliance upon the Divine, became an inspiration to Hubert during their talks, and a rock on which the boy found himself resting amid the storms of his problems.

Though unworldly in one sense, Dr Challoner, he found, was eminently practical when it came to the needs of his flock, undertaking all his arduous duties, both literary and administrative, to supply the want of the moment. In his plain, bare room at Mrs Hanne's he was always to be found surrounded by books and papers, busily scratching away with his quill, but laying it down instantly to receive a caller. Once he rebuked Hubert quite sharply when the boy, having complimented him on the success of his published works, added something about his elegance of style, thinking to please him.

"I hope my style is not elegant, Sir Hubert, and, thank God, I know it is not," said the Bishop. "I write for the simple, who do not want elegance but plain instruction."

He was now engaged, he told Hubert, on no less a task than a revising of the Douai version of the Scriptures.

"It needs," he said, smiling, "a committee of Catholic scholars, but since this is impossible I feel I must undertake it, though I have no Hebrew. It will not be the best, but the best I can do in the face of so crying a need; and as for my having no gift for writing noble English, why, the beauty of the king's daughter was from within, you remember. I would have the Sacred Scriptures within the reach of all, so long as they are properly annotated; but what simple soul can understand such phrases as" – he reached for the Bible lying on his desk and turned the pages – "as this, for example: 'And beneficence and communication do not forget, for with such hostes God is promerited'? Our worthy translators of the sixteenth century were so scrupulous in their faithful following of the Vulgate, that they even invented Latinisms if they could not find a word equivalent in English."

One evening when Hubert called on the Bishop he found him unusually idle. The day had been chilly and Mrs Hanne had lit a fire in her lodger's room, but Dr Challoner had forgotten to make it up, and it had sunk to a heap of dull ashes. He greeted Hubert with his customary kindness, but seemed a little abstracted. After a while he gave a small sigh, and said:

"I have heard some very sad news today, Sir Hubert. The Gascoignes of Hampshire, one of the most ancient and hitherto most staunch of our Catholic families, have conformed, and are to be rewarded with a peerage. God forbid that I should judge them, but such families are the mainstay of the Faith in England, and whole districts are lost when one apostatises."

He turned to Hubert and laid a hand upon his knee.

"I know that the pressure upon you and your like, my dear son, to violate your conscience in order to avoid ruining yourselves altogether is well-nigh irresistible. Sad examples are all around you of those who, by an exterior conforming, have rid themselves of the dreadful frustration to which the constant are subjected, and have enriched themselves to boot. It is a time for heroic virtues. In the past our enemies made war upon us with the rack, the noose, the disembowelling hook. It was hard to die by such cruel means; yet I know not whether to live as outcasts, to stand fast under ridicule and calumny, is any easier."

Then he smiled in a way that was almost mischievous as he added:

"They hope to make us die a natural death. They forget that the Faith is supernatural."

There was a long silence. It seemed to Hubert that in this poor room, inhabited by a shabby, middle-aged man who was so powerless and so lacking in the ordinary qualities of leadership, the supernatural was indeed very near. After a while, Dr Challoner took up the poker and began to stir the grey ashes on the hearth.

"See," he said with his puckish smile, "it is not quite out. There is still a live ember in the ashes. And so it is with the Faith in England; that fire will never lack its glowing ember."

### (iv)

By the end of a few weeks the simple faith of Dr Challoner and the friendship of Barbara Masson had so fortified Hubert that he had become again the steadfast and spirited young man he was by nature. But he could not linger in town indefinitely; he was needed at Old Park. If there was news to be had of Robin, Dr Challoner had promised to send it to him there, though both the Bishop and Hubert himself were certain by this time that the boy was dead.

There came a day when Hubert walked up Holborn towards the garden in Lincoln's Inn Fields for the last time. The sky was overcast, with a threat of rain, and his heart matched it. The Catholic associations in which this district was so rich depressed rather than consoled him this morning; here St Hugh of Lincoln had died; the Angelic

89

Doctor had trod its stones on his one visit to London; up this ill-paved street had been jolted on their hurdles the long procession of martyrs whose names and histories Dr Challoner so assiduously had rescued from oblivion. And now that glorious company was represented by a saintly, ageing man lodging under an alias in a poor house, by a handful of priests, good and bad, and here and there, in little pockets, by a few folk who heard Mass behind locked doors and listened to the Word of God while they pretended to drink beer.

But he knew that his depression this morning had its root, not in the fallen state of his religion, but in a personal matter. He was just a boy of eighteen who had formed a friendship with a girl of his own age and now must say goodbye to her.

Even though he dreaded this last meeting, he dreaded even more not finding her here today. But there she was, sitting on her usual bench by the fountain, watching the wind blow the silvery mist of water this way and that; and before she saw him, he stopped for a moment to look at her when she thought herself unobserved.

If you had asked him to describe Barbara, he would have launched into an enthusiastic account of her comradeship and her courage, her intelligence and her sense of humour. She was the complete antithesis of his sister, the only other girl he had known; Magdalene dramatised everything and everybody; Barbara saw them as they were and accepted them. It had never occurred to him to pay Barbara compliments or to rehearse the sort of pretty speeches which, so he read in books, young ladies seemed to expect. He had talked to her exactly as he had talked to his school friends at Douai.

But as he stood here in the garden now, looking at her, as he thought, for the last time, he realised with a kind of shock that Barbara, for all her masculine mind and her camaraderie, was a woman, a pretty woman, a woman who surely must have admirers.

This last thought made him jib interiorly like a shying horse; yet he forced himself to look at Barbara under this new aspect. And though, even now, he could not have told you whether she was short or tall, or the colour of her eyes, something in his heart trembled on the brink of revelation. Before he had more than glimpsed it, she turned her head, and saw him; and her smile made him actually glance up at the sky, thinking the sun had broken through.

"I was afraid you might not be here today," he said, after making her the courtly bow he had learned at Douai, "for it is going to rain, I think."

She motioned him to sit beside her. They observed perfect, even formal, good manners, these two; except that somehow or other, as if by mutual consent, they had dropped the 'sir' and 'madam' which was *de rigueur* among the well-bred. On the other hand, neither had once used Christian names.

"I like rain," said Barbara "except in the streets where the coaches and waggons splash you so. And I love to watch the fribbles when it rains; you'd scarcely believe how horrified they are if they feel a spot. I suppose it makes their paint run."

"What will you do when the winter comes on your free day?"

"I shall walk here and keep myself warm. And I do *hope* it snows. Snow is so exciting and so pretty, with every twig putting on a little white fur coat. But I shall miss being in the country, as we were at home. It was noisy during the day, with so many stage-coaches and pack-horses passing, but at night you heard nothing but owls, and there were ponds to skate on."

It was the first time he had ever known her make anything approaching a complaint, and in his sensitive mood it touched him deeply.

"What will you do?" he burst out again, sounding oddly angry. "I mean, you can't go on being a governess all your life. It's preposterous! I suppose – I suppose you'll marry some day."

"I shouldn't think that's very likely," replied Barbara in a considering sort of way. "I have no portion, and I'm a" – she leaned towards him and whispered into his ear with a kind of mischievous solemnity – "a Papist."

"Papists do marry, each other, I mean," mumbled Hubert, drawing a pattern on the gravel with his riding-whip and appearing quite absorbed in it.

There was a slight pause.

"You look as though you are dressed for a journey," Barbara remarked in an even tone. "Are you leaving London, sir?"

He winced at the sudden formality. A sort of barrier seemed to have come down, and for the first time he was embarrassed in her company.

"Yes, I'm going home. I – I have to. I'm needed at Old Park."

They were both silent again, and it was not one of their old companionable silences. He had the extraordinary feeling of wanting to say a hundred things to her and not being able to think of one of them. It was time to go or he would miss the coach, yet he seemed rooted to this familiar bench which had become a little private world of peace and comradeship and laughter.

At last he almost leapt up, made her a most abrupt and stilted farewell, and walked rapidly towards the gate. He had got within a few yards of it when something seemed to explode inside his head, and he found himself walking as rapidly back towards the bench again. He looked so fierce that a beggar who had been going to whine for alms thought better of it, and slunk away.

Barbara was sitting where he had left her, with her head downbent under the little gypsy hat, so that he could not see her expression. Her voice sounded just a trifle strained as she asked, without raising her head:

"Have you forgotten something, Sir Hubert?"

"Yes!" said Hubert loudly. (He felt hysterical, almost drunk.) "I have. I forgot to tell you that I love you; and I forgot to ask you whether you could possibly find it in your heart to marry me. All I have to offer you," he galloped wildly on, "is a decayed estate which at any moment might be taken from me under the penal laws. There are weeds everywhere and the house is damp and there are not enough servants, and I'm ostracised by my neighbours and my sister is very difficult to get on with. I'm telling you the worst, you see – but no, I'm not. The worst is this: when I came to London I was on the point of ratting from my faith. I felt I couldn't go on. My chaplain was taken away, and there didn't seem any point in – in… That's the kind of man I'm asking you to marry. It isn't fair to tell you that if I can't have you to fortify and inspire me, I might even now – "

"Please."

He stopped dead. He stood there blinking at her, aghast at himself. He looked distracted and very young, and at the same time pitiably older than his years.

"Please excuse me for interrupting you," said Barbara, in a little thread of a voice, "but what seems a long time ago you asked me a question. You asked me to marry you. And the answer is, Yes, dear Hubert, I would like very much to marry you, if you please."

He found that his mouth was opening and shutting in a ludicrous manner like a fish's, but no words came.

"And before you asked me that question, you said something. You said, 'I love you'. Please, would you very much mind saying that again, because, you see, no one has ever said that to me before, and I haven't wanted them to, but when you say it I could go on listening for ever."

He flung himself down on the bench beside her, and grabbed her hands so roughly that she winced.

"I love the freckles on your forehead," gabbled Hubert ridiculously, "and that darn in your glove and that rather silly little hat, and the way you wrinkle your nose sometimes, as you did at the sparrows the first day we met, and the way you munch an apple like a child, and your giggle, and your wide eyes, and your sweetness, and your courage. I love you, dear, darling Barbara! I could make a whole litany of it! And I shall go on loving you *in sæcula sæculorum, Amen.*"

"I think that's slightly profane, isn't it?" said Barbara shakily. "Oh dear, I can't find my handkerchief, and I don't like our sparrows seeing me cry."

"There's one thing our sparrows have got to get used to," said Hubert, taking out his own handkerchief and wiping her eyes with clumsy tenderness, "and that's to doing without you. Because today we're going to dine at the most expensive ordinary in London, and as soon as possible I'm going to take you home to Old Park – my Lady Thorne."

# Chapter Seven

Magdalene was leaning on the green gate into the lane, waiting for the passing of the post-boy.

The worst of poses is that they are extremely difficult to give up without loss of face when one has tired of them, as Magdalene was discovering. She had posed from so early an age, taking refuge from a world in which no one seemed to want her, that the habit had become second-nature, and by now she was honestly very largely unconscious when she was acting. Yet even her elaborate grief for Robin had had an element of acting in it. It was true that those brief months of excitement, when life suddenly had become colourful and full because her twin had made her his confidante in his determination to fight for Prince Charles, had been her most vivid experience. Yet at the bottom of her heart she had suspected that Robin had merely been making use of her because there was no one else at hand.

And so her frantic watching for his return had been to a large extent escapism. To pretend to be broken-hearted for her lost twin had warded off for the time the hateful knowledge that she was back again to her old unimportant self, seventeen now, a woman, with no chance of marrying, of ever being necessary to anyone, with nothing to look forward to except 'making herself useful about the house'.

By her pose of the distracted sister at least she had forced herself on Hubert's notice, and even had caused him to make a journey to London on her account. But it was beginning to be extremely difficult to go on with this watching-and-waiting business, and equally difficult to give it up.

With the fatal ease of the self-dramatising, however, Magdalene had begun to see herself in a new role. There was no real doubt in her mind that Robin was dead, and that henceforth, at least until that distant day when Michael returned from Douai, she and Hubert would be alone at Old Park. She had always been slightly in awe of Hubert, though she had plucked up courage to be extremely offensive to him when she had had Robin to support her. Now she was about to romanticise Hubert, just as she had romanticised Robin; he was to be her new god, and she was to be the devoted younger sister on whom he would come to depend for everything. She had imagined little scenes; Hubert in despair and saying that he would have to conform because he could not bear any more frustration, and herself strengthening his faith, reminding him of the proud record of Thorne constancy. The pair of them riding into Newtown, she his support in the company of surly tradesmen and unfriendly neighbours, while folk whispered how wonderful was that pretty Miss Thorne's devotion to her brother.

It was not an entirely satisfying role, but it seemed the only one left her. She had never, she realised now, seriously contemplated suicide; she was horribly healthy, and it was unlikely that she would die young; and the dream of a dramatic martyrdom had vanished with adolescence.

So now when she came as usual to wait for the post-boy at the green gate; it was not for news of Robin but for a letter from Hubert telling her he was coming home. Coming home battered in spirit from that dreadful strange place called London, to weep on her shoulder and to tell her how much he needed her.

Above the drowsy cawing of the rooks in the 'cathedral trees' she heard the post-boy's horn, and slipped nervously into the shadow of a great oak near the gate. Poor Magdalene was terrified of people, even of post-boys. The horn sounded nearer, and her spirits rose. She had been telling the cards last night (a mortal sin according to the Catechism, but she couldn't go to confession now, and, anyway, God would understand her anxiety), and the knave of diamonds had kept on turning up in company with the queen of hearts: unexpected news and heart's desire. It was true that occasionally the ace of spades had made its ominous appearance; but when Nana, who had taught her the forbidden art, was not present at the fortune-telling, Magdalene cheated, managing at the same time to persuade herself that the ace of spades had got there by mistake.

The hoof-beats on the lane slowed to a walk. There *was* a letter! To be found lurking here under the oak would be worse than being found waiting at the gate; she strolled forward as though merely taking a little walk, and affected surprise when she saw the boy.

"Letter for Miss Magdalene Thorne," said the post-boy, taking it out of his bag. He was a cheeky youth, reminding her sometimes of that other impertinent youth who had tried to kiss her in the shrubberies long ago. She had never quite forgotten that incident, though Stephen Vickery had disappeared from Old Park. "Come in the London bag, it did; grand, ain't you, miss, having letters from London."

She flushed angrily. It was only because she was a Catholic that post-boys dared to be so familiar. She took the letter, which, it seemed, was prepaid, and without a word turned back along the drive.

In the manner of those unaccustomed to receiving letters, she studied its outside as she walked. It was quite a fat packet, not like the brief little notes which Hubert had sent her since his going to London a month previously. But it was in his handwriting. Perhaps, after all, there was news of Robin; she was conscious for a moment of a genuine emotion, and Robin became vivid. Oh, supposing he was safe after all! They had had such times together, conspiring in the garden-house, exchanging secret signs in public; he had been so ecstatically grateful when she had sold her jewels to finance him on his great adventure. And he would hear when he returned of how she had watched for him, never had despaired of his coming home, yet had nearly lost her reason in her frantic anxiety.

Walking along, avoiding the boulders by the side of the drive where adders were wont to bask in the sun, Magdalene went off into one of her day-dreams, planning what she should wear, what she would say, exactly where she would greet him, when her hero returned from the wars. So romantic was this imaginary scene that she had almost reached the house before she remembered that she had not yet opened Hubert's letter. She was passing the solarium, the little court enclosed within high living walls of yew into which windows had been cut. There was still half an hour before dinner, and this would be a pleasant place, she thought, in which to read her letter. She sat down on the edge of the fountain, never mended, rusty and encrusted with lichen, and broke the seal.

'My dear Sister, I have some most happy and unexpected news for you. I am going to be married... '

(ii)

"Oh, there are the rooks!" breathed Barbara, craning out of the window of the coach. "I've been waiting to hear them.

And those must be your 'cathedral trees'; they *are* just like pillars in a great church. Hubert, do you think we could send the coach on and walk the rest of the way? I want so much to see this part for the first time quite alone with you."

She had been very silent on the journey from London, first in the stage to Newtown, and from there in the shabby family coach which had been sent to meet them. She was like a child who has been told about fairyland and actually finds itself in that enchanted country.

"The green gate on which you used to swing – and oh, the motto!" She ran her hand over the inscription carved beneath the heraldic beasts on the gate-posts. " 'Thorne guards the Flower of Honour'; I must learn to read it in the old French. I do like that beast on the left post; he's lost an ear and looks so friendly, like a woolly lamb I had as a child."

"I can't understand why this drive hasn't been tidied up," said Hubert, frowning. "I sent such particular instructions to Magda about what I wanted done, and there has been plenty of time."

"Is that the roof of the Dower House over there?"

"My mother had to sell it to pay her taxes."

"I know; you told me; but it doesn't matter. Nothing matters today except that we've come – home. Wait, oh do wait, Hubert! Isn't it from here that you can first see the sea?"

"Yes, it is, but of course there would have to be a mist on this day of all days when I wanted everything to look its best for you."

She put her arm through his and asked presently:

"Are you listening for something."

"I'm listening for the fountain. I particularly asked Magda to have it mended because you told me you loved fountains. I wanted you to hear it on your homecoming," he cried, like a disappointed child.

She hugged his arm.

"Never mind. Oh, how lovely those flowers are!"

"They are weeds, my darling."

"They are lovely, all the same. Magda must teach me gardening. Poor Magda will have to teach me a lot of things. Oh!" she caught her breath sharply. "There is the house!"

Magdalene was not at the door to greet them, and neither was she in the withdrawing-room. Nana, witch-like, sly-eyed, malodorous, brought the tea-things, and, scanning Barbara with avid curiosity, muttered that Miss Magda was sick; the poor lamb was stricken with so bad a migraine that she could not lift her head from the pillow.

Magdalene's room was darkened, but a night-light burning in a basin guided Barbara to the bed. A languid hand was extended in response to her soft greeting, and she felt something hard and cold transferred to her own.

"The housewife's keys, madam," came a faint voice. "I regret I was not able to present them in proper fashion, but I wish you joy of them."

Barbara swallowed down a sudden irritation. She had been warned by Hubert that his sister was 'difficult', but this stilted talk which sounded as though it had been borrowed from some book was surely unnecessary. But she was too happy to let even so cold a welcome upset her. She began chattering about her journey, of how wonderful it was to come home, and of how Magdalene must show her all the treasures of Old Park when she was better.

"I wish you could have come to my wedding, but I suppose the journey would have been too much for you, since you're not well."

Magdalene gave a small hollow laugh.

"I have no clothes for going to London."

"Oh, it was very quiet. Of course it had to be as it was a Catholic marriage. It was rather sad not having any of my own family there, but they wouldn't have come even if I'd asked them, and it wouldn't have been safe. But it was wonderful, all the same, to be married in that poor little attic in the Ship tavern where I was received into the Church. And we dined with Bishop Challoner afterwards. If only you could have been there, Magda – "

She stopped abruptly. The face on the pillow was looking at her, and she was shocked by the naked hostility in the eyes.

"Only my own family call me Magda. My name is Magdalene."

### (iii)

I must give her time, thought Barbara. It was natural that she should resent the advent of a stranger as the mistress of Old Park, but by and by Magdalene would adapt herself to the new situation and make friends. And though Barbara detested self-pity, she was naturally tolerant, and it soon became plain to her that it was very largely Magdalene's upbringing and circumstances which made her so difficult. Hubert, on the other hand, deeply in love, raged against his sister's unreasonable hostility.

"I'll not allow her to make you unhappy just because she's miserable herself. And, in any case, why should she be miserable?"

"She is lonely and frustrated, Hubert."

"She need not be lonely now she has you. And as for being frustrated, I don't know what you mean."

"She never goes anywhere or sees anyone, only because she's a Catholic."

"And what about the sacrifices you made for religion? You were turned out of your father's house and had to take a menial post."

"I'm a tradesman's daughter," said Barbara, smiling. "Working for a living is in my blood. But Magdalene and I will make friends, you'll see."

She was wrong. She did not understand how warped had become the character of this girl of her own age. If Magdalene could not have a hero in her private dreams, she would have a villainess, and she had cast Barbara for that role. And in her determination to make things difficult for Barbara, she found a dangerous ally. While young Lady Thorne's charming eagerness to fulfil her new duties endeared her to the other servants, she fell foul of Nana, and there came to be two rival camps at Old Park. Nana might be an institution here, but she had an evil reputation. In the servants' hall they talked darkly of how she could turn the milk sour and cast a spell on a spinning-wheel so that it would not revolve, and of what would have happened to her in the days before witchcraft ceased to be a capital offence. They feared to cross Nana; but Barbara, who knew nothing of the ways of old family servants, and who saw Nana merely as a dirty, malicious old woman, treated her without fear or favour.

"Threw out my adder-broth, she did," grumbled the crone to Magdalene. "Said it stank. Eh, she don't know no country lore. And sharp she was with me when I told her, your ladyship mustn't bring them flowers into the house, not if you don't want Sir Hubert to take the falling-sickness. She laughed at me. Eh, she may laugh, but you mark my words... "

And as the months went by, Nana began to comfort Magdalene and indulge her own grudge against the new Lady Thorne by other dark predictions.

"Got out the old cradle, I did, what I rocked all you dear childer in. But there won't be more babies to lay in it. Barren she is. Didn't I say so to meself first time I ever saw her? Ah and a spider running over me hand that very morning. A sure sign, that is, of meeting a barren woman. Sir Hubert'll be the last of his line. Eh, and this house will be yourn some day, my dearie; I seen it in the cards."

But that day, if it ever came, was too distant to be of comfort to Magdalene. Her dream of keeping house for Hubert, of being his cherished and only companion, had been shattered like all her other dreams. Hubert did not need her; nobody needed her or ever would. Her future was as it had ever been; she was doomed to grow into an old maid and 'make herself useful about the house'. And not even her own house now. Its mistress was Barbara, the daughter of a horse-coper. Those were Barbara's clothes hanging in the best bedroom; that privileged arm-chair in the withdrawing-room must be given up to Barbara; Barbara must be allowed to precede her sister-in-law who must open the door for her; it was Barbara to whom the servants came for orders; Barbara who wore the precious keys, the insignia of the housewife, on a chain at her waist.

And worst of all was Barbara's happiness, her voice singing as she went about her duties, the loving exchange of glances with her husband, the sight of them, arms entwined, heads close together, walking in the gardens of an evening.

Magdalene's bitter jealousy rebuffed all the attempts of her sister-in-law to win her over. If Barbara wished to sit in the garden-house, naturally she could; the whole estate was at her service; but Magdalene found it too full of sad memories now. The lily-lake must be cleaned because it smelt? Perhaps it ought to be; it had always been well enough for Magdalene and her family as it was. New tapestry hangings for the morning-room? Of course, if

Barbara liked to work them. For Magdalene, these old ones, tattered though they were, were sacred as having been stitched by her great-grandmother. Wasn't it lovely to hear the fountain? Magdalene supposed it was; Hubert had never thought it worthwhile to have it mended for her, and she had grown used to not hearing it.

If there were any little gaucheries Barbara committed in her new role, Magdalene was on them like a hawk. Barbara would excuse her, she was sure, if she told her that it was not usual to shake hands with farmers' wives; naturally, London tradesmen had their own customs. It was not etiquette, though of course there was nothing actually wrong in it, to invite the bailiff into the withdrawing-room; if one wished to speak to him, the steward's room was the place.

Barbara was no plaster saint, and occasionally there were scenes.

"Life is lonely and hard for all of us here, Magdalene. Why do you insist on making it harder?"

"Lonely for you? I thought you had a husband."

"You know what I mean. The world outside either hates or despises us; we need to stand together."

"Hubert and I were not lonely before you came."

"You knew he would marry some day, just as your father did. I don't know why you decided to disapprove of me even before we met."

"My father married a Darell of Kent, one of the oldest families in England. And I wasn't asked to approve of you. My approval isn't important to anyone, never has been nor ever will be. But yes it was, to my dear brother Robin; Hubert went to London to seek for news of Robin, and instead he got caught by – "

The look on Barbara's face stopped her; she had gone too far, and what she had said, or had been going to say, might be reported to Hubert. Barbara swallowed her anger and said in a low voice:

"I can't make you understand, Magdalene, that I need you. I know I am more fortunate than you, having a dear husband, but I have no child. I need your friendship and your prayers. Pray, oh please pray, that I may give an heir to Old Park."

(iv)

A pose of some kind was essential to Magdalene; and as the years crept past she began to realise the extreme suitability of the religious devotee.

Here again there was no conscious play-acting; she was genuinely unhappy, tortured by her jealousy, and reproached by her conscience; it was natural that she should turn for comfort to the religion which was in her blood and bones. But then she began to feel a sense of superiority when she lingered long over her prayers, she referred rather often to the dreadful implication of the unlit lamp in the Sanctuary, she observed with a sad smile that naturally Barbara would not understand, she having been bred in heresy. It was only a step from this to fancying she saw visions and heard voices, to wearing an abstracted look, and to be seen pacing the garden with Dr Challoner's new translation of *The Introduction to the Devout Life*.

Hubert, harassed by material cares, tormented by the un-happy atmosphere, and secretly grieving for his wife's childlessness, rejoiced in this development, and not only because it would mean Magdalene's leaving Old Park. He did not for a moment doubt his sister's sincerity, and to him vocations to Religion were signal favours. Young Michael's vocation to the priesthood had persisted, and the letters which came regularly from Douai were now from a 'divine' who was studying philosophy and Theology, and whose correspondence was read with becoming respect. It would be an added comfort to have a sister in Religion, and to receive the benefit of her prayers in his many problems.

And so one day in the summer of 1752, Magdalene took an emotional farewell of her family and her home, and went off to 'try her vocation' in the little hidden convent at Hammersmith, where Queen Catherine of Braganza had established a small community of teaching nuns.

# Chapter Eight

(i)

Though Magdalene did not know it, an old acquaintance of hers was in London, having preceded her thither by several years. His name was Stephen Vickery.

When Stephen left the Grammar School at Newtown, his masters, unanimous in their admiration for this lad's brilliant brain, had made various suggestions for the future. It was a thousand pities that his religion closed the Universities to him, for undoubtedly he would have got a fellowship in due time, but the Grammar School would be only too happy to take him on its teaching staff, or if that did not please him, the post of clerk could most easily be obtained for him with some topping tradesman in the town.

Stephen had paid no heed to any of this advice. Long ago he had decided what he would do when he left school; he would go to London and make his fortune. This was no romantic notion, for Stephen was anything but a romantic youth. It was simply that only in London, that city of fabulous wealth, could his talents be appreciated and his ambitions realised. To his old father's offer to consult Sir Hubert Thorne, who so largely had paid for the boy's education, Stephen replied shortly that he did not need the advice of an impoverished landowner. What he needed was a small capital sum to maintain him until he had found a suitable post. It was the story, in fact, of the Prodigal Son, though in this case there was no elder brother with whom the substance must be divided, and Stephen did not propose to waste his portion in riotous living.

So with his father's reluctant blessing and the greater part of the old man's savings, Stephen took the stage-coach to London, riding economically on the roof.

The first thing he did on arriving in this strange city was to drive a very hard bargain with a bookseller to whom he sold half a dozen handsome volumes which he had received at school in the shape of prizes. With his nest-egg appreciably increased, he hired an attic in a cheap lodging-house, and proceeded to make a survey of his chances of climbing fortune's ladder. His assets were an iron tenacity, a flair for discovering the weaknesses of others, an entire lack of scruple, a talent for figures amounting to genius, and an old grudge which served him as a goad.

It did not take him long to discover the interesting fact that the preoccupation of all classes in London was to make money fast and spend it as rapidly. Sitting in a coffee-house, where he could have a dish of coffee, a share of the fire, and a perusal of the newspapers, all for one penny, Stephen read of great personages who gambled away fortunes in a single night, of men who were fabulously rich one day and the next had lost everything on some ridiculous wager. Gambling, it seemed, had become a mania; he could not go into a tavern without hearing bets being laid on the dissolution of Parliament, the length of the King's life, whether the earth was round, or the Isle of Wight a peninsula.

And, above all, there was the lottery. Stephen's close-set eyes studied notices in shop-windows, notices promising undreamed-of gold; at the barber's and at the eating-house the proprietors pestered him to buy tickets which, if the number turned out to be fortunate, entitled the holder to so many free shaves or free dinners. Even at his humble lodging-house the 'morocco men' called regularly, wheedling the inhabitants to buy tickets in the private lotteries known as Little Goes. Everyone with whom he spoke was infected with the urge to get something for nothing; everyone had imbibed a contempt for business honesty and hard work. If you were lucky, you could make your fortune in an hour without doing a hand's turn, and then you could buy a seat in Parliament, a Government office, an invitation to a royal Drawing-room, a title, a great lady's favours, or what you would.

But Stephen did not invest his little capital in lottery tickets. He trusted not to luck but to his own sharp wits to make his fortune. The town was full of fools who frittered away their money as soon as they made it, fit prey for a bright lad like himself. And he had not been in London more than a few weeks before he discovered one such fool, so to speak upon his very doorstep.

The ground-floor front of the tenement in which he had his attic was an apothecary's shop, and Stephen's keen eyes had noticed several things about this shop which interested him. The principal commodity advertised for sale was something labelled 'Colick-water', and it appeared that the inhabitants of the district were chronically afflicted with colic, for whenever Stephen looked through the window, the proprietor could be seen selling bottles of the stuff. Yet though the business appeared to be flourishing, the apothecary had no apprentices or assistants, and looked half-starved. There was some mystery here, possibly a lucrative mystery; so one day in went Stephen and bought a bottle of 'Colick-water', for which the apothecary demanded the exorbitant price of half a crown.

109

So costly a potion was not to be wasted, even though Stephen had no colic. It bore the instructions, 'Take two or three spoonfuls five times a day, or as the fit takes you.' He sniffed at the stuff, and found that it gave forth the same queer sickly odour that he had smelt on the breath of the lower sort of people since he had come to London. He took a spoonful, and felt as though his head was on fire. The solution of the mystery immediately occurred to him. This 'Colick-water' was gin.

Since gin was pre-eminently a London vice, it was new to Stephen, but he had read in the newspapers various diatribes against the fact that though the Government had at last been forced to pass laws restricting its sale, there were illicit stills all over the town, so that the men and women to whom this fiery opiate had become more necessary than food could continue to buy it under fancy names. Undoubtedly the apothecary was one of these unlicensed distillers; but why, then, was he so poor?

To find the answer to this interesting question the apothecary's acquaintance must be cultivated; and here Stephen had a stroke of luck. He strolled into the shop one day and was about to ask for something, when a slatternly woman entered and made some sort of sign to the proprietor who, ignoring Stephen, ushered her into the back room and closed the door. He had been at work on his accounts, and Stephen, left alone, curiously inspected the crude slate and tallies. When the apothecary emerged from the back room alone, Stephen said to him:

"Lucky for you, master, you left this slate where I couldn't help seeing it. For you've been cheating yourself, you have. Done yourself out of no less than four shillings and fivepence by miscalculations."

The man stared at him in open-mouthed astonishment.

"You done that sum while I was out? Damme, it took me days to add up that row of figures, and it never came out the same total twice."

"Figures are a pastime with me," said Stephen grandly. "See here, I lodge abovestairs, and if you like I'll get your ledgers put shipshape by this evening. I got nothing to do."

That was how Stephen had laid the foundations of his fortune. In this down-at-heels apothecary he had discovered the type of fool he could use until he could fly after higher game.

(ii)

The shop was a façade. The real business was carried on in the back room where there was an illicit still in which were concocted the raw spirits masquerading as 'Colick water', 'Tonic for the Hair', and 'Lady's Delight' in the window. And in that back room other business was transacted. The apothecary was a pawnbroker, a receiver of stolen goods, an agent for those who kidnapped young men and sold them to the Plantations. He was in with the press-gang and the crimps; he was engaged in a nefarious traffic of offering false bail; he dabbled in the horrible trade of the resurrection-men.

Yet with all these irons in the fire he was perpetually on the brink of ruin, because, like everyone else in London, he frittered his money away in drink and gambling. He belonged to a punch-club, a sixpenny card club, a free-and-easy, and a club in which the members went shares in betting on horses. He spent half his time considering which agent and which number he should choose in a lottery, feverishly consulting fortune-tellers. Three was lucky, and so was twelve; seven must be avoided like the plague, and the number must not be divisible by seven. A friend he had met, who knew someone who was acquainted with someone who had won the twenty thousand pound prize in the last Government Lottery strongly advised him to stick to twelve or to one of the multiples of twelve. And would Stephen work that out for him?

The sober, industrious Stephen had become indispensable, ensconced in the back room, taking from his employer's shoulders the burden of keeping the accounts, and greatly improving trade.

Indeed, in the competent and ruthless hands of young Stephen the business became a little gold-mine, and transactions became ever more ambitious. Stephen was familiar now with ladies' boudoirs and gentlemen's closets, where he advanced money on heavy and still heavier interest to pay gambling debts or blackmail. Merchants' wives were no longer content with one new gown a year; shopkeepers turned up their noses at ale and demanded Indian madeira; after all, they were sure to win a prize in the next lottery, or they were going to make a fabulous profit by speculating in this or that venture. And when they didn't, they must pawn or borrow, and there was Stephen with his little book and his bulging purse.

When he had been with the apothecary for four years, the childless old widower died, leaving him the business. Stephen was now nearly twenty-one, already old in the gentle art of preying on the weaknesses of others, and knowing his way about the seamy side of London life as well as if he had been born in that city. He was possessed, too, of a fair capital, and it was time to go after higher quarry. He sold the shop, engaged a lodging in a more genteel part of the town, and turned his talents to the lending of money on a larger and a larger scale.

His clients were now of the fashionable world, but he did not feel out of place there, for this was the era of the 'mushroom men', the hey-day of the *nouveaux riches*. West

Indian planters, speculating builders, stock-jobbers, manufacturers, East India Company officials, nobodies who had made a fortune during the South Sea Bubble or by winning some enormous prize in a lottery, all were buying themselves country estates, seats in Parliament and the entrée to Court. With such men Stephen felt at home. His under-sized figure with the regrettable 'cheese-cutter' legs was often to be seen at Mr Handel's oratorios, at Ranelagh and Vauxhall, in the gallery of the House of Commons, at routs and masquerades, his keen ears pricked for scandalous secrets, for whispers of who was in debt, for rumours of the rise and fall of stocks. He made no friends and desired none. He wanted only the power that money brings.

But locked away in his isolated heart there was a secret, even more sinister ambition. Someone had humiliated him in his childhood, and that someone's family was going to pay for it to the uttermost farthing.

(iii)

On a certain fine June morning in 1753, Stephen drove out to Hammersmith in his smart chariot, feeling particularly pleased with himself. He was going to put the screws on a client who, though a respectable City merchant, Stephen rightly suspected of being a Catholic. The merchant, a Mr Phillimore, had suffered of late certain misfortunes in his American trade (for France was encroaching on the American colonies), and in his difficulties had applied to Stephen who, it had become known, was less tiresomely strict about securities than were the bankers. And Stephen dearly loved the chance of embarrassing by usury any member of the faith he had deserted.

He had completed his business to his own satisfaction, if not to Mr Phillimore's, and was walking back along Brook

Green Lane to the Bell and Anchor where he had left his chariot, when he noticed a young woman going in the same direction some dozen yards ahead of him. He noticed her first because of the oddly irritable gesture with which she snatched off her hood and began to swing it in her hand, for she was dressed in so prim a manner that the gesture seemed incongruous. And as he watched her, a memory began to stir in him. There was something familiar about her walk and the set of her shoulders and her glossy black, unpowdered hair.

He was still observing her when she stopped and unlocked a door in a high wall. Just before entering she half turned, so that he caught a glimpse of her profile; and though it was eight or nine years since last he had seen her, he instantly recognised Magdalene Thorne.

He stood stock-still on the side-walk, staring at the door which she had closed behind her, and smiling all over his face. It was extraordinary, he thought with a kind of awe, how everything went right for a man who knew exactly what he wanted in life and allowed nothing and nobody to divert him from his goal. He had come to London at sixteen and made his fortune by the time he was twenty; he had cherished the ambition of revenging himself on the Thornes, for whom he had slaved and one of whom had thrashed him in public in front of this very girl. And now fate had crossed his path with hers again; whatever it was she was doing in Hammersmith, she had come within his orbit, and he would find the means to satisfy his grudge through her who had always been lonely, emotionally unstable and vulnerable, and who had aroused his adolescent lust.

He had intended to drive straight home, but instead went into the Bell and Anchor and ordered a whet. There were no other customers in the coffee-room, and Stephen got into conversation with the waiter who served him.

After some small talk, he asked the man in a casual manner who was the owner of the house behind the high wall in Brook Green Lane.

"School for young ladies, sir," replied the waiter. "Lady in charge a Mrs Simpson. Leastways, that's what she calls herself."

He leaned over the table towards Stephen, prepared to gossip.

"Open secret, sir, they're Papists that keep that school. We call 'em the Jesuitesses, for would you credit it, sir, they're nuns. They don't wear no fancy dress, of course, but that's what they are, and it's a crying shame, I say, sir, to the neighbourhood."

"H'm," muttered Stephen non-committally.

"I won't say but they seem harmless bodies," continued the waiter, struggling to be fair, "and good teachers, they say; 'tanyrate most of the quality hereabouts sends their daughters there and have done this many a year. Portuguese Ambassador has his country seat, Cupola House, next door, and I s'pose they feels safe under the protection, you might say, of that Popish foreigner. But what *I* say is, 'tain't right to have female Jesuits teaching good Protestant children, and it's against the law and all."

Stephen went home in an even happier mood than that in which he had set out. So Magdalene Thorne was earning her living as a school-teacher; things must be bad at Old Park. And her manner, when he had caught that glimpse of her in the street, was of one who was dissatisfied with life. Eating his solitary dinner at Pontack's, Stephen pondered upon various vague but exciting possibilities.

(iv)

Mother Mistress was reading aloud to the Community at dinner from one of Dr Challoner's books on the martyrs.

Her harsh, monotonous voice matched the dry style of the author; the man had a positive genius, Magdalene thought bitterly, for leaving out any vivid touches even when, as now, he was recounting the martyrdom of Mary, Queen of Scots.

She let her glance wander from the view through the window of the nuns' graveyard to the meagre gathering in the austerely bare refectory. When first she had come here there had been fourteen in the Community; now there were only eight. For though the school had continued to prosper since its foundation nearly a hundred years previously, the Community had dwindled almost to the point of extinction, and some said that secular teachers would have to carry it on. In any case, she thought irritably, the whole thing was a farce. The Institute of Mary had been suppressed by Urban VIII as being opposed to the spirit if not to the actual decrees of the Council of Trent; and so far as Magdalene was concerned, it was a pity that Clement XI had restored it in a modified form fifty years later.

For how different was it from the convent of her dreams!

She had imagined herself clothed in a picturesque habit, her beauty enhanced by a white veil; but the Institute of Mary wore no habit; its dress, secular in cut, was a very plain, unbecoming black gown and white cap. In fancy she had paced an ancient cloister, wrapped in contemplation, and had tended flowers in an old-world garden. But the Hammersmith convent had no cloisters; its garden was devoted to the growing of vegetables; and when she paced, it was in the graveyard where she was expected to recite the Office of the Dead.

And oh how she had dreamed of those occasions when she would confide the secrets of her visions and revelations, and would overhear the Sisters whispering that a saint had come into their midst. Instead of which, Mr

Stokes, the nuns' confessor, had absolutely forbidden her to mention such things, talking sternly about them as being a trap to her humility; and Reverend Mother, whom she had been so sure would be sympathetic, had merely ordered her to read St John of the Cross. This had appeared encouraging, for was he not a great mystic? But St John of the Cross, she discovered, had a perfect horror of visions, which, he declared, were either of the devil or the result of spiritual pride.

It had been pride of a sort which had been largely responsible for her not leaving the convent after the first few miserable, disillusioning weeks. She could not face the humiliation of admitting to herself and others that her vocation to Religion was but another empty dream. Nor could she face a return to Old Park, though homesickness made her feel physically ill. Until she was twenty-three she had known no other world, and though she had often longed to penetrate beyond it, now that she had done so she felt as though torn up by the roots. The shabbiness, the frustration, the monotony of that past life, all were seen now through the lens of nostalgia, and even to hear the cawing of a rook or to pick up a fir-cone in the garden was enough to bring the hot tears to her eyes.

But Old Park had been invaded and usurped. In the place of the rightful mistress of the house – herself – there reigned a stranger, an ex-governess, a convert, the daughter of a dissenting horse-coper. She could not contemplate a return to her home as the unwanted spinster sister, the reluctant observer of a married love.

There had been times during this past year when she had tried to accommodate herself to the life she had chosen. She was prepared to accept the physical hardships, the domestic work combined with teaching duties, the long hours in the chapel, the frugal and monotonous meals, the cold, the discomfort; even the silence, strictly observed whenever possible, was not too galling, for her upbringing had made her a solitary. But the lack of the romance she had expected made her desperate in her black moods, bewildered and miserable in her better ones. She was the bride of Christ, but the phrase was meaningless; she was just a girl who had turned to Religion because she had despaired of finding human love. That was the stark and bitter truth.

Apart from her pride, what had kept her here was the adoration she had conceived for Reverend Mother, known by the alias of Mrs Simpson. Always seeking someone to romanticise, Magdalene had turned naturally to this woman who was not only a strong personality but had shown her from the first the maternal love she had lacked since childhood. But even Reverend Mother could be disappointing. She was tenderness itself if one were really in trouble; she was extremely formidable if one were at fault. She had a most uncomfortable way of diagnosing the secret weaknesses of those under her care; and though she did so with sympathy and humour, she preached always the same hard doctrine – acceptance, detachment, war to the death against self-love, and the conquest of the feelings by the will.

As the reader's harsh voice ceased this dinner-time and the Community rose for Grace, Reverend Mother glanced at the novice and her shrewd eyes were troubled.

"I wish to see you, my dear child," she said quietly, as Magdelene opened the refectory door for her. "Come to my room after Vespers."

It was a business-like room without any personal touches. A gaunt crucifix dominated it from over the hearth, facing a portrait of the pious Foundress of the Institute, Mary Ward, who seemed to frown disapprovingly at Magdalene as she entered. Reverend Mother was correcting the senior girls' exercises at a table piled with school books, and did not glance up for a moment or two; Magdalene watched her hand, distorted with arthritis, laboriously writing comments, and speculated nervously on the reason for the summons.

Reverend Mother laid down her pen, indicated a low stool near the desk, and began in her usual brisk manner:

"My dear child, I do not have to remind you that the time of your Profession draws near, for I am sure that the taking of such solemn vows occupies all your thoughts and prayers."

"Yes, Reverend Mother. At least, I – I do try to pray."

"We have a body as well as a soul, Magdalene, and we make it harder for ourselves if we do not dedicate the one as the other to our vocation. All those little outward acts which appear so arbitrary are intended to help us to inward recollection. And here, I am afraid, you fail. You do not observe the guard of the eyes; I noticed you at dinner, and have done so many times before. And yesterday, when Mother Mistress sent you on an errand, Sister Portress saw you re-enter the convent with your hood in your hand. We have not the privilege of wearing the holy habit, and for this very reason we should be meticulous in our modesty of dress and deportment."

"I was hot, Reverend Mother," said Magdalene defensively. "And what harm can there be in – I mean, I don't see – "

"You mean, my dear child, that you do not see the use of holy obedience. Then how can you offer yourself for Profession?"

There was a pause. Magdalene's eyes begged for comfort and love, but the face looking down at her from under the stiff white cap was very grave.

"I think you must not do so, my dear child. I have thought for a long time that you have no vocation."

"Reverend Mother – "

"No, listen to me. You have tried gallantly; you have persevered for a full year. That is long enough, perhaps too long. I know our Order is a very difficult one for certain souls; we have dedicated ourselves to active work in the world with all its distractions, and we live in a climate of heresy. Interior recollection is doubly hard for us. But I do not think, my child, that any of the older Orders overseas would accept you. I have prayed much and observed you closely, and I am sure that Our Lord has not called you to serve Him in Religion."

"Then what will become of me?" cried Magdalene, before she knew what she was going to say.

The penetrating eyes held hers.

"Ah! I suspected that was the reason why you stayed with us – no, Magdalene, I am not angry."

She held out a crippled hand, and the girl slipped to her knees.

"I know that you shrink from returning to your home; we have often spoken of this, and though I have tried to convince you that you are needed there (for I am sure you are), and that though the conditions may be hard they should be accepted as being either willed or permitted by Our Lord for your salvation, you cannot bring yourself to face it. But this I know, my dear child; I cannot permit you to take your solemn vows only because you feel that no other life is possible or tolerable."

"Don't send me away!" begged Magdalene, crying bitterly. "I'll try again, really try this time. I'm sorry about taking off my hood in the street and not keeping the guard of the eyes, and banging the door of the Chapter-room the other day, and I will observe the Rule in future – really I will!"

Reverend Mother put an arm round the shaking shoulders. She had come to love this girl, difficult though Magdalene was.

"No, my child," she said firmly, "it is no use. We do not choose to serve God in Religion; He chooses us. But since the thought of going home is so distressing to you, I have a suggestion to make. You have a certain gift for teaching, and if you would try to conquer your moods, you could develop it. As you know, we depend more and more on our secular teachers, and if it pleases you, you may become one of them and not have to leave us. The salary is very small and the work hard, but you would have freedom to go out when you wished – and to take off your hood in the street," added Reverend Mother dryly.

Magdalene leapt at the offer; and straightway began to see herself as the perfect teacher, adored by her pupils, invited to their homes, and perhaps one day meeting there a fairy prince in the guise of an elder brother.

(v)

It did not take more than a few weeks to shatter such dreams. Her pupils were wary of her moods, and took advantage of her lack of self-confidence. Her colleagues, though willing to make friends, were bored by her egotism; and now that she had no Office to say, she felt an outsider in the convent, and time hung heavy on her hands. Not until the end of July did she receive a solitary invitation to a pupil's home, and when it came it did not sound promising. A wealthy Catholic merchant of the name of Phillimore summoned her to take tea with his wife, for the purpose, it transpired, of impressing upon her the talents and accomplishments of his unattractive little daughter, and his own nobility in sending the child to so modest a school when but for his religion he could have sent her to some fashionable academy for young ladies in town.

All this was conveyed to Magdalene in a monologue by Mrs Phillimore, whose spouse, it appeared, was closeted

121

with a business friend. Sipping her tea, Magdalene glanced enviously about the luxurious room, though her native good taste informed her that it was vulgar.

"It is difficult for you to understand, Miss Thorne," patronised the merchant's wife, genteelly using her back-scratcher, "what trials we of the *beau monde* endure for conscience's sake. You will scarcely credit it, but my black-girl, whom I whipped for some fault, threatened to inform against us for not going to our parish church. And what a cross it is for Mr Phillimore to know that he can never be Lord Mayor, when with his fortune he ought – "

She was interrupted at this point by the entrance of her husband, whose complexion seemed to indicate that though its owner might be debarred from the mayoralty, he was not unacquainted with City feasts. But Magdalene did no more than glance at him, for he was followed into the room by a young man.

If this young man was a fairy prince in disguise, the disguise was a very effective one. A plain though expensive suit clothed a weedy figure; partridge silk stockings encased a pair of bandy legs; a snowy wig tied back with a black silk bow sat above a narrow forehead and very close-set eyes. He was not a young man one would want to look at twice, yet Magdalene's glance lingered; for he reminded her of someone she had seen somewhere before.

The merchant, bowing to her with a nice mixture of politeness and condescension, immediately afterwards turned to his wife, and with a very different air begged to present to her Mr Vickery.

"Vickery!" exclaimed Magdalene, too startled to remember her manners.

Mr and Mrs Phillimore frowned at this impertinent interruption, but the young man, with a smile which seemed to beg Magdalene to keep a secret, murmured that that indeed was his name. As Mrs Phillimore proceeded to make a fuss of a guest who seemed to be an important one, Magdalene sat silent, observing him. Was it possible that this expensively dressed person, who crooked his finger so genteelly as he handled his tea-cup, who took snuff with such an air, and who patronised a rich City merchant, was really Stephen Vickery, the gardener's boy at Old Park? The boy who long ago had tried to kiss her in the shrubberies, who had told her she was pretty...

She felt herself blushing and rose hurriedly. She must beg to take her leave; she was so much obliged to Mrs Phillimore for her kind hospitality; such delicious tea; so refreshing.

"May I be permitted the honour of escorting you to your chair, madam?" enquired Mr Vickery. (There was not the trace of a rural accent; surely it could not be he.)

"You came by chair, Miss Thorne?" enquired her hostess woundingly surprised.

"No, madam, I walked," bit out Magdalene, hating her. "I have a positive passion for walking."

"But it begins to rain," said Mr Vickery, glancing through the window and sounding pleased. "I should be infinitely honoured, madam, if you would allow me to drive you home."

It's just a dream, she kept thinking, as she sat beside Stephen in a calash drawn by a pair of spanking horses, with two liveried footmen clinging on behind. Again and again she glanced covertly at him sitting there beside her with the air of one who has driven in smart carriages all his life; it was incredible that he had once been a scruffy boy who had dug up weeds in the gardens of Old Park. For some minutes he said nothing, and his silence gave her a queerly excited feeling of intimacy.

"It was mighty kind of you, Miss Magdalene," he murmured at length, "not to tell on me."

"Then it is you! But tell on you – I don't understand."

"If a man's made money, he likes to forget his humble origins. But I can't pretend with you, now can I?"

"But how did you – Oh lord! how ill-mannered of me to ask."

He smiled at her. When he smiled he was not so very unattractive, she decided.

"It's a long story, Miss Magdalene, and you'd find it but dull. But you, madam; it's strange to encounter you so far from home."

"I am earning my bread as a school-teacher," said Magdalene distinctly. "You have gone up in the world, Stephen – I mean, Mr Vickery – and I have gone down. There is where I live and work, that hideous red-brick house among the trees. Oh, I – "

She broke off, biting her lip, horrified to find that she was near to tears.

"You what, Miss Magdalene?" asked Stephen softly.

"Meeting you has made me so homesick. And being patronised by that fat merchant and his odious wife, when my own family... Here is the gate. Thank you for the drive, Mr Vickery."

Again he said nothing, but tapped on the glass to order his coachman to stop; and waving aside the footman, himself handed her out and walked beside her to the gate in the high wall. But while she fumbled for her key he said hesitantly, with a flattering, respectful eagerness:

"It would be doing me a real charity, Miss Magdalene, if you would permit me to see you again, and tell me how master does, and her young ladyship and all. I heard tell master was married before I left the Grammar School, but no news of Old Park since, and I'm homesick, too, sometimes. But there! you wouldn't want to be seen with the likes of me – "

"Of course I would!" Magdalene interrupted impulsively. "And I want to hear how you have made your fortune; it's quite a romance. Well, you know where I live now, and – and how to get in touch with me."

He stood looking after her as she hurried up the drive; and he was smiling. It was the kind of smile one could imagine on the face of a cat which has sat patiently by a mouse-hole for a long, long time. And when he had re-entered his smart calash, he began to laugh silently, rocking to and fro with an unpleasant delight.

# Chapter Nine

It was wisest to tell Reverend Mother of the encounter; for Mr and Mrs Phillimore would be sure to mention to their daughter that her school-teacher had driven off all alone with a young man, and the child would spread it round the convent.

"I had such a pleasant surprise today, Reverend Mother. I met a – a friend from home, a young gentleman whom I have not seen since we were children. He was calling at Mrs Phillimore's when I took tea there. And he has asked if I would permit him to see me again."

Reverend Mother was pleased. Her private opinion had always been that Magdalene needed a husband, and here perhaps was the gentleman.

"But of course you must have a chaperone, my dear child. You could ask one of the other teachers."

Mr Vickery wasted no time. The very next day a liveried footman called with a note; it bore an address in Welbeck Street, was excellently written and phrased, and begged the honour of Miss Thorne's company to take tea at the Chelsea Bun House. Magdalene asked Nancy, who was plain and a trifle deaf, to chaperone her; and on the day appointed Stephen arrived with an elegant nosegay, and was inspected through windows by half the convent. But

126

Magdalene was too exhilarated to care what impression he made. She was going out with a young man, a rich young man, someone from home, and someone who really desired her company.

Nancy, her friend, was astounded by the change in her. Gone was the moodiness and the look of discontent; her face was radiant, and one suddenly realised how pretty she was. Too pretty, Nancy thought, to waste her charms on such an unattractive admirer; though Nancy had to admit that this Mr Vickery was pleasant enough and seemed quite at home in the fashionable world.

Mrs Hands, who kept the Bun House, had a special table ready for them, and served them herself, showing them with pride the silver mug presented to her by Queen Caroline, and telling them exactly how the famous buns were made. What with this and an inspection of the little museum with which the place was fitted up, time passed so quickly that no news was exchanged between Magdalene and Stephen. But another appointment was made, this time to see Mrs Salmon's waxwork show; and while Nancy was gaping at the latest exhibit, a representation of Sir Robert Walpole, Stephen enquired tentatively of Magdalene whether she thought she would be allowed to give him the pleasure of taking her and her friend to Vauxhall one evening.

Vauxhall! The most fashionable pleasure-garden in London; and Stephen, it seemed, had a silver ticket which cost twenty-five shillings and which admitted him throughout the three months' season. Reverend Mother was indulgent; yes, Magdalene might go, but she must not be home late.

It was a wonderful evening. The thousand lamps illumined the gaily dressed throng who strolled through the groves; if only, thought Magdalene, I had such pretty dresses to wear! They admired Hogarth's *Four Times of the Day* painted round the walls of a pavilion, in which they listened to the marvellous voice of Mrs Bland, a leading actress from the Haymarket, singing *My Pretty Jane*, and watched Mr Handel conducting one of his own works; they ate the famous thin slices of ham and a whole basket of peaches, sitting in a banqueting-house made entirely of glass, with fountains playing, and afterwards they drank a bowl of arrack punch under the trees.

Stephen pointed out celebrities. There was my Lord Bute with his guard of prize-fighters, without whom he never stirred because he was so unpopular. And there was the Prime Minister himself, wrapped as usual in at least two greatcoats even on this warm evening, so terrified was he of catching cold.

"You see that lady holding court there," whispered Stephen. "That's the great Italian singer Mingotti, who refused to sing the other night because the King was not in the Royal Box as usual. And so Mr Quin, the actor, who so inveighs against the Italian opera, wrote a squib on her:

> 'Ra, ru, ra, rot ye,
> My name is Mingotti,
> If you worship me notti,
> You shall all go to potti.' "

The ladies laughed at this until they cried; but Nancy, unaccustomed to wine, was beginning to nod. This was precisely what Stephen had hoped, and drawing his chair very slightly nearer Magdalene's, he said with a small sigh:

"I find myself somewhat depressed whenever I come here Miss Magdalene. You see that great oak near the music-house? It always reminds me of the Hiding Oak at Old Park, and that makes me really homesick."

"But surely," said Magdalene, whom the heady punch had stimulated, making her feel at the same time natural and sentimental, "you can't regret the old days when you were so poor."

"A man can be lonely, madam, even though he's rich."

"You promised to tell me how you made your fortune," said Magdalene, oddly excited by the implication of his words.

He told her; not, indeed, all, but the respectable part. And he made the most of his early struggles. With considerable skill he conjured up a picture of an ambitious, penniless boy, a sort of Dick Whittington, who had come to this great city to try his luck.

"It's a cruel place, London, Miss Magdalene. Honest trade's out of fashion; a man must live by his wits."

He had not, he hastened to add, descended to dishonesty, but he had been forced to some hard dealings. He did not say so, but he hinted that this was chiefly because he had lacked the influence of some good woman, adding that it was his deepest sorrow that his beloved old father had died before Stephen could set him up in comfort. He had no one now; he was turning into a sour old bachelor. She laughed a trifle hysterically; why, he could not be more than twenty-three, she reminded him. Stephen did not laugh; he sighed again, this time more deeply, murmured something about a foolish, presumptuous, secret dream, refused to enlarge on this, and changing his subject abruptly, begged for news of Old Park.

So Magdalene began.

The wine and the flattery loosened her tongue, and she made no attempt to be fair. Sir Hubert had gone to London to seek for news of her beloved twin, and had been tricked into marriage by a livery-keeper's daughter, who was now the mistress of Old Park. Her old jealous hatred of Barbara grew hotter with every word. Sir Hubert had been sorry for this woman, she cried, because she had told him some tale about being turned out of her home by her father for becoming a Catholic. A Catholic indeed! Why, she didn't know the responses to the Office of Holy Cross, and actually she had asked what was meant by the Vernacle, the picture of Christ's face impressed on St Veronica's cloth, which hung in the chapel at home.

"I've always believed she was a spy," whispered Magdalene.

Stephen sympathised and probed further. There was no child of the marriage, it seemed; and though Magdalene, with the prudishness of some passionate natures, hurried away from the subject, he gathered that such an event was unlikely now. Robin had never been heard of again; Michael, the youngest boy, was studying for the priesthood at Douai. One day, therefore, the estate might pass to Magdalene herself; and since the male Thornes were notoriously short-lived, that day might not be so very far distant. It was all very interesting.

"She poisoned my brother's mind against me," Magdalene raged on, "and turned me out of my dear home. Old Park was everything to me, and now I may never see it again. And my sister-in-law doesn't really care about it; and how should she? – a tradesman's daughter! She's quite content to see it neglected; she even likes the weeds; she said so. But if I had money, I would – oh lord! how silly I am to talk like this. I shall never own Old Park, and I shall never have any money because of my religion. And yet since I've been in London I've found that some Catholics do have – oh, I beg your pardon," stammered Magdalene aghast. "I meant Mr Phillimore; I didn't – "

Her voice petered out and she blushed furiously. But Stephen, far from taking offence, appeared to be hanging his head in shame. It was not that he had conformed, he told her, but he confessed that he had found ways of dodging the inconveniences of his religion. And the fact of it was, he had been drifting away from the Faith of late years; that was what came of living among heretics. But it was not fitting that he should trouble a young gentlewoman with such matters, he added; sighed heavily again; and suggested that it was time they woke Nancy.

(ii)

Stephen had good cause to feel pleased with himself as a result of that evening at Vauxhall. For by now he had decided that he was going to marry Magdalene Thorne, and he did not think the wooing would be difficult.

Her grudge against Barbara, her loneliness, her discontentment with her uncongenial life, her obsession with her lost home, all had combined to make her reckless; and she had no chance of marrying a man of her own class. And this evening he had started the most promising of all flirtations, a spiritual one. He had left her with the impression that he was in trouble about his soul, and would like to consult her but was too humble to do so. A girl who had believed herself to have a religious vocation would see herself as a sort of good angel in such circumstances; and as such Stephen was very willing that she should see herself, until he had got her securely on the hook. Until after his marriage he would have to pretend to be a devout Catholic, for it was unthinkable that Magdalene would marry him unless she thought she had reconverted him. But he had not the slightest intention of practising his religion once he had married Magdalene; apart from the fact that he despised it, it would do him infinite harm both financially and socially.

There were two reasons why he had decided to marry her. She had a considerable physical attraction for him, and he was cunning enough to realise that she would never

131

consent to an illicit relationship; and by marrying her he would satisfy his old grudge against the Thornes. To go down to Old Park, he, the ex-gardener's boy, as a member of the family, to contrast their poverty with his wealth, to watch Sir Hubert's face when he called him 'brother', to boast his grand acquaintances, to stroll about the grounds where once he had trundled a barrow, to see the very servants who had cuffed and scolded him pulling their forelocks and bobbing curtsies – oh there indeed were the sweets of revenge!

And after his *tête-à-tête* with Magdalene at Vauxhall, an even greater ambition had been born in his mind, though he was sensible enough to realise that the chances of its being fulfilled were remote. Yet the fact remained that if Sir Hubert died childless, Magdalene would become the mistress of Old Park and Lady Thorne merely the dowager. And if he, Stephen, married Magdalene and she inherited, it would not be a case of going down there on a visit, but actually of owning the estate. Owning Old Park! Giving his orders, turning out tenants and servants at his pleasure, pulling down and rebuilding the place if he chose, sleeping in the best bedroom, receiving the visits of the County. His mouth watered at the mere thought.

But he was not the man to waste time building castles in the air. After years of patient nursing of a grudge, fate had given him a chance of striking a mortal blow at the Thorne pride. Sufficient unto the day was the good thereof.

Stephen was right in believing that his giving Magdalene the impression that he was in some spiritual distress had done his business for him.

Already, after the first few meetings, she had indulged in some new dreams. Marriage, wealth, and security, those blessings to which, it seemed, she could never look forward, suddenly had come within the realm of possibility; and though her pride revolted from the idea of marrying a man who had been a menial in her own home, such revulsion was largely offset by the fact that he had acquired good manners and was accepted by London society. Moreover, there was on her side, too, a definite physical attraction, dating, though she did not know it, from that evening long ago when a skinny arm had entwined her waist in the dark of the shrubbery.

But Stephen's hints that he had been drifting away from the Faith for want of a friend to keep his feet upon the right path lifted the affair from the sordid to the romantic, and without romance Magdalene could not live. Here indeed was a most becoming role, and one she could play with genuine enthusiasm; she was to be the wife who led her husband back to religion. She had a vocation after all; it was not just a question of marrying for money, or of escaping from the terrifying prospect of growing old unloved, of getting hairy-faced like Mother Mistress. It was a question of the saving of a soul. In the happiness engendered by this thought, she became meticulous in her own religious devotions. She wanted to make it up to God for all her past indifference and rebellion.

Reverend Mother watched the affair with some misgivings. Stephen when presented to her was at his most respectful, but she was a shrewd woman, and she suspected a hidden malice beneath his honeyed words, his veneer of good manners. Yet she could find nothing definite to object to in him, and she was of her age in believing that unless a girl had a religious vocation, marriage and children were what God had ordained for her. As for Stephen's lowly origins, so far as the English Catholics were concerned social barriers inevitably were breaking down.

Debarred from the professions, many of the noble families were being forced into trade.

Stephen proposed to Magdalene in writing, the most approved method of his day. It was a letter modelled on those in which the heroes of popular romances sought the hand of their lady-loves, a nice mixture of passion, propriety, and extravagant humility.

Magdalene's answer, the composition of which occupied all her leisure hours and wasted a great many sheets of paper, was in the same style; she said 'Yes' in a whole tangle of stilted phrases. The accepted suitor, wearing a proper expression of bliss, straightway called at the convent, and was ushered into the parlour, where he kissed his fiancée under the benevolent eyes of Reverend Mother. After compliments and congratulations, Reverend Mother opened the question of the marriage ceremony, explaining the perplexity into which the recent Marriage Act had thrown the Catholics.

For many years past the fact that marriages could be solemnised without licence or banns in any church or chapel not subject to the jurisdiction of a bishop had given rise to very scandalous abuses. The clerical debtors in the Fleet, the Marshalsea, and the King's Bench fitted up rooms within the liberties of these prisons, and sent out touts to bring in couples. It was no uncommon thing to see in these neighbourhoods the sign of a male and female hand joined, with a notice 'Marriages performed within', a clock kept always at a canonical hour, and a parson, in a tattered plaid nightgown, prowling up and down outside, ready to marry anyone for a dram of gin or a roll of tobacco.

To stop the evil, the present Lord Chancellor had just brought in a Bill which enacted that henceforth every marriage must be solemnised with the full rites of the Established Church, the only exceptions being in favour of

Quakers and Jews. The penalties for evading the Act were extremely heavy; the parties could be convicted as felons, the officiating clergyman was liable to four years' transportation, the future children would be considered illegitimate, and on the death of the husband the widow might find her property seized on the grounds that she had never been his wife in the eyes of the law.

"Dr Challoner has spoken with me several times upon the dilemma into which this Act has put us," continued Reverend Mother. "It was suggested by some that a memorial be drawn up, petitioning for an amendment to the Act, whereby those who are not members of the Established Church might be excused from the religious service. But Dr Challoner, always so prudent, has refused to countenance such a memorial fearing to draw attention to ourselves and thus to risk a renewal of persecution."

"But I could never be married with Protestant rites," cried Magdalene. "It would be sacrilege!"

"Some of our priests say," went on Reverend Mother, "that we are now under the compulsion of the law, that the heretical rites may be treated as a mere civil ceremony, and the officiating minister as no more than a civil officer; all agree, however, that the parties must not kneel to receive the minister's blessing or take part in the prayers. But those after Dr Challoner's own heart are the ones who heroically accept the very grave risks involved by refusing to go to the Protestant church at all, and are married secretly with our own ceremonies as heretofore."

"And that is how we will be married, Stephen and I," Magdalene said proudly, taking her fiancé's hand.

Stephen nodded his head in solemn agreement, and Reverend Mother's opinion of him was considerably improved. Shrewd woman though she was, she did not understand the tortuous processes of a mind such as Mr Vickery's. To fulfil the law and go to a Protestant church while refusing the minister's blessing would advertise to the town that he was a Catholic. As for the risk of incurring penalties by not doing so, he could afford to laugh at it, for he had every intention of repudiating his religion as soon as he had satisfied his grudge against the Thornes.

(iii)

Life for Magdalene became a whirl of delight.

Stephen was most generous, insisting on giving his betrothed a substantial sum of money so that she might buy herself a trousseau, and showering expensive presents upon her. Her gratitude to him knew no bounds, not only for the gifts but for the love she was sure had prompted them. For the first time in her twenty-five years she was the most important person in somebody's life and had become the object of envy to others. Her bare little room at the convent was always full of teachers and pupils admiring her hoop of the new oval shape, her clocked silk stockings, her head-dress *en cabriolet*, a huge cap in the form of the one-horse chairs just introduced, her furred mantuas, her little jewelled watch. She was to have a maid of her own as soon as she was married, and even a little black page.

Dr Challoner himself officiated at her wedding in the convent chapel, which the nuns had decked with flowers; and in her triumphant happiness she thought with contempt of Barbara, who had deemed it 'wonderful' to be married in a wretched little tavern garret, with no admiring congregation, no silver bride-cup, no expensive wedding-dress. But of course a horse-coper's daughter might well have been content to be married anywhere when she had caught a baronet for a husband.

A few days later the newly married couple drove down to visit Old Park. They went in style in one of the new perch-phaetons, the very last word in carriage design, with the graceful swan-necked perches painted yellow and the high wheels picked out with red, and a cart piled high with luggage following on behind. A small retinue of servants, in new liveries and well armed because of the danger from highwaymen, accompanied them; and trotting on ahead a running-footman, picturesque in velvet cap and silver-fringed drawers, cleared the way with his huge staff, in the ball of which was a mixture of white wine and eggs with which he might refresh himself while he ran.

Stephen was in a perfect ecstasy. He imagined them waiting for him at Old Park, seeing them by turns nearly mad with mortification and trying to ingratiate themselves with him, even to borrow from him. But no, they would snub and ignore him; they would be extravagantly sympathetic to Magdalene in his presence, and furiously reproachful in private for having brought this disgrace on the Thornes. They would get out the best plate and pretend they used it every day; they would make pathetic efforts to conceal their penury. They would try to humiliate him by references to his humble past when he had been their drudge.

And he, how he would patronise them! How plain he would make it that he had conferred a favour on Magdalene by marrying a penniless school-teacher when he might have picked and chosen from the cream of London society. How tongue-tied he would make them by talking familiarly of public men and the affairs of Government, pretending to take it for granted they would understand when he referred to Ministers by their nicknames…

"Hello there!" cried a voice, a voice he had not heard for many years, interrupting his day-dream.

He looked over the side of the phaeton, and saw a man on horseback pushing his way along an overgrown path on to the drive. The horse was old, the rider shabby and without wig, hat, or gloves. Sir Hubert Thorne! Oh, this was better than his wildest dreams! He had come upon his aristocratic brother-in-law before the latter had had time to doll himself up. And what a glorious contrast they made, the pair of them, the owner of Old Park dressed like a labourer, the one-time gardener's boy in silver-buttoned suit and lace cravat, with a gold watch in his fob and a snowy wig built up in front in the very latest fashion. Before Magdalene had time to greet her brother, Stephen, surveying Hubert through his quizzing-glass, drawled:

"Did you want something, my man?"

He was startled by a shout of laughter.

"Gad, that's droll! Yes, brother Stephen, I wanted to greet you. But small wonder you don't recognise me after all these years. Here, you, fellow, hold these horses' heads. Magda, my dear, lean down from that perilous perch of yours and give me a kiss."

'You, fellow!' To Stephen's running-footman! He wanted to snarl at the footman, 'Let the horses be'; but the man, at the command of someone who looked like a tramp, instantly had obeyed, and one of the liveried outriders had jumped down to assist in quieting Hubert's horse, which was inclined to shy at the phaeton.

"He's all right," laughed Hubert. "(There, old beauty; never seen such a contraption, have you?) I hope those high wheels don't get stuck in our ruts, Stephen. You'd best lead the horses, man," he added to the running-footman, "and could do with a quiet walk yourself, I fancy; you look dead beat."

Silent with fury, Stephen observed his brother-in-law, as Hubert walked his horse beside the phaeton, chattering cheerfully to his sister.

Memory called up a grave-faced lad, whose forehead was creased with an anxious frown, whose firm, authoritative voice concealed the basic uncertainty of youth. This young man, though he looked much older than his years, was not grave and did not frown, and his voice had a happy, self-assured ring. Above all, he was perfectly natural; there was not the faintest trace of that embarrassment and defensiveness over which Stephen had gloated in anticipation. There was no attempt to explain away the shabby dress, the ungloved hands, the ill-groomed horse.

The bitterly frustrated Stephen could find only one comfort. Despite his cheeriness and the happiness in his eyes, Sir Hubert Thorne looked ill.

Stephen needed comfort, for his darling dream of revenge, nursed through so many years, faded rapidly during his stay at Old Park.

Like all egotists, he had taken it for granted that his former employers had been as preoccupied with him as he had been with them, that the poor gardener's boy who had made good would be vivid in their memories. But the grudge had lived, he discovered, only in his own warped mind. From master to servant they welcomed him as the husband of the daughter of the house; no more, and no less than that. They were either too well-bred or too indifferent to make any reference to his astonishing rise in life. There were no congratulations, except one which he did not relish.

"You're quite a wonder" remarked Hubert at dinner, "if, you'll excuse me saying so. A wealthy Catholic. But I suppose there are quite a number in London."

This gave Stephen an excuse for launching upon a description of his grand acquaintances. He often met the Duke of Norfolk at White's, and despite his religion his Grace had been an intimate friend of the late Prince of Wales. And then there was Lord Petre, who was a relation of the Vicar Apostolic, and a member of the Beefsteak. Hubert interrupted with a pleasant laugh.

"You forget what a country bumpkin I am," he said, sounding as though he liked being one. "I've never heard of these clubs, for I was never in London but once."

"To enquire for news of your missing brother," said Stephen meaningly.

"Yes. I wondered if you remembered Robin. It seems so long ago."

"I have cause to remember him. He thrashed me. On the terrace there. It is not a thing one forgets – brother."

Hubert threw back his head and laughed.

"Isn't it? You must have a good memory. Goodness knows how many times I was flogged as a boy, and damme if I can remember any particular occasion. And I expect we both deserved it."

Thus airily did he dismiss the subject, setting the seal on Stephen's thwarted malice. But you wait, thought Stephen; I'll find the means to make you pay for that thrashing, if it's the last thing I do.

Oblivious of these dark thoughts, Hubert and Barbara were doing their best to entertain him. They feigned polite interest in their guests' description of the latest play and the Italian opera, of excursions to Belsize to eat breakfast in the famous gardens, of Mr Foote's scandalous mimicry of public men in his unlicensed theatre in the Haymarket. And they took it for granted that in return Stephen and Magdalene would want to hear of their own affairs.

"My brother Michael hopes to be ordained next year," said Hubert. "It seems so strange, for I remember him only as a small boy down among the babies at Douai. But Dr William Green, the new President, writes me that Michael has done extremely well in his Higher Studies, and is going to make a very good priest."

"I have dreamed of his coming to his old home as chaplain," said Barbara, "but if he is sent as a missionary priest, I suppose he will be needed in London. How fortunate you are to be able to hear Mass. We have never been able to replace Mr Maribon, Magdalene, but sometimes a priest who is travelling from one part of the country to another stays with us for a night or two."

She turned to Stephen and asked eagerly:

"I wonder if you have ever come across my parents in London. I dared not even tell them I was married, because my father is so bitter against the Faith that I was afraid he might go to the length of informing against Hubert."

"I fancy I once hired a horse from a person of the name of Masson," drawled Stephen, still hoping to wound. "But it was such a wretched screw that I have never patronised the stables since."

"Poor Father," said Barbara compassionately. "I'm afraid that when he put on the wedding-garment of faith, as he termed it, he shed the workaday garment of sound business sense."

"Fancy having a father you fear might turn informer!" Magdalene cried spitefully.

Hubert was about to give her a sharp rebuke, but, encountering his wife's eyes, refrained. Throughout the meal and afterwards over the tea-table, Stephen noticed how often they glanced at one another, and how full of love were those glances. As the four of them went out for a stroll in the gardens, Barbara put her hand through her sister-in-law's arm, and whispered:

"Come to the garden-house, Magda, where we can talk."

Magdalene stiffened at the use of the diminutive, but allowed herself to be persuaded, for she was looking forward to impressing Barbara with her own self-sacrifice in marrying beneath her in order to save a soul.

"I must lend you one of my aprons the next time you pour out tea," she said as they walked along. "No lady in London ever dreams of pouring out without one."

141

"But I am not a fine London lady," laughed Barbara, "and I wear an apron for so much of the day that I'm glad to take it off sometimes. I'm afraid those pretty shoes of yours aren't suited to our mud. Oh, Magda, I am so glad to see you!" And she pressed the other's arm.

She was obviously sincere, and Magdalene was both irritated and puzzled. She had noticed from the first that Barbara seemed to have a new bloom about her, a new lilt to her step, a new happiness that bubbled in her voice and danced in her eyes.

"I hope you won't find the old place too much changed," said Barbara, opening the door of the garden-house, "but I've got rid of all those pagan figures your grandfather put here; I couldn't bear them, especially just now."

There was a shy significance in the last three words, but Magdalene did not notice. How full of memories was this place, how sacred to the Thornes! So many games had been played here; and later, so many secrets whispered and romantic plans made, when Robin had resolved to fight for Prince Charles Edward. Nostalgia had been growing in her ever since she had passed through the entrance to Old Park, reviving her hatred of the intruder, and this usurpation of the garden-house set an edge to it. She turned to glower at Barbara, and was in time to see something which increased her jealous hostility. It was just a little loving glance by Barbara at a crucifix she had nailed up on the wall where a bust of Apollo had stood; no pious play-acting, but something quite instinctive. Barbara, it seemed, had the best of both worlds – the love of God and man.

"I wanted to tell you how happy Hubert and I are," said Barbara, taking in a work-roughened hand her sister-in-law's artificially whitened fingers, "that you are married. It was such a surprise – "

"That I should marry? My dear sister, one would think I were old and ugly."

"You know I don't mean that, Magdalene. But we thought, you see, your vocation – oh, I don't quite know what I'm saying today! I'm so very, very happy. For I have a surprise for you, Magda. Dear Magda, I'm going to have a child."

There was a hissing breath from the stiff figure beside her, and the hand she was holding wrenched itself free, but she did not notice.

"At last! After all these years of marriage. It's like a miracle. I've hoped and prayed and tried to resign myself, but now God has been good to me, and with His blessing there will be an heir to Old Park. I'm sure it will be a son. I'm so joyful and grateful that I – "

Her voice choked, and the tears poured down her face.

"*Your* child to inherit Old Park!"

Barbara raised her head and blinked. Her sister-in-law's face was contorted, her voice was like a whip.

"And Hubert's child – why, Magdalene, don't look like that, don't speak so. What is the matter? Magda, sit down again, let's talk… "

"Let me go!"

"No, I won't. Not until you tell me why you are behaving in this strange fashion. I know you always disliked me, but you must be glad for your brother's sake. He has been so patient, so uncomplaining, and now he is so happy. Magdalene, you cannot be so wicked as to – "

"Wicked! How dare you call me that! It's you who are wicked, robbing me of my rights. Yes," she cried, beside herself with fury, "after Hubert, Old Park should come to me! Michael can't inherit; Robin's dead; this is my home. You drove me from it once and now you'd keep me from inheriting it one day. But you shan't, you shan't! I'll find a way to prevent you; I've a husband now, a rich man, a clever man of the world. I'm not poor and friendless any longer; and I won't see the grandson of a horse-coper lording it at Old Park!"

Then she was gone and the door slammed behind her.

# Chapter Ten

The woods of Old Park lit their autumn torches, the sea mists isolated the ancient house still further from the outside world, blurred the windows and crept damply into the rooms. Hubert coughed a good deal as he rode round his estates and worked at his husbandry, and often he looked grey and drawn when he came home of an evening. It was nothing, he insisted; he would be well in the spring. But old Nana muttered dark hints in the servants' hall, brewed magic potions in her still room, and saw nothing but sickness and death in the cards.

The last leaves carpeted the lily lake and Christmas came. Barbara hung the house with bay and holly, and Hubert and Mr Filton carried in the yule log. From the attics the old crib was fetched down and put in its usual place in the chapel; often Barbara knelt there, finding a new sweetness in the battered figures, the Holy Child lying so helpless and appealing in the manger, and the ass and the ox, one of them without a head, of the same size as the shepherds.

But Barbara, for all her happiness, had the nervous moods of the pregnant woman, and for the first time since Hubert had met her wept easily.

"If only we could hear Mass," she said, listening to the joyous pealing of the church bells in the village. "And how is my child to be baptised without a priest?"

He comforted her as well as he could. Though the whole purpose of his life seemed to have been taken away with the going of his chaplain and the gradual lapsing of his tenants, his inner life had deepened and intensified, even though the framework of it had been withdrawn. Lacking a human guide, he had turned to the spiritual writers, and he had penetrated far into that mysterious country of which they wrote. Throughout the ages, thousands of men and women, through no fault of their own, had been cut off from Mass and the Sacraments, and it seemed that God had chosen him to be among that company who must depend on prayer alone.

And at least he was no longer solitary as he had been when first he had returned from school. The post-boy's horn sounded at regular intervals in the lane of the 'cathedral trees', announcing a letter from Michael, a Michael who, it seemed, was also an inhabitant of that world of the spirit which had become so real to Hubert, and who was able to guide his elder brother through some of its more difficult tracts. And for human companionship there was Barbara, his dear and only love, Barbara who was about to give him a child, perhaps a son to carry on his name, perhaps even, one day, to make Old Park a centre of Catholic life again.

Often, sitting by the fire of an evening, reading aloud from Dr Challoner's latest book, *Meditations for Every Day in the Year*, while Barbara stitched at her baby-clothes, Hubert would let the volume slip from his hand, and would fall into a reverie, staring into the fire and remembering that strangely comforting remark of Dr Challoner's:

"There is still a live ember in the ashes."

146

But often lately Barbara would interrupt his musings by saying things which suggested that she was being foolishly fanciful.

"I wish we could get rid of Nana," she burst out one evening.

He laid down his book, bewildered.

"Get rid of Nana! Why, she is part of Old Park."

"She is evil, Hubert. She is for ever plaguing me with her old wives' tales, seeing ghost-lights in the woods and mumbling about a death in the family because a robin came into the house one day. She pesters me to wear the dried dead body of a toad about my neck, or otherwise I shall die in labour. And I cannot bear to think of her delivering my baby; she is so foul, and she has that terrible birthmark. They say that sometimes a child is born with a like disfigurement if – "

"It is you who are being superstitious now, my love," interrupted Hubert, laughing at her gently, taking her hands. "Nana brought us all into the world; she has her little ways, I know, but she's an experienced midwife."

"I would rather have a doctor."

"But there is none of our religion in the whole of the county."

"A Protestant one would not make my child a heretic," objected Barbara with unusual tartness.

"You don't understand. None of the Protestant physicians would consent to attend a Papist; it might do their practice harm."

She dismissed this as nonsense. Throughout the years of her married life she had met very few Protestants; and as for her father and his bigotry, she thought of him as an exception. After all, did not the local parson always raise his hat to her most courteously whenever she encountered him, booted and spurred, on his way to a meet?

It was the Feast of the Epiphany. Barbara had seemed her old self that day, full of courage and hope. They had added the figures of the Magi to the others in the crib, and had knelt side by side at a prie-dieu, beseeching the Holy Child once more to manifest Himself to the world. And Barbara had laughed as she cut the traditional cake, and the slice Hubert took had been found to contain the bean for the knave. But immediately after supper she said that she was tired and would go to bed, bidding him remember to take his hot posset which was keeping warm in the cup of one of the fire-dogs; for his cough had been made worse by the foul weather.

He watched her ascend the stair, her movements heavy, one hand grasping the banister. He had an impulse to run after her and help her, but she disliked being fussed, and presently he saw her kneel down as usual before the picture of Blessed Michael Thorne. By some odd trick of the candlelight the sad face of the Martyr seemed to contort itself, as it must have done on the scaffold when the noose tightened about his throat. A thrill of fear tingled in Hubert; and next moment his nerves jangled and his heart leapt, as from the figure beneath the portrait there issued such a scream as he had never heard in all his life before.

He was beside her in an instant, shouting for the women, scarcely recognising his wife, with her starting eyes and her mouth a-snarl with agony. They got her to bed, and Nana came hobbling, malodorous and senile; and Hubert saw her suddenly for what she was, a creature more fit to lay out a corpse than to bring a child into the world. Pacing the gallery, listening at the bedroom door, he heard her cackling laugh, her unsteady footsteps, her voice gabbling some incantation, mingling with Barbara's moans. He knew nothing of the mysteries of childbirth; there were only dim memories of being wakened by Nana, the safe, familiar Nana, and told that he had a new baby brother. And later being led on tiptoe to this very bedroom, so grand and mysterious to him then, to kiss a little something wrapped in shawls, while his mother lay relaxed and smiling on the pillows.

It was a bitter night and the gallery was icy; his cough racked him, seeming now to tear his chest, but he could not go down to the fire. There was a huddle of maids outside the door, whispering, exclaiming, knocking; he scarcely noticed them until the cook, the mother of a large family, came up to him and pulled his sleeve.

"Nana won't let us in, sir. She will have it that we'll bring my lady bad luck. She's a witch, sir; I always said it; weigh her against the family Bible, and you'd see! But she's right when she swears we can do nothing, for my lady is past the skill of midwives. For Jesu's sake, master, get a leech!"

He brushed her aside, flung down the stairs, and ran to the stables to get his horse.

(ii)

As soon as he was away from the shelter of the trees, the wind, blowing dead out of the east, cut him across the body like a lash. He had not stayed to put on his old riding-cloak, and the blast went through his threadbare suit as if it had been paper. But presently he was in a sweat and had to dash his hand across his eyes to clear his vision. For some days past he had felt a curious weakness in his limbs, and now when he tried to guide and urge on his horse he found he had no strength to do so. But the horse seemed to sense his urgency, even to know his destination, for without need of heel or rein it galloped breakneck through the darkness of the familiar lanes towards Newtown.

He roused himself when a feeble light or two announced the little town. It was nearly midnight and the streets were deserted. The doctor. Where did he live? What was his name? This buzzing in his head, this horrible pain in his chest which made him think of the painted knife stuck in the breast of the Martyr...Gregson, that was the name... three doors down from the White Hart...the White Hart, Robin drinking to Prince Charlie there, getting foxed, forcing passers-by to pledge his Royal Highness... No, no, Robin was dead... Gregson, a little man with a mole on his chin, a good doctor it was said...three doors, two doors... this was the one.

The thud of his fist on the door was drowned in the shriek of the wind down the empty street. He shouted; he kicked at the panels. It seemed an eternity before a light appeared in an upstairs window, and by that time other windows had been flung open and dim heads craned out up and down the street.

"Well, what is it, what is it?" demanded a fretful voice.

Hubert stepped back into the road, so that the light in the window shone upon him. He cried hoarsely:

"Mr Gregson, sir, I implore you to come to my wife. She is fallen in labour and the midwife needs your assistance."

The candle was moved to and fro as the doctor sought to identify his caller, and in the pause could be heard an undercurrent of voices from the townsfolk whom Hubert's shouting had aroused. Then the light vanished; a few moments later there was the sound of a bolt being withdrawn, the door was opened, and the doctor, in nightcap and bedgown, stood there shielding his candle flame from the wind.

"Sir Hubert Thorne," he said curtly. "I thought I recognised you. I regret I cannot come."

"You cannot – "

"Tut, sir, you have worked yourself into a fine state. Your wife will do well, never fear. Why, by the time you return you will find her safely delivered – "

"Mr Gregson, you don't understand. She has only my mother's ancient nurse whose skill is long gone. I conjure you by your profession to ride with me immediately. I will pay you any fee you care to name."

"It is not a question of a fee, sir," snapped the doctor. "You know very well why I cannot come, and I am amazed that you ask it of me." He lowered his voice. "Had you not wakened half the town by your knockings and hallooings, I do not say but I might have risked it. But to be seen going on a professional visit in your company – gad, sir, tomorrow my rival would have all my patients."

"You will not come to save two lives?"

"It is not I will not, but I dare not. There you have it blunt, sir. You have only yourself to blame," he went on, speaking loudly now for the benefit of the ears straining at doors and windows. "So obstinate in your Papistry have you and your family shown yourselves, and now you come whining for aid to a good Protestant. If you were consistent, sir, you would fall upon your knees and enlist the help of the Virgin Mary and your other idols. And now, sir, have the goodness to take yourself off and allow me to return to my bed."

He rode home in a phantasmagoria. There seemed to be people with him, Robin, his mother, old Mr Maribon. He kept hearing his brother Michael's voice begging him not to be sad at home. On the saddle with him sat one of the heraldic beasts from the gate-posts, the one which had lost an ear and looked so friendly, like a woolly lamb Barbara had cherished in childhood. In his chest, twisting and turning, was the knife from the picture of Blessed Michael Thorne.

And all the while the face of Barbara looked at him from the darkness, now smiling her wide comradely smile, now contorted with agony, now gallant and courageous and bright as a beacon.

But when his horse stopped of its own accord at last, and he stared through the open doorway beneath the cracked Corinthian pillars of the porch, a real sound broke through the walls of his fever. The cry of his infant son was the last thing he heard before he plunged into unconsciousness.

(iii)

Barbara came of a good yeoman stock, and the knowledge that she was needed gave her added strength. Despite the difficulty with which he had come into the world, her son was a healthy babe, but her other loved one was dangerously ill. She was up in a few days, and, driving Nana from the sickbed, took charge.

At first her native optimism held at bay her fears for his survival. He was only in his middle twenties and had lived an outdoor life; devoted nursing was all he required. But the bright red blood in the basin when he coughed told a different story, and presently it did not need the scared faces of the servants and Nana's dark mutterings to warn her of what she must face. Old master had gone the same way, whispered the crone, and his father before him; fair-lived but short-lived, the male Thornes.

That he himself was aware of the dread shadow that darkened over him was plain from Hubert's talk. In intervals of consciousness he devoted the little energy that remained to him in instructing his wife in the affairs of the estate, and, his face bathed in the sweat of the effort, laboriously dictated his will. As this would have to be admitted to probate in the Prerogative Court of Canterbury, he communicated verbally to Barbara what he wished to have set aside for charity and for Masses for his soul, asking her to seek the help of Dr Challoner in arranging such matters.

"He will be a friend to you, my love; whatever happens, you may rely upon his friendship."

Neither of them ever mentioned that ghastly night of their son's birth and the refusal of the doctor to come to a Popish mother's aid. To Hubert it was just one more penalty he had had to pay for adhering to his religion. Even the knowledge that he must be buried, according to law, with Protestant rites, drew no complaint from him, for so it had ever been since the Reformation. But once he murmured wistfully that he wished he could have had his chaplain with him still, to give the absolutions over the coffin before it was carried to the parish church; and again, wringing Barbara's heart, he said, waking from sleep:

"I dreamed a good dream, my love. A priest came into the room; I thought it was Michael. He told me he had come to give me shrift and housel; perhaps you won't understand those ancient, hallowed terms. The Last Sacraments – how they must fortify the soul at its passing!"

That passing came when his son was but a few weeks old. It was a clear, soft winter's day, and Hubert seemed better, lying quietly in his bed, propped with pillows so that he could see through the window his favourite trees, five tall pines which were, he had thought in childhood, five old women enveloped in coarse black lace, who bent and whispered together in a wind, and caught the moon in their web on a clear night.

But as evening fell, Barbara noticed a change in him, a change which made her heart beat thick and her mouth dry. He was not in pain now, and he was fully conscious, but he seemed suddenly withdrawn. He did not respond to the pressure of her hand; it was as if a part of him were already somewhere else, and that he was preoccupied with something which made him aloof even from her and her desperate grief.

In the small hours of the morning he spoke suddenly, his voice clear and strong.

"My people. My servants. Please call them. And the candles and the Manual; fetch them, please."

She had prayed for strength for this hour when he would need her supremely, but he did not need her. He laid his hand for a moment in blessing on the head of his son, then signed peremptorily to Nana to carry the child from the death-chamber; he spoke to each of the servants, from butler to scullion, as they knelt about his bed, thanking them for their faithful service, asking their forgiveness for any harshness of which he might have been guilty towards them, begging them to respond to the prayers his wife would read. His strength was nearly gone now; only his eyes, sunk deep in their sockets, implored his wife to begin the Commendation for a Departing Soul.

Her hands were shaking so violently that she could scarcely find the place; but as she began the Litany, and the voices round her, husky and choked, responded with *Ora pro nobis*, she realised clearly the meaning of the Communion of Saints, and the long honour-roll of the Blessed was no longer a mere string of names.

The Litany was ended, and she began the Church's splendid valediction:

" 'Go forth, O Christian soul, out of this world, in the name of God the Father who created thee; in the name of God the Son who suffered for thee; in the name of God the Holy Ghost who sanctified thee...in the name of angels and archangels, thrones and dominations; in the name of the virtues and of the cherubim and seraphim; in the name of the patriarchs and prophets, of the holy apostles and evangelists, of the holy martyrs, confessors, monks and hermits, of the holy virgins, and of all the Saints of God... ' "

It seemed to her that his soul, like a grounded ship, was beginning to lift to gentle waves that came to free it. The flames of the tapers held by all present fluttered this way and that, as from the movement of an unseen company, his face had an august dignity, but his eyes, wide open, were full of a childlike wonder. When they glanced her way, she knew they did not see her; he was not hers any longer; he belonged to the heavenly beings she invoked.

" 'When your soul shall leave your body, may angels in their splendour come to welcome you. May the Apostles rise from their twelve thrones to meet you; may the triumphant army of martyrs give you greeting. May the holy men who have served Christ gather round you, dazzling in their glory, lilies in hand... May Mary the Virgin Mother of God, kind comforter of all in distress, be to you at this moment a true mother; and thus may you overcome the fear of death and go forward, happy and in her company, to the place you have always longed for in your heavenly home... ' "

The first bird twittered in the eaves, as though saying, 'Amen'.

# Chapter Eleven

(i)

St Cuthbert's Church was filled to overflowing for the funeral of Sir Hubert Thorne.

His neighbours who had ostracised him in life flocked to his obsequies, less out of respect for the dead man than to exchange opinions and to indulge in gossip. It was an open secret that Sir Hubert's desperate ride to summon Dr Gregson to his wife's accouchement had hastened if not caused the young baronet's death, and views on the doctor's conduct were sharply divided. Some spoke indignantly against him; others maintained that he was right and had acted only as a good Protestant should. In any case, young Lady Thorne had not needed him, as it turned out; and perhaps this would teach those obstinate Papists that the only sensible thing to do was to conform and to lay aside their absurd superstitions.

"It is a very shocking thing to think," the Vicar had remarked at a recent Hunt breakfast, "that Sir Hubert died without ghostly comfort simply because his wife was too bigoted to send for me when he was dying. And there can have been no secret Popish mummery, since they have no chaplain now. I remember how shocked I was when I heard from one of my churchwardens of how when her ladyship was buried the chaplain came at dead of night to sprinkle holy water round the hearse in the Thorne chapel."

Intoning the beautiful phrases of the Anglican burial service, the Vicar experienced a kind of pious exasperation, which quite honestly had little to do with the fact that he was missing an otter-hunt by moonlight. It could have been such a splendid funeral; he would have been so completely in his element if he could have officiated here tonight in the grand style befitting so ancient a family as the Thornes. Genteel funerals were so very consoling for the bereaved, with the hatchments and the torches and the paid 'weepers', the distribution of mourning-rings and scarves, the subdued feasting afterwards.

There was only one occupant of the pew which in ancient times had been sacred to the Thornes, and many were the curious glances directed at this occupant; indeed, it was chiefly to get a good look at him that the County had come here in force. For really it was quite a romance how he, once the gardener's boy, had made such a fortune and had married the daughter of the house, though one could not approve of any Papist making a fortune. But was he a Papist? He was attending this Protestant funeral. Altogether he was something of an enigma, this Mr Stephen Vickery.

Those who had hoped to learn something of him or from him were disappointed. As soon as the coffin had been lowered into the vault beneath the floor of the chapel, once a chantry, from which the altar endowed by the Thornes for their Requiems had been removed, Mr Vickery, without exchanging a word with anyone, rode back to Old Park in the mourning-coach carved with death's heads and other emblems of mortality. Directly he was away from the prying eyes, his expression of conventional grief gave way to one of cheerfulness; he

157

chuckled once or twice, took snuff, and tossed out of the window the sprig of rosemary he had held during the service.

When the Darell relations who had come for the funeral left Old Park, Stephen and his wife still stayed on, though there appeared to be no reason why they should not return to town. They avoided the widow who, clean contrary to custom, had emerged from her mourning-chamber instead of staying in seclusion there for a whole month. She was quietly busy, attending to her child, and closeted often with Mr Filton, the bailiff.

Her guests appeared quite able to amuse themselves without her. While Stephen went off by himself on mysterious errands, Magdalene indulged in an emotional revisiting of her childhood haunts, filled with self-pity for the lonely child who had been herself, who so often had contemplated suicide in 'My Little Bay' because no one loved or wanted her, who, roaming solitary in the woods, had heard the cheerful voices of the neighbours who shunned her. But now she was the wife of a rich man, with a house in Welbeck Street, and a host of fashionable friends; and soon...

Stephen stopped as he entered the hall and drew back into the shadow of the porch. From here he watched Barbara, in her black gown and crape headdress, come down the stair; turn to the left, and enter the room which had been her husband's study. He wanted to come upon her unawares, to take her by surprise. Walking softly to the door of the study, he listened, and hearing no sound of voices went in without knocking and closed the door firmly behind him.

Now though he would sooner have died than admit it, Stephen had never felt completely at his ease with Barbara. It was ridiculous that he should not; she was low-bred like himself, a tradesman's daughter, and he ought to have been able to dominate her without any such effort as he had to make when he patronised the grand Thornes. And yet, perversely enough, when he had come down to Old Park immediately after his marriage, it had been Barbara and not her husband who had given him some moments of discomfort when he had boasted of his wealth and his grand acquaintance.

He looked at her now. She was on her knees, lifting papers out of the drawers of a bureau and beginning to sort them into piles. He was pleased, and at the same time vexed with himself for needing to be pleased, to notice that she looked plain; dead black did not become her, and her face was pale and pinched. The soles of her shoes, blackened according to custom, needed repair he saw as she knelt there; the hands sorting the papers were those of a working woman. And that was what she was, by upbringing and even as Lady Thorne: a plain working woman. He turned the phrase over in his mind, drawing comfort from it.

"You'll excuse this interruption, sister," he began, trying to remember exactly what he had planned to say, "the more readily since it seems you have no use for the fiddle-faddles of the gentry into whose ranks you married and whose widows shut themselves up in mourning-chambers. I've given you ample time to – er – recover from the shock of Hubert's death and now we must have some talk."

"I am very sorry indeed," said Barbara, sitting back on her heels and speaking with an obvious effort, "if I have neglected you and Magdalene. But there are so many matters to settle, and only myself to deal with them. And then there is my child. I have not yet, I'm afraid, even thanked you for going to the funeral. You are a born Catholic, and so will know better than I what the Church

159

allows on these occasions; I think I've heard that a man is permitted to attend a funeral with heretical rites if it is a question of charity. But it must have been painful for you; and I do thank you most sincerely that Hubert had someone of his own faith to see him – buried, and to say a prayer over his grave."

She blinked back her tears and added hurriedly:

"Are you and Magdalene returning to London today? Have you come to bid me goodbye?"

"No," said Stephen, more loudly than he had intended.

He was not a man who ordinarily needed Dutch courage, but he found himself suddenly longing for a drink. He pulled out a chair from its place against the wall, and made a rough gesture towards it.

"Sit down, sister. You and I must have some talk."

There was a second's pause before she rose and sat down and her expression, though faintly puzzled, daunted him by its underlying composure. But it was better when she sat down; she had done what he had told her to do, and he himself was standing. He was in command.

"A sensible woman you are; I've always said so; and we can speak blunt, you and me. First now, I have to ask you a question. Are you intending to bring your son up a Papist?"

He was standing by the window, looking out over the ragged lawns. That myrtle tree; he'd cut it down. He'd always hated it, he remembered. He had kept seeing it, seeming as though it mocked him, when Robin had thrashed him on the terrace. A thousand pities that Robin had not lived to see this day.

"A *Papist*? I thought only Protestants used that term. And I can't understand why you should ask me such a question. Of course I am going to bring up little Hubert in the religion of his fathers, which is mine, and yours also."

160

"Question I had to ask. For I mean to stand strictly by the law."

With the myrtle tree removed, there would be quite a tidy view of the sea. But he would not cut down the shrubbery yonder. Oh no, not that. That was where he had made Magdalene scream.

"I am afraid I am a little stupid today, Stephen, or else you are talking in riddles. Of what law do you speak?"

He wheeled round and faced her. This was it.

"One you should know by heart – 11 and 12 of William III. No? Let me refresh your memory. 'Persons educated in, or professing the Popish religion, to be disabled from inheriting or taking lands, tenements, or hereditaments within this kingdom; and during such persons' lives, the next of kin, being a Protestant, to enjoy their lands, without being accountable for the profits.' "

He had a sudden uncanny feeling that he was addressing a statue, so still she sat, so unblinking were the eyes looking straight into his.

"There was a further clause in that Act. 'Whoever shall convict a person of sending his child beyond seas to be educated in Popery, shall receive the whole penalty of £100 inflicted by the Act of James I.' But you and I can forget that clause, sister; I don't quibble over a paltry hundred pounds. You can send your boy to Douai like his father, so far as I'm concerned, and I'll wink at it. Only I was obliged to ask you if you intended to rear him a Papist in order to discover whether I had a just claim."

She merely looked at him.

"Damme, sister!" He smacked one fist into the other palm, and was mortified by the feeble sound it made. "You're not so dull as you pretend, y'know. A claim to Old Park. As the husband of the Protestant next of kin. For I

161

forgot to mention that I've conformed to the Established Church, and so has my wife Magdalene."

(ii)

He had rehearsed it all so often. He had relished in anticipation a storm of weeping, furious denunciations, attempts to argue, a dramatic summons to the servants to throw him out, even, best of all, Barbara on her knees, pleading with him. But he had not reckoned on exploding his bombshell and finding a woman who just sat perfectly motionless, and looked at him and said nothing whatsoever. It was like finding a fellow actor 'dry up' in the most vital scene of the play. He went on talking; he had an odd feeling of struggling against an unseen current, and to his horror found himself almost making excuses.

"Now, lookee, young woman, you may think this hard, but come one day and you'll thank me for it. See all them papers" – (why the devil was he reverting all of a sudden to his old rural mistakes in grammar?) – "those papers, that tease you so; you don't have to worry no more about rents and debts and so forth. You don't belong here; a London wench you are, and must have found it dull being buried in the country."

He stopped; a sort of flicker had passed over her face at his last words, but she said nothing.

"And living under a leaky roof, half smothered with all them – those trees, with the rats squeaking behind the wainscot, and scarce knowing how to pay your way. Aye, I know your husband loved the old place, and because of that he'd have been glad to see it put into shape and redded up, as I intend to do; in fact I'm bound to do it by law, for the Act says I may enjoy the lands but not waste 'em. When Magda and I have made it fit to live in, you must come down and visit us some time," he said with ghastly jocularity.

Still she neither moved nor spoke, and because her silence was so daunting, his anger flared.

"Seems you don't believe me. Think I'm trying to bubble you." He plunged a hand into his pocket and brought out a document. "Here," he said, thrusting it at her; "copy of the Act of King William I got on purpose in Newtown this morning; Clause 10, that's the one. And I've been to two lawyers, *and* taken counsel's opinion, and they all tell me that according to this Act, Old Park properly belongs to Magda – "

Again he broke off, this time with a start. For she had risen, and it was like seeing a statue come to life. She moved steadily to the fireplace and pulled the bell, standing there in silence with her back to him until old Braithwayte came hobbling in answer to the summons.

"Braithwayte," said Barbara quietly, "would you ask Mrs Vickery if she would be kind enough to come here?"

Stephen gave a snort of laughter, and began to hum a tune to himself. He had no fear of an appeal to his better half.

"Magdalene," said Barbara, as soon as her sister-in-law had entered and closed the door, "I have to ask you if what your husband has told me is true. That you are seizing Old Park from your nephew?"

"Now you won't do no good by talking that way – "

"I am speaking to you, Magdalene."

"It's true that I'm the rightful heir now that Hubert's dead."

"And that you have apostatised from your religion?"

Magdalene's face flushed with fury.

"How dare you speak to me like that! Don't you dare to preach to me about religion, you who only pretended to be converted so that you could catch a husband above your social station. As for conforming Hubert would have done it long ago if it hadn't been for you, and not beaten his head against a stone wall and lived as a recluse and seen our dear home go to rack and ruin. You don't care what happens to Old Park so long as you can live here and call yourself Lady Thorne."

"Are *you* going to be able to live here, Magdalene? Won't you be afraid that every stone will cry out against you? Will your feeble poses be proof against the sight of your family motto carved above the door? Will you feel easy when you attend the heretical services in the church your Catholic ancestors built and endowed, sitting there above the bones of so many Thorne confessors, above the body, scarcely cold, of the brother you have betrayed? And will you never fear that the man you married, who for all he talks of the law, is no better than a common robber on the highway, will betray you in your turn?"

"Get you abovestairs, wife," broke in Stephen furiously, "and leave me to deal with this virago."

"You have forgotten something, Magdalene," said Barbara, as he hustled his wife from the room. She unfastened from her waist the housewife's keys on their chain, and laid them on the table. "Your thirty pieces of silver."

"I took you for a sensible wench," snarled Stephen, slamming the door behind Magdalene and rounding on his sister-in-law, "but I see I was mistaken. That kind of stageplay talk won't do you no good, and won't move me or Magda. I was thinking of offering you a few bits and pieces from the old place – not that I'm obliged to, mind, and don't begin to prattle about your late husband's will, for he could make wills till he's black in the face, he still can't leave nothing, having died a Papist. But if you'd asked me as a favour – "

"Yes, Mr Vickery," Barbara interrupted. The restrained passion which had come into her voice when she had been addressing Magdalene had gone again, leaving it utterly impersonal. "I have, in fact, two favours to ask you. One is that I may take with me from Old Park some things which you term bits and pieces – "

"Nothing valuable, mind. The law says – "

"I don't think you would count the things I ask, valuable. I would like to have for my son the portrait of Blessed Michael Thorne, and a certain manuscript book which contains a record of all the fines and penalties inflicted on the house of Thorne since the Reformation. I do not think that you and Magdalene would be very – comfortable – living with these things."

He gave a short laugh.

"Oh, you can take that trash and welcome. And the other favour?"

"That while I am still mistress of Old Park, you will relieve me of your presence. For I presume that not even the Act of William III lays it down that the Catholic heir, who happens in this instance to be a baby a few weeks old, is to be turned out of doors without due notice."

Without waiting for him to reply, she pulled the frayed bell-rope again, and while she waited, turned back to the papers she had been sorting when Stephen had come in, her hands perfectly steady. Thwarted malice boiled within him. He wanted to strike her, to kick the furniture, anything to pierce this woman's armour, to break her self-control. She was cheating him, as she and her husband had cheated him on a former occasion, of the sweets of revenge.

"If you please, Braithwayte," her voice said evenly, "show this person to the door."

Stephen made one last effort to assert himself.

"This person, Braithwayte," he said with savage pleasantry, "had better be treated with respect by you, for he's your new master."

He brushed the old butler aside and walked out with an exaggerated swagger.

Braithwayte stood there flaccid, his rheumy eyes gazing blankly at his mistress.

"He's mad, my lady," he whispered fearfully. "He's mad!"

She rose from her papers. Her face was stony, and she did not seem to see him. She said, as one thinking aloud.

"No, not mad. Wicked. I never knew, you see, that men could be wicked. Weak, stupid, greedy, but not... I don't think I ever believed in positive evil before. Not even when I read the prayers for the dying at my husband's bedside, and prayed that the devil and his angels might be forced to make way for him."

She bent to pick up a paper, and all of a sudden her hand began to shake as if with palsy.

"My lady," faltered the old man, "let me fetch you something. Let me call the women."

"No, Braithwayte. Ask all the servants to come into the hall; I'll speak to them there – presently. And I shall do what I can to provide for you and the others; I promise you that. But just for a little while, please leave me by myself."

She wandered to the window when he had gone. A gull, blown against the colourless sky, laughed mockingly; a great holly from which she had cut sprays only a few weeks ago for Christmas, rustled its dark pointed leaves, and the south wind brought the thunder of the breakers as they crashed against the ancient, half-built landing-place known as the Thorne Folly. Not one of those dear familiar sounds had power to move her. It was as if her heart was dead.

But then from upstairs there came another sound, the lusty crying of an infant. She swayed; the relieving tears burst forth; and she crumpled to her knees among her husband's papers.

# PART TWO

# Chapter One

On a September morning in the year 1777, Michael
Thorne, alias Michael Clare, missionary priest, stepped out
of the Six Cans and Punchbowl where he had stayed the
night, into the roar of Holborn. He was now forty-one
years old; he had not seen his native land since he was
eight, and he had never been in London before.

He stood hesitating, an inconspicuous figure in his
snuff-coloured coat of a slightly old-fashioned cut, his
plain neck-cloth and neat brown wig tied at the back with
a small ribbon. In one hand he held a shabby valise; it
contained, besides a few changes of clothes, one precious
personal possession, a stout, leather-bound notebook, in
which during his five years as a 'divine' Michael had taken
down the lectures in Philosophy and Theology slowly
dictated by his professors, which 'Dictates', according to
the custom at Douai, were designed to serve the future
priest as works of reference when it should seem good to
his superiors to send him to the mission-field of England.

So this was London, he thought, trying to adjust himself
to the bewildering noise and bustle, the jostling of porters
who offered to carry his valise, the constant cry of "Chair!
Chair!", the rumble of coach and wagon wheels over the
flat Purbeck stones of the street, the ceaseless footsteps, the

snarling of stray dogs in the gutter, the bawling of apprentices and street-vendors, the hoof-beats sounding like heavy rain, the monotonous invitation of the shoe-black on the corner to "Clean your honour's shoes!"

He turned eastwards, looking anxiously for the street names which, for a decade now, had been placed at the corners. Ah, there it was, Red Lion Square. The houses here were new; the site had been occupied by Red Lion Fields until a speculating builder had run up, with bricks made on the spot from ashes and scavengers' filth and only just warmed at the fire, a square of poor houses which already looked ready to collapse. Their wretched appearance was enchanced by the number of windows boarded up to evade the window-tax. Stray children fastened on the stranger like flies, whining for alms, waiting for an opportunity to pick his pocket. What a neighbourhood, he thought, for the residence of Bishop Challoner, now Vicar Apostolic of the London District!

No. 15, however, displayed marks of self-respect. The sidewalk in front of it was swept, there were neat curtains at the few unblocked windows, and he could see his face in the door-knocker. Having applied this, he found himself confronted almost immediately by a middle-aged woman who seemed to have been poured into her clothes, so closely did they encase her stout person. She had a buttoned-up mouth, sharp eyes, and a formidable manner.

"Another of them!" exclaimed this tight sort of lady. "You'll have to take your turn like the rest."

"My name is Clare," said Michael, puzzled by seeing the little hall crowded with poorly dressed folk who stood or sat with the bored but patient air of people in a doctor's waiting-room. "I believe Mr Fisher is expecting me."

"Oh indeed, sir, yes he is, and I beg your pardon," said Mrs Hanne, Dr Challoner's landlady, bobbing a curtsy. "Please to come this way. I took you for one of them that comes here night and morning pestering the old gentleman, wanting this and wanting that, and all to be admitted; them's the orders, and how the old gentleman says his prayers and writes all them books of his, I don't know, and him so frail too. I'll tell him you've arrived, sir."

She returned presently with a message from Dr Challoner, who begged Mr Clare's pardon, but since he had so many callers to see this morning he must postpone the pleasure of greeting the newcomer until dinner at two o'clock. In the meanwhile Mr Clare was to be shown his room, and was to be sure to ask for anything he required. While Michael unpacked his valise, Mrs Hanne entertained him with a description of the Bishop's routine and her own comments thereon.

"Rises at six, sir, summer and winter, and has done ever since he's done me the honour to lodge with me, and that's near forty years. (I've moved a time or two; I've had to, when them beastly informers got on his scent.) Then he says his Mass in my best parlour, and spends near an hour in thanksgiving ere I can serve him with his breakfast, and a poor one it is, by his orders, and I've heard his chaplains grumble at it many a time, but, says the old gentleman, the humbler we fare the more we shall have to give in charity. Ay, and as like as not, just as it's ready someone calls, and by the time he comes to it it's a perfect heretic, burnt to a cinder. And for the rest of the day, sir, save for dinner and a bite at nine at night, he's saying his office or visiting the poor or writing his books, and the door-knocker going every few minutes – (there it goes again! well, they can wait) – with women come whining about their souls or men wanting him to find 'em some post, and all to be invited in and treated respectful."

She paused to draw breath.

"I've said to the old gentleman many a time, I've said, Mr Fisher (for he's very strict, sir, about us calling him by

his cant name even in private), Mr Fisher, I've said, you'll
come to an early grave, sir, and what shall we do then? Mrs
Hanne, he says, with that smile of his that puts you in
mind of a mischievous boy, Mrs Hanne, you remember
where it says in the Bible that the life of a man is threescore
years and ten, and how old do you think I am, Mrs Hanne?
And true enough it is, sir, though I can scarce credit it, that
he's rising eighty-seven."

It was indeed a very frail old figure who came hobbling
into the dining-room where Michael waited an hour or so
later. The Bishop wore his own hair, which was like fine
white silk hanging on his bent shoulders; he had lost all his
teeth, and the skin of his face, wrinkled as an apple too
long stored, was stretched tight over the bones. But the
eyes were still bright and keen, and despite the frail
appearance there was something about him which
instantly suggested strength.

He greeted Michael with an endearing fatherly kindness,
asked eagerly for news of Douai, and sympathised, though
with a twinkle, with the President for having to part with
so valuable a member of his College. (For several years past
there had been a battle royal between Dr Challoner and the
President on Michael's account, the former insisting that
Mr Clare was needed in England, and the latter declaring
that he was even more necessary as Professor of Philosophy
and Prefect of Studies at Douai.) But during the meal when
Mr Bolton, one of the chaplains, set out to entertain the
newcomer with comments upon the American war,
Michael observed the old Bishop lapse into a kind of
apathy, as though the affair which was engrossing the
attention of all England had not the slightest interest for
him.

"The mistake each successive Ministry has made," pro-
nounced Mr Bolton, a cheerful, vigorous person with

horse-like teeth, "has been to treat the Colonists either as savages or as naughty children. The Governors we sent them were mostly decayed courtiers, and their despatches were frequently unopened. And to tax them again after their friends here had carried through the repeal of the Stamp Tax was plain madness, for they had tasted power, and from that time it was clear that they were determined to throw off all allegiance to the motherland. As soon as they had established their United States of America we ought to have accepted the situation and made them friends, for we shall never beat them, and this war which drags on and on is causing terrible hardships at home."

"Which will lead to more riots, I'm afraid," remarked the other chaplain. His name was Hindle, and he was a quiet, tired-looking little man. "There was a mob gathering outside Lord George Germaine's house – (he's Secretary of State for the Colonies," he said in an aside to Michael) – "when I passed by there this morning, breaking his windows and flourishing banners with a crude representation of the Massacre of St George's Fields painted on them. I – "

He broke off and glanced swiftly at his silent superior. Michael, following his glance, noticed that the Bishop had a queer look on his face, his mouth sucked in and his bright old eyes troubled.

"St George's Fields," murmured Challoner. "I do not know why, but the very mention of that place has always filled me with a strange foreboding. I beg your pardon, gentlemen, I interrupted your talk." And he sank back into his seeming apathy.

"I must explain, Mr Clare," said the cheerful Bolton, "that during the riots over Wilkes and Liberty in '68, when he was in the King's Bench Prison in Southwark, the mob became so threatening that the Riot Act was read and the Guards fired upon the rioters, killing twenty of them, hence the lower sort always speak of that incident now as the 'Massacre of St George's Fields'. They have never forgotten it, and bring it up whenever they have a new grievance. And neither has the Government forgotten it, for it led to a horrible kind of mob war, with ships lying idle and hearths empty of coal. I don't think the authorities would ever dare to take such action again."

The Bishop roused himself, and changing the subject began to talk eagerly of his success in persuading the new Pope Pius VI to restore some twenty-two English saints to the Missal and Breviary, saints whose very names had been forgotten when the Sarum Missal had fallen into desuetude after the Reformation. This, it was plain, was of far more importance to Dr Challoner than was the American war.

When Grace had been said, Mr Bolton announced that he had visiting that would occupy him till supper, adding with his usual exuberance:

"Thank God I have said my office!"

Michael, who was holding open the door for the Bishop, saw an almost roguish smile light the old man's face.

"I thank God," gloated Dr Challoner, "that I have that pleasure still to come."

Inviting Michael to his room for a talk at five o'clock, when he hoped to be at leisure, he hobbled out, leaning heavily on his stick, and Michael was left alone with the tired-faced Mr Hindle.

"It was very strange," mused the chaplain, "how he looked when I mentioned St George's Fields at dinner and how that place has always seemed to haunt him."

He hesitated a moment and then went on:

"There is no man more reticent, Mr Clare, upon the subject of spriritual favours than our Vicar Apostolic, but we who know him intimately have observed upon occasions that he seems to have the gift of prophecy. And so when I am in a fanciful mood I sometimes wonder whether we may not look to see a sort of Armageddon fought out one day upon St George's Fields in Southwark."

(ii)

Michael decided to employ the time before his appointment with the Bishop by calling on his sister-in-law, the dowager Lady Thorne.

He had heard from her occasionally during the years which had elapsed since Hubert's death; she had sent him an unemotional, matter-of-fact account of her forcible leaving of Old Park, and of the kindness of Dr Challoner in finding her a post as housekeeper to a Mr Ashmall, a Catholic attorney of Clement's Inn. At long intervals she had written him other news. The Bishop had arranged for little Hubert to be educated at his expense at the only Catholic boys' school in England, Standon Lordship in Hertfordshire; on leaving school, Hubert had become a law student under Mr Ashmall himself; and at eighteen had married that gentleman's only daughter, Alice. That was more than four years ago, and since then Michael had heard nothing from his sister-in-law. But on enquiring of Mr Hindle, he learnt that the Thorne family still lived with Mr Ashmall at his house in St Clement's Lane, but the afternoon being fine he would be almost certain to find the dowager Lady Thorne in the garden in Lincoln's Inn Fields, a place for which, it seemed, she had a particular affection.

Rehearsing the directions given him, Michael turned down Great Turnstile, a narrow passage inhabited almost entirely by booksellers, and saw before him a large square, bounded on three sides by rows of substantial houses, and on the east by a mellow brick wall shaded by the elms of Lincoln's Inn Gardens. Around the square was an iron palisade in which were gates, and entering by one of these he found himself in a very pleasant place, laid out with lawns, flower-beds, and gravel walks, and in the centre a Corinthian column supporting a sundial, beneath which infant tritons spouted water into stone shells.

How in the world was he going to identify his sister-in-law, he wondered, among all these folk who were strolling about in the sun. Hubert's letters, though they had been full of Barbara, contained nothing but a lover's hyperbole when it came to her physical appearance, and now she must be nearly fifty. Preoccupied with his problem, he was startled by a sharp exclamation, and turning, encountered the gaze of a lady who had half risen from a bench near the fountain and was staring at him as though he were an apparition. She was so pale that, thinking she might be ill, he raised his hat and was about to ask if he could be of any assistance, when she cried:

"Oh, forgive me, but you are so like Hubert!"

He stared at her in his turn.

"Hubert? I had a brother of that name, madam, but he is – is it possible that you can be – "

"Barbara. And you must be Michael. You are *so* like Hubert. May I call you by your Christian name, please? For discretion's sake I can't address you according to your – your profession, and I'm afraid I've forgotten your alias. I shall remember it in a moment, of course, but it was such a shock seeing you walk towards me."

"I am so very sorry that I distressed you," he said, sitting down on the bench beside her.

"It was foolish of me, for I knew you were expected. But isn't it strange that we should meet here, on this very spot where first I met your brother? I thought I was seeing a ghost. This bench on which we're sitting became 'our' bench; we were quite ridiculously annoyed if we found other people occupying it. It was here he asked me to marry him."

He found himself staring at her almost rudely while she talked, deeply touched by what he saw. Her pallor had given place to a rosy flush, increasing her quite extraordinary look of youth, and despite the little lines which suffering had traced around her eyes, the face of this widow in her late forties was stamped with a strange innocence. She had a positive though quite unconscious dignity, but at the same time she was so perfectly easy and natural that he felt he could talk to her as though he had known her all his life.

"There is so much to say that I don't know where we are to begin," said Barbara happily. "But first of all I must present to you your great-nephew. I'm ashamed that I never wrote to tell you that I had a grandson; I've grown so lazy of late years. He's rather an odd little boy, quite a character, and has imaginary companions, but he's so good. Hubert darling!" she called softly.

A small boy still in petticoats, who had been playing some mysterious game by himself near the fountain, came toddling up in answer to her summons, wearing a very solemn expression. He permitted himself to be kissed by the strange gentleman, but immediately afterwards explained to his grandmother the progress of his game.

"Mr Bear called Miss Gunner a rude name, and she 'served it, too, and it was a good name really 'cause it came from the Bible. He called her," went on little Hubert, looking hard at Barbara to make sure she would be properly impressed, "a Pro'gal swine."

"And what kind of a swine is that?" asked Barbara gravely.

"You *must* know about the Pro'gal Son," exclaimed the child reproachfully. "Well, he tended Pro'gal swine. Anyway, Miss Gunner's so cross that she's brought up all her armies, and Mr Bear and I have got to fight her again." He paused, scraping one foot on the gravel and contemplating his great-uncle. "Did you ever live at a place called Old Park?"

"A long time ago," replied Michael.

"It really belongs to my Papa, but there's a Beast living there, so we can't go home. Is it true there's a monkey-puzzle tree there, but no monkeys? Then I don't see the use of puzzling monkeys if there aren't any monkeys to be puzzled."

With that he returned to his imaginary companions and their battles.

"Old Park," said Barbara, after a pause. "How painful it must be for you to hear that name."

"But how much more painful for you! I scarcely remember it, and had grown used to the thought that I might never see it again."

"It has become a place inside my mind," said Barbara, "full of only happy memories now." She was silent for a moment. "I went through a very bad time inside myself after it all happened. Everyone thought me so self-controlled and calm, and that I was behaving beautifully. But the calm was really shock, and far from behaving beautifully I was feasting on a horrible sort of satisfaction out of infuriating Vickery by accepting the situation when he had hoped I would argue or storm or plead. I really descended to his level, and I hated him in my heart."

"I think only a saint could have done otherwise."

She wrinkled up her nose like a schoolgirl.

"Hate is such an *uncomfortable* thing to live with. And then I began to feel ashamed of myself, because I remembered how much Hubert had suffered for his religion, and he never complained. I know Vickery's seizure of Old Park was an extreme case, but it was the sort of enforcement of the penal code which might happen at any time to those of our religion, a sword of Damocles which has got to be accepted. And really, you know, I've been very fortunate; I have a home again where once I was only a housekeeper, and my son was too young to remember the home that is his by inheritance."

"Yes, you are very fortunate," said Michael; but he did not mean in her material circumstances.

She turned to him impulsively.

"Here have I been talking about myself when you must be so anxious for news of someone else, someone so unfortunate. Your sister."

"And what is the news of her?" he asked quietly.

"Except that she has no children, I suppose she has most things to make her happy in a worldly sense, an enormously rich husband who has bought himself a knighthood and a seat in Parliament, a fine house in Welbeck Street, the entrée to Court – and Old Park. We don't meet, of course, but now and then I catch a glimpse of her driving by in a smart chariot, or walking in the Park with her footman and her blackboy and her little dog carried in her muff. Sometimes I've almost plucked up courage to speak to her; but she never liked me, and to be honest, I never liked her."

"I remember her only as a lonely little girl."

Barbara caught her breath.

"I know! I was too young to understand, I suppose; that's my only excuse," she said. "Magdalene was lonely and frustrated; I could have done so much more than I did do to make friends. She has been on my conscience for years. Because she's a Thorne, she must feel so dreadful sometimes, about forsaking her religion and robbing her own nephew of his inheritance. I did once go to someone I thought might help, someone I believe she really loved; Reverend Mother at the convent at Hammersmith where Magda was for a time."

"And what did she say?"

Barbara smiled ruefully.

181

"She told me, in the kindest possible way, not to interfere. That's what it amounted to. And then she began to talk about the parable of the Prodigal Son, and she made me see it in a new light. The point was, she said, that the father must have known all about the famine in the far country, but made no move to send relief to his son or beg him to come home. And Reverend Mother told me that she, like the father in the parable, would never stop watching and praying, but that Magda must make the first advance before she could run out to meet her. And she said something else, too, which I've always remembered. 'I think,' she said, 'the most comforting part of the story is that the Prodigal's very low motive for returning completely satisfied his father; there was no question of perfect contrition, but merely an empty belly and the thought of all the good food being eaten in the servants' hall.' "

(iii)

That same evening Michael went by invitation to sup with Barbara and her family, so that he might make the acquaintance of his nephew.

Mr Ashmall, with his daughter and son-in-law, lived in a tall wooden house on the south side of St Clement's Lane which ran past Clement's Inn and so through an archway into the Strand. Barbara herself opened the door, and explaining that Mr Ashmall was supping with a client, took Michael upstairs to the parlour where her son and his wife were waiting to receive him.

His nephew reminded him instantly of his brother Robin. There were the same flaring nostrils, the same air of impetuosity. One could well imagine this Sir Hubert, like the dead Robin, throwing himself into romantic enterprises. His wife Alice was a fresh-faced, wholesome-looking girl who, from the general appearance of the room, appeared to be a somewhat formidably efficient housewife. Michael received the impression that while she plainly adored her husband, she kept her mother-in-law and her little son in some awe of her. He sensed further, while compliments were exchanged and general questions asked and answered, that his nephew's attitude towards himself was very slightly frosty; and when the talk turned to the state of English Catholics, it became apparent that Hubert was infected with a mild anticlericalism.

"A great chance was missed in '74," Hubert declared vigorously, "when the quarrel with the Colonists was approaching a crisis, and saving your presence, sir, I blame the clergy. The Government were terrified lest the Irish should take the opportunity to revolt; after all, the maxim of the Colonists, 'No representation, no taxation', applied very awkwardly to the state of things on the other side of St George's Channel. Besides, the Government were desperate for recruits, and therefore were inclined to allow the Irish Catholics to take the Oath of Allegiance, thus at least acknowledging their existence as subjects. In fact, the victims of persecution were to be permitted to swear fidelity to the persecutor."

He gave a short barking laugh.

"It was the moment to apply for some concessions to English Catholics, but our Mr Fisher would not hear of it, though several prominent Catholic laymen asked his permission to petition the King. Only by staying quiet and waiting for better times, he said, could we avoid persecution."

"By staying quiet at least we have survived all these years," said Barbara quickly.

"Oh, Mama! How *you* can be content with our appalling conditions I never can imagine," cried her son. (Evidently this was an old argument.) "How has this staying quiet advantaged us? We don't exist in law; to the nation at large we are a sort of jest, except when the Government wants something to divert public attention from their own misdeeds and corruption, when they are sure to work up the old fear of Popery. And in time of war they fear us because, having oppressed us for so long, they believe us ready to league with any foreign foe."

He tossed his head in a manner very reminiscent of the dead Robin.

"All right, then. If they won't tolerate us out of love, let them be made to do it out of fear. We should take advantage of their poor opinion to clamour for some measure of relief, and then we'll show them that their fears were groundless."

"There are several well-informed gentlemen who think with my husband on this matter," observed Alice, sweeping up the already spotless hearth.

"And who were appalled by the seizure of Old Park," said Hubert. "That could have been made a test case if handled properly at the time. It might have been possible to have appealed to the Court of Equity, which, after all, was designed to grant redress of grievances and to moderate the rigour of the Common Law."

Since it was plain to him that the subject distressed his sister-in-law, Michael made an effort to change it, but Hubert was not to be diverted. Obviously he was on his hobby-horse.

"I have spoken with many Protestants, sir," he said to his uncle, "who, while they would not for an instant approve of real toleration were so shocked by Vickery's action that they would be glad to see that particular Act of William III repealed. And now is the time to attempt it, while we have Lord Mansfield as Lord Chief Justice. He is acknowledged as one of the greatest judges we have ever had, and he has shown in the case of both Catholic and Protestant

Dissenters that he is utterly opposed to the persecution of a man for his religion. And Mr Dunning, too, who was Solicitor-General in Grafton's Ministry, though my Lord Mansfield's opponent in politics entirely agrees with him in this."

"My husband is acquainted with Mr Dunning," Alice put in proudly.

"I met him through a great friend of mine, Mr Sheldon, a Catholic attorney – "

"He was 'cated by Jesus," interrupted a voice from under the table. "He must be very old."

"He was educated by the Jesuits," corrected Alice. "Really, my son, you must learn not to clip your words."

"Mr Bear says – "

"And if you must talk to imaginary persons, you should talk to your Guardian Angel."

"My Garden Angel isn't imaginary," objected little Hubert emerging from his retreat. "And I couldn't talk to my Garden Angel as I talk to Mr Bear; it wouldn't be rev'rent. Was you 'cated by the Jesuses?" he enquired of his great-uncle.

"No," said Michael gravely. "But I used to clip my words just like you when I was young."

"And now we must go up the stairs to Bedfordshire," Alice interposed brightly, but with a reproachful glance in Michael's direction. "So ask a blessing, and say good night."

"I'm going to be 'cated by the Lord in Hertfordshire," announced little Hubert, getting the last word.

Michael mentioned during supper that while he was at Douai there had been reports of some new outbreak of persecution in England a few years previously, but the constant opening of letters in the post had compelled Dr Challoner and his colleagues to be so guarded in what they wrote to their friends abroad that the latter had remained in ignorance of the real extent of the trouble.

"Oh, it was just one of those mysterious outbreaks of anti-Catholic hysteria which have always infected certain sections of the people from time to time," Hubert said hurriedly. "And there was only one conviction; a priest named Maloney was given the maximum sentence under this abominable Act of William III, life imprisonment. But his sentence has since been commuted to banishment, and the petty persecution has died a natural death."

Barbara laid down her fork. There was a heightened colour in her face, but her voice was steady enough.

"You forget, Hubert, that your uncle is a priest, and now that he has come to England is in the same sort of danger. There was another force at work besides the anti-Catholic hysteria, Michael. A band of common informers led by a man named William Payne, commonly known as the Protestant Carpenter, were setting the law in action in a business-like way in order to gain the £100 reward for the conviction of a priest. And – and my father was one of them."

"But not for the sake of the reward, Mama," said Hubert, leaning over and taking her hand in an affectionate gesture. "You have never believed that of him."

"No, I have not," she said, pressing his hand, "and never will. He was always a perfectly sincere man, and would never stoop to making traffic of his prejudices. Yet his very sincerity may make him the more dangerous. I have not seen him for years; none of my family will have anything to do with me, and didn't even let me know when my mother died; but I have heard that Papa has given up his business and has become a great preacher of the Calvinist persuasion, holding forth in a little chapel near St George's Fields. Why do you look like that, Michael?"

"It is nothing," he said hastily. "It was only that someone happened to mention St George's Fields this morning."

She had troubles enough, he thought, and so he did not tell her then that during his interview with Dr Challoner, the Bishop had mentioned to him that after he had spent a few weeks lodging in Red Lion Square and learning something about the life of a London missionary, his superior would like him to take charge of the Catholics of Southwark, who lived mostly in the neighbourhood of those same St George's Fields.

# Chapter Two

Magadalene was beguiling the time while her 'head' was having its fortnightly redressing in the powder closet, by drinking a dish of Hyson tea (at twenty-five shillings the pound) and glancing through the *Fashionable Magazine*.

There was something here for everyone's taste, 'News from the Seat of War in America' sandwiched between acrostics, odes, reviews of current plays, domestic intelligence, and the popular *tête-à-tête* which, under fanciful names, gave the history of the latest intrigues. There was also J Harman, who wrote weekly astrological forecasts, and who described himself as a Student in the Celestial Science. He was rather ominous today. Apparently the planet Saturn, which was Magdalene's significator, was just entering Libra, the Sign of Justice, and she must beware of someone she had once wronged.

She flung the magazine aside and began practising the art of the new folding fan, the angry flutter, the amorous flutter, and so forth. What should she wear at Lady Carlisle's rout this evening – the blue tabby embroidered with silver or the gold tissue faced with peach-coloured satin? The *Fashionable Magazine* was hinting that the hoop was about to undergo one of its periodic banishments and that the train was coming back. She had never been able to acquire the art of the train; to turn round was such a difficult and lengthy business. And some dim instinct from the days of poverty made her secretly shocked by having to discard fifteen yards of expensive taffeta after it had swept the public walks for a few days.

So she cogitated, desperately fighting a familiar depression. It was nearly noon, and there had not been a single caller at her toilette levee. Only a few years ago, how delightful those morning hours had been, reclining in bed with her hair and nightgown in carefully arranged disorder, while a little stream of visitors, male and female, came to talk scandal and read her the latest lampoons and pay her extravagant compliments. But now her only callers were her frisseur, her milliner, and her professor of quadrille. Once or twice she was sure she had intercepted glances between her servants (so insolent nowadays and demanding such high wages), glances which said, 'My lady is getting old, losing her looks; no more admirers to give vails; time to be looking for another place.'

This bedroom which once had been her delight had become like a luxurious prison. The black furniture with the lac-work panels and rich gilt mounts, the genuine Chinese ware crowding the shelves, the picture of herself by Sir Joshua Reynolds, depicted as a shepherdess, crook in hand, reclining gracefully against a tree trunk and listening to the mournful ditty of her current lover masquerading as a rustic swain, the ceiling asprawl with plump gods and goddesses, the wallpaper colourful with peacocks, the toilet-table painted with temples and dragons, all were grown stale; her appetite for luxury had been blunted, and she had nothing to put in its place.

There was Old Park, of course; but she could not go down there at this time of the year, she thought hastily, shying away in her mind from its new grandeur, not daring to think of it as it once had been.

"A little of the cordial in my tea, Hanson," she said languidly to her woman. (She was as secretly afraid of Hanson as she had been of post-boys in the remote past.) "I find myself somewhat indisposed this morning."

Drink might help; sometimes it did, and sometimes it only made things worse. Like a nervous invalid, she was continually flying from one opiate to another – from amours to astrology, from strong cordials to a whirl of shopping, anything to stifle the thing in her mind that ached like an old wound, impervious to anodynes, rising at moments, especially when she was alone, to screaming pain. Not even her last and desperate weapon could kill it; I am lost, excommunicated, damned, she would tell herself; I could not get back to the Faith even if I wanted to (which of course I don't); it is madness, therefore, to think of it...

The day was cold with a slight fog. What should she do? She could not walk in the Park; she had already seen the show at the new marionette theatre in St James'ss Street, and she was not in the mood for the excitements of Astley's circus in Westminster Bridge Road. She might go to Doiley's warehouse in the Strand and see what new stuffs they had; but then she remembered that her jeweller in Holborn had said that by today he hoped to have ready an exact replica, of her little diamond watch; it was all the rage now to wear two.

Holborn. She did not like going into that street. More than once she had caught sight of Barbara there, and on one occasion of someone with Barbara, a tall young man who had reminded her of Robin... Nonsense, of course she would drive to Holborn. Why should she fear to encounter Barbara? Barbara looked perfectly happy, and she, Magdalene, had done her a good turn really, by sending her back to London and to the modest mode of life which was her natural environment.

"My chariot at one, Caesar," she said to her blackboy. (He was growing rather ungainly, that child, and it was time to replace him. She had seen an advertisement in the *London Evening Post* yesterday, offering for sale at Salter's coffee-house a little negro who spoke English; she might call in there after she had been to the jeweller's.) "And, Hanson, see that the card-tables are set out in the salon; I have a faro-party at three."

It was one of those days when everything seems to go wrong.

Jasper, her monkey, was in one of his moods, and bit a footman, who promptly gave notice. The fog thickened as she drove eastwards, penetrating through the glasses of the chariot and preventing passers-by from admiring her newly dressed 'head'. Her jeweller had not her watch ready; the blackboy at Salter's had already been sold. Mrs Edgeley was coming to the faro-party, and would be sure to talk about Sir Simon Littleton, who had been such an ardent lover of Magdalene's and now was as attentive to a younger mistress. In the Strand she passed a cart carrying a coffin on its way to the poor-hole, and that was a most unlucky omen.

When she came out of the coffee-house the fog was so thick that the link-boys were touting for custom with their flaring flambeaux. She was hesitating whether to engage a couple to walk beside her chariot (it was risky, for they were often in league with the footpads), when in the smoky glare of a torch she saw a man coming down the street towards her.

Her heart began to beat with quick, sickening thumps, and despite her furred *coqueluchon* she felt suddenly ice-cold. That walk, that turn of the head, those features, distinct for an instant in the link-light…it was the ghost of her dead brother, Hubert.

Then the apparition vanished down an alley-way, and Magdalene stood there crying out something, with a footman running to her aid.

Michael went briskly down the alley, unconscious of how nearly he had missed an encounter with his sister, intent on his duty of attending a committee meeting of Dr Challoner's Benevolent Society for the Aged and Infirm Poor.

(ii)

Stephen was sitting in the Blue Drawing Room at Welbeck Street, lolling on a couch in his dressing-gown and turban while he listened to an inflated dedication addressed to himself and read aloud to him by a wretched hack poet whom he had deigned to take under his patronage.

"Your easiness of humour, or rather your harmonious disposition, is so admirably mixed with your composure, that the rugged disturbances that public affairs bring with them does scarce ever ruffle your unclouded brow. And that above all is praiseworthy, you are so far from thinking yourself higher than others, that a flourishing and opulent fortune, which seldom fails to affect other possessors with pride, seems in your case as if only providentially to enlarge your humility... "

Allowing for the high-flown language used by these half-men, it was all very true, Stephen decided. He was always composed because he could always get what he wanted; if by 'public affairs' the hack was referring to the war, far from disturbing him it had increased his fortune; and he was humble in the sense that he was quite content with a borough bought on the Stock Exchange and a knighthood which had cost him a modest £9,000 when he might have had a Government office and an earldom. He was a very unique man was Sir Stephen Vickery; he had attained all his boyhood ambitions. By his own efforts he had corrected the wrong done to him by Providence in making him the son of a gardener; by marrying Robin's sister and dispossessing Robin's nephew, he had avenged the thrashing Robin had given him as a boy; and by transforming Old Park into something the Thornes would have hated, a 'gentleman's estate', he had indulged both his snobbery and his malice against that family.

The transformation had cost him a good deal of cash, but after all he had got the estate for nothing. He had pulled down the old kitchen wing and built a new one underground, connecting it with the main block by a subterranean passage; for it was *à la mode* to pretend that menials did not exist. He had engaged the services of the great landscape gardener, 'Capability' Brown, to redesign the gardens, filling them with shelleries, follies, bridges and pagodas, in accordance with the present rage for the Chinese. The lake he had cleared of lilies and had it turned into a bathing-pool, with dragon boats moored to marble stairs; the common-lands he had enclosed, turning out the copyholders; and the woods he had cut down, except for a few dead trees which gave, he was told, a 'natural' air to the landscape.

It was true that his seizure of Old Park had brought him a few minor annoyances such as even very rich men unhandicapped by scruples cannot always escape. Some of the older County families, notably the Lessings, had refused to have anything to do with him because of his treatment of the late Sir Hubert's widow and infant son; and there had been at first a petty revolt on the part of his new tenants. Rustic maledictions had been scrawled on his doors, a stone or two flung at his coach as he drove by, and the marine temple he was building on the site of the old arbour had kept on being pulled down by unknown hands at dead of night. But he had had no cause to complain of his reception by the County generally; the Vicar ate out of his hand; and as for his impertinent tenants, he had either ruined them by rack-renting or taught them a lesson by getting a local justice to fine them the statutory one shilling each time they failed to appear at their parish church, going to the length of distraining the goods and chattels of those who could not pay.

In London his wealth made him courted by nearly everyone who mattered, including his Sovereign. His popularity with King George dated from the year 1765 when his Majesty had suffered his first attack of insanity, and Parliament, alarmed by the fact that there were no provisions for carrying on the Government while the heir to the throne was still a child, had rushed through a Regency Bill, which very pointedly had excluded the dowager Princess of Wales and her detested favourite, Lord Bute. On his recovery King George had been so furious at the insult to his mother that he had determined to get rid of George Grenville's Ministry, and had spent public money running into six figures to ensure that his own nominees would win the next election. They had; but the Opposition naturally kicked at being asked to make good the deficit in the revenue caused by bribes, demanding particulars of the debt incurred.

Encountering Lord Rockingham, the new Prime Minister, at White's while this row was in progress, Stephen had made a suggestion. A loan could be raised, said Stephen, upon terms so liberal as to give the copyholders a return of ten per cent; but instead of following the usual course and inviting the Bank to become the subscribers, the much-desired stock could be divided among the supporters of the Government in both Houses. And he, Stephen, would be happy to open the list in any sum the Prime Minister cared to name.

Next day Stephen had received a summons to attend his Majesty at a private audience at Buckingham House, which King George had persuaded Parliament to settle on the Queen, and where this dull couple lived in economical seclusion, going to St James's only for levees. And his Majesty, who never unbent even with his Ministers, actually had embraced Stephen in his fat little arms, had offered him a glass of barley-water, and in the strong Westphalian accent of his race had praised Stephen's loyal ingenuity, inveighing against the insolence of his faithful Commons. He did not, raged his Majesty, build palaces, or lavish large sums on pictures or other such trash, or throw away pensions on popular heroes, or keep an extravagant Court. All he asked was to be a king and to have his friends in Parliament, and to do that he was compelled to pay their election expenses.

From that time Stephen was often at Court, even being invited to Richmond Lodge where his Majesty pursued his agricultural hobbies, selling skim-milk to the villagers and ordering the local farmers to try out his own inventions in the way of cattle-food and the curing of bacon. They got on very well together, did 'Farmer George' and Stephen Vickery. Both had a contempt for men of wit and genius; both took themselves very seriously; and both were exceedingly vindictive. Never doubting that they were in the right, they agreed in regarding as legitimate punishment what to others seemed revenge.

Thus through the years had Stephen Vickery flourished like the green bay tree.

And yet, though no one guessed it, he had a secret torment. He had thought of revenge as a servant; he had discovered that it was a master, a thing insatiable, feeding upon itself, relentless in its demands. It had become with him that which drink becomes to the drunkard; he must have more and still more. Somehow or other he felt that he had been cheated so far in the acts of vengeance he had performed; he had not humiliated the Thornes by marrying Magdalene; and it had been Barbara and not he who had dominated the scene when he had turned her and her son out of Old Park. He felt for her and for all her family the peculiar hatred experienced by those who deeply wrong another and find themselves faced with an armour they cannot pierce, and therefore he still had a score to settle with the Thornes. But revenge against individuals was no longer enough; he longed for the day when by some means or other he could strike a blow at the faith he had forsaken, at the remnant of the downtrodden Catholics.

(iii)

Stephen had an appointment with a confidential agent of his this morning, after he had dismissed his tame writer; there was a snippet of secret political information he could turn to good use on the stock market. As he lounged up the stairs towards his study, he was approached by his wife's woman, who whispered to him that my lady wished to see him at once.

"Such a state she's in, sir," breathed Hanson, obviously relishing the upset. "Come back from shopping as white as a sheet, and has sent to say that she can't receive for faro this afternoon."

"I shall come when I am disengaged," said Stephen tersely, dismissed Magdalene from his mind, and went on thinking precisely how he would use that inside political information.

It was an hour later when he strolled into his wife's bedroom. He was dining out, and was in an apricot-coloured coat with frogged buttonholes and the new cut-away skirts; his black ribbon solitaire was fastened at the throat with a jewelled pin, he had his tall, gold-knobbed cane in his hand, his tricorn hat under his arm, and his wig sticking out in two stiff pigtails behind him.

"You drink too much," remarked Stephen, careless as to whether any servants were hovering, and sniffing the odour of cordials. "And don't tell me it's orangeade, for all you contrive to make it look like it."

The baiting of Magdalene was one of his minor pastimes, a sop to his thwarted malice. His power over her was complete; he had made her no marriage settlement, and she had not a penny of her own. And she was so vulnerable; he could always make her weep. On the other hand, she was useful; even in this paradise of the *nouveaux riches* her breeding carried a certain weight, and had opened doors to him which otherwise would have remained closed. And she was beautiful – or had been; she, like the works of art bought wholesale, the Chippendale furniture from the great factory at Moorfields, and the piano in the salon (never used but the very latest novelty), adorned this town house of his designed by Robert Adam. Moreover, it was only through her that he could claim Old Park.

Ordinarily, like any other fashionable couple, they went their several ways, he to his mistresses, she to her lovers, and for days together they never met. But there were occasions, growing more frequent of late, when her moods and her attitudes, her fits of depression and nervous storms, provided his sadism with a satisfactory outlet. Such an occasion, it seemed, was the present one.

She was still in her morning gown, her skirts and fichu rumpled from lying huddled on the couch, her enormous wig, redressed only that forenoon, as untidy as a bird's nest. The sunlight streaming through the windows pitilessly exposed the ravage which tears had made of her face-paint, and there were streaks of black on her cheeks where the dye from her eyelashes had run. With enormous contempt, he looked down on her and took out his snuff-box.

"Stephen! Something terrible is going to happen!"

He took a pinch from the gold box, dusted nostrils and hand with his lace-edged *mouchoir*, and very deliberately yawned.

"The same old stuff! Remarkable news from the stars by Dr Somebody, and too many secret swigs from the brandy bottle."

She scrambled off the couch and gripped him by the shoulders.

"Stephen, you must listen to me. This morning in Holborn I saw – Hubert."

He glanced at her sharply. The heir he had dispossessed, and who all these years had been growing up, sometimes rather uneasily intruded into his thoughts in the guise of a secret foe.

"And so the sight of a poor law student, your nephew, has given you the vapours," he sneered.

The grip on his shoulders tightened.

"It wasn't my nephew," she whispered fearfully. "It was my brother, Hubert; it was his ghost!"

The terror in her eyes was genuine enough, and just the very faint shadow of it infected him. Complete realist and man-of-the-world though he deemed himself, he was of his age and therefore superstitious. Then he metaphorically kicked himself for being such a fool, and gave a loud, brutal laugh.

"And you desired my presence to tell me this. You actually expected me to put off a business appointment to listen to your drunken ravings."

"I'm not drunk. I've only had one tiny dram this whole day. I saw him, I tell you! And then there was the coffin; I passed it on a cart in the Strand, and it was a sign. And you may laugh at Mr Harman's prognostics, but they always come true. And he said that those born under my sign must beware today of someone they had once wronged."

"And what message did your ghostly brother come to bring you?" enquired Stephen, twisting free from her grip and propping one bandy leg upon the fender.

"He vanished without speaking, but I know why he came. Stephen, we must give Old Park back to his heir – no, listen to me! We don't want it; I hate it now; we can buy another country seat; it's a long way from town, and you have often complained of the bad roads and the danger from highwaymen. And it's much more modish now to have a seat at Chelsea or – or Hammersmith," she gabbled, imploring him, trying to sound reasonable, terrified by his stony face. "And then perhaps God will – "

"God! I thought we should have God brought into it sooner or later. Lovers and the brandy bottle have palled, it seems, and so you're turning to religion again in your old age, are you? But I wouldn't, you know, if I were you. I've stomached a lot from an ageing, barren wife I married out of pity, but I won't have that."

She covered her face with her hands. What a spiritless bitch she is, he thought. For all her wonderful fine breeding, she never finds the guts to hit back.

"And so we must return Old Park to the rightful heir," he went on, savagely playful, "like characters in a novel. And what Old Park are we to return, pray? Not the tumble-down, overgrown ruin in which you Thornes grew up; that's vanished; what's taken its place is a gentleman's seat on which I spent good money."

She had a flicker of spirit then. She spat at him:

"And at which you were the gardener's boy."

His close-set eyes narrowed. He said, dangerously quiet:

"You are very, very foolish to provoke me, Magdalene. In case you have forgotten them, let me remind you of some facts. As a spinster past your first youth, a school-teacher earning a pittance, you leapt at the chance of marrying the ex-gardener's boy. In return for a rich husband and a fine establishment, and in order to indulge your spite against your sister-in-law, you were perfectly willing to renounce your religion and dispossess your brother's heir. You're such a born play-actress that one can't expect you to lie contentedly on the bed you made, but don't try my patience too far, m'dear, or otherwise I shall be obliged to remind you of one other fact you appear to have forgotten."

He paused. He wanted to savour to the full the playing of a card he had been holding up his sleeve for many a long year.

"Of the fact, my dear Magdalene, that you are not my wife."

The clock on the chimney-shelf, held in the jaws of a gilt dragon, ticked away several seconds in its elegant little voice before her hands dropped slowly from before her face. Her swollen eyes stared at him blankly.

"Not your wife?"

He was sucking the gold knob of his cane like a child with a lollipop. He spoke between sucks.

"Where is – the record – of our marriage? Do, pray – name the church register – which contains – that interesting event."

She made a distracted gesture, throwing her hands together, and clutching them till they shook.

"Such a devout Papist you were at the time, m'dear," went on Stephen, twirling the cane now, savouring every word he spoke. "The new Marriage Act? Oh, Reverend Mother, it would be sacrilege to be married with Protestant rites! You were willing to accept any risk rather than violate your precious conscience. And now one of those risks has overtaken you. Our marriage is invalid in law and always has been; you are no more my wife than is the pretty little whore with whom I amused myself when I had an hour to spare yesterday."

Her grey eyes moved, but no sound came.

"You are a kept mistress; that is your only advantage over the pretty little whore. Everything you possess (and you possess a great deal, my sweet Magdalene), I could take away from you like that" – he snapped his fingers – "if I so chose, and could show you the door without a penny. And if I have much more of your tedious drivelling I shall do it. It's merely out of the kindness of my heart that I continue to maintain in luxury a silly, barren woman who is losing her looks. And now if you will excuse me, madam" – a deep, ironic bow – "I must be gone about my affairs, having given you, I trust, a remedy for the laying of ghosts more effective than your cordial bottle."

(iv)

She sat perfectly still for a whole hour after he had left her. She was seized with that strange numbness of mind and body which follows shock. A disconnected sentence kept repeating itself in her head, like a tune one cannot get rid of: 'Everything you possess…everything you possess… everything you possess… '

For a while it made no sense at all. Then presently it seemed to her that it was not the echo of a brutal voice, but a phrase which contained a message quite other than Stephen had intended. Everything I possess, she thought; my wardrobe of fine gowns, my jewels, my chariot, my blackboy, all the things without which life would be intolerable. All the things for which I sold myself; Old Park…

201

"No," she said aloud, getting the message at last. "Not Old Park. That's mine; not Stephen's."

She still sat motionless on the couch, but now the numbness was passing, and a cold, deadly hatred was taking its place, giving her a cunning quite uncharacteristic. Old Park was to Stephen a sort of trophy; he valued it as a savage values the head of his enemy stuck on the pole of his tent. And she could take it from him! But wait, wait, warned the Magdalene who was no longer a romantic girl but a woman unable to live without luxury. If she made such a gesture, undoubtedly Stephen would make good his threat of turning her out, their marriage being invalid in the eyes of the law.

But there was something else she could do, not so satisfying, but providing a secret armour against Stephen's cruelty, perhaps even an assuagement of her own tormented conscience. Before her natural infirmity of purpose had time to weaken her, she rang the bell and ordered her chariot.

Mr Gaffrey, Sir Stephen Vickery's lawyer, was rather surprised when a servant informed him that Lady Vickery had called and wished to see him on urgent business; for the office was closed and Mr Gaffrey had just sat down to a game of quadrille. But he rose from the game to attend the wife of so valuable a client; and was even more surprised when her ladyship, who looked, he thought, very strained, cut short his polite greetings by saying abruptly:

"My husband does not know I have come to see you, sir, and I do not wish him to know. I believe that over twenty years ago he consulted you as to whether, as the Protestant next of kin, I could claim possession of my ancestral home of Old Park in Southshire."

Mr Gaffrey assented in a somewhat gruff manner. In his heart of hearts he had always thought it a preposterous law, but there it was.

"I wish to understand this clearly," went on Magdalene. "Has my husband personally any claim to Old Park?"

"Indeed he has not, my lady," energetically replied the lawyer. "The law is extremely strict on this point. Such – er – claims can be made only by the genuine next of kin."

She smiled to herself in a secret sort of way, and told him that she desired to make her will. It proved to be an odd kind of will for a lady in her position; there were no legacies, there was no mention of her husband; there was nothing at all except the simple statement that she, Magdalene Thorne, gave and bequeathed absolutely the house and estate known as Old Park, in the County of Southshire, to her nephew, Sir Hubert Thorne, baronet.

Mr Gaffrey, wondering greatly, pointed out one rather strange mistake; she was not Magdalene Thorne; she was Magdalene, Lady Vickery. In a toneless voice she explained the situation; she had been married with Catholic rites, and though she had conformed since then, there had been no legal ceremony, and the union remained invalid in law. The look in her eyes prevented him from commenting. He turned the thing into legal language; the document was folded; two clerks were called in to witness it; and it was left in the care of Mr Gaffrey, locked safely away in a strong-box.

But so sober an act could not satisfy the emotional Magdalene. When she got home to Welbeck Street she had recourse to the brandy bottle, and with the help of this composed a letter to the nephew she had so deeply wronged, pages and pages of maudlin contrition; a letter which, after she had sealed it, she inscribed, 'Not to be opened until after my Death', and hid romantically at the bottom of her jewel-case.

# *Chapter Three*

(i)

On a fine spring morning in the following year, Sir Hubert Thorne sat over his midday pint of ale in the 'snug' of the Ship tavern in Little Turnstile, reading the newspapers.

In character as in looks, Hubert bore a striking resemblance to his dead uncle Robin. He was headstrong, charming, slightly irresponsible, and much given to the riding of hobby-horses. And it was natural that his favourite hobby-horse should be the sufferings of his fellow Catholics. He had never forgotten the story of how a doctor had refused to come to the assistance of his mother at his own birth, and how this indirectly had killed his father; nor was it likely that he could forget that his patrimony had been seized under an iniquitous law. But in his ragings against such wrongs he was not indulging a personal grudge; he was honestly convinced that it was the duty of his co-religionists to fight for their rights, and the non-resistance attitude of Dr Challoner and the clergy generally infuriated him.

It had been Challoner whose influence had prevented the Catholics from rising in force for their rightful King in '45; had they done so the Stuarts, and the Faith, might well have been restored. And again, when the Government, desperate for recruits on the eve of the American war, had been in the mood to make some slight concessions, Challoner would not hear of asking for them. It was all very well to say how holy Challoner was; what was needed was a leader. Suppose, Hubert would argue, our ancestors had sat tamely down in the days of Elizabeth, as they would have done but for the Jesuits, there would have been an end of the Faith in England.

Both in his longing for action and in his irritation with the cautious Vicar Apostolic, Hubert had found a kindred spirit in his friend, William Sheldon, a man ten years older than himself and of a very forceful personality. He had an abiding grievance – he would have made a brilliant barrister, but the penal laws forbade his practising at the Bar. Apart from this, he had a grudge against Bishop Challoner; Sheldon had been educated at the Jesuit College of St Omer, and when the French Government had expelled the Society, an action followed shortly afterwards by its suppression by Clement XIV, Challoner and the other secular prelates had accepted the Jesuit Colleges abroad rather than let them be lost to the Church. Sheldon was wont to say flippantly that the only good thing Challoner had achieved was to persuade Rome to reduce the thirty-six holy days of obligation to eleven.

Sitting over his ale-can this morning, Hubert was waiting for Sheldon, who usually joined him here for a whet, beguiling the time by reading the *Westminster Journal*, which paper, though all reports of parliamentary debates were most strictly forbidden, contrived to give its readers the gist of them under the heading, 'Proceedings in two Political Club Rooms', and by designating Members merely by their initials.

As usual nowadays, the paper was full of the war. In December the nation had been thunderstruck by the news of the surrender of General Burgoyne at Saratoga; and the General having returned to England had just made an impassioned speech in the House, throwing the whole blame for his defeat on the unpopular Lord George Germaine, Secretary of State for the Colonies. The *Westminster Journal* added a colourful account of how the veteran Lord Chatham, who appeared to be kept alive only by his fury at the Government's misconduct of the war, had been carried into the House wrapped from head to foot in flannel, for the purpose of issuing dire warnings and condemnations 'like a venerable spectre', said the *Journal*. It really looked, thought Hubert, as though Lord North's Ministry might fall at last.

Presently he heard the outer door open and slam and a familiar firm footstep come along the passage. He looked up with a welcoming smile as his friend Sheldon strode into the room. The mere presence of this magnetic personality always heartened him, and this morning Sheldon's vitality seemed almost feverish. He said not a word until he had shrugged himself out of his greatcoat, come to the table, and spread his hands flat upon it. Then:

"I've told the landlord to let us have this room to ourselves for half an hour. For I've news for you, my boy, the best news you ever heard in your life."

He made a dramatic pause.

"The Government are minded to offer us some relaxation of the penal laws."

"Now wait till I tell you," went on Sheldon, waving aside Hubert's astonished exclamations. "I was walking down Holborn this morning when a chariot drew up beside me, and a gentleman who was a stranger to me called me by name. He introduced himself as Sir John Dalrymple, and said he had often seen me in Westminster Hall; would I, he asked, do him the honour of taking a whet with him, as he desired to consult me on weighty business. I told him rather curt that I was engaged, but then he whispered to me that what he had to say concerned my own interest and that of all those of my religion."

"Dalrymple. Is that the man who wrote the Memoirs which made such a sensation a few years ago?"

"Full of probably spurious anecdotes of public men. The same. He's one of the Barons of the Scottish Exchequer and a lay member of the General Assembly."

"Then why – "

"If you'll have a bit of patience I'll tell you. It seems that the Prime Minister and the Colonial Secretary are driven into so tight a corner by their own mismanagement of the American war, and now are alarmed by a rumour that secret negotiations are going on between the Colonists and France, that a month or so back they dispatched Dalrymple to Scotland to see if he could get recruits in the Highlands. And in order that he might do this, he was empowered to approach Bishop Hay, the Vicar Apostolic of the Lowlands, to ask what concessions the Catholics would expect if they were allowed to enlist."

Hubert slapped his thigh.

"Ireland all over again!" he chortled.

"Not if we can help it. There was no question of any of the penal laws being repealed in '74; merely the condescension of allowing the Irish to take the Oath of Allegiance. Well, Hay, it seems, told Dalrymple that he must apply to Challoner, for he would have no concessions made to Scottish Catholics unless we English had the like. And what do you suppose Challoner said?"

"Oh no – no! Don't tell me that – "

"I *am* telling you, my boy. I am telling you that that old woman deemed the whole matter 'imprudent if not dangerous', raising a dozen feeble objections. We do very well as we are, he quavered; any proposed relief would arouse the jealousy of the Dissenters; we should see persecution flare up again; and so forth. And so Dalrymple decided, against Hay's express order, to consult the Catholic laity. Thank God he did! He'll get a very different answer. Relief is as much a matter for us as for the clergy – more, in a manner of speaking."

Sheldon paused to gulp some ale. His eyes were dancing and his air that of a fighter on the eve of combat.

"Mind you, I don't trust Dalrymple one inch; there are all sorts of rumours about him, that he's a spy of the Colonists, of the Government, even of the French. But there's no doubt that North and his colleagues are at their wits' end for recruits, and that they're terrified of what we persecuted Catholics might do if the French invade. It's the chance of a lifetime, and we must seize it."

"We? You mean – "

Sheldon laughed joyously.

"Oh, I don't mean just you and me, dear old Hugh. I mean the Catholic laity in general. There are half a dozen prominent men now in town, the Duke of Norfolk, who's in the King's favour, since His Majesty was born at his house after George II turned out the Prince of Wales, and Lord Petre and the Earl of Shrewsbury, and Sir Edward Swinburne, and so on. I told Dalrymple I'd wait on them and discover how they felt about it, and if they are of our mind, we'll arrange a general meeting."

"I can't believe it!" Hubert murmured with a kind of awe. "I just can't believe it. After more than two centuries… "

Sheldon clapped a kindly hand upon his shoulder.

"And after all you've suffered, old Hugh, you and your family in particular. Oh, you won't get back Old Park – "

"I don't want it," said Hubert, laughing rather shakily. "I can't think of anything Alice and I would dislike more than being buried in the country."

"But we're going to make sure that our children can never be subjected to that sort of villainy. And we can interest John Dunning in any proposed appeal for relief by reminding him of your case. Stout heretic though he is, it's always been like a red rag to a bull to him. And lookee, Hugh, we're going to be very moderate; we're not going to ask for complete tolerance or anything like it; that *would* put the fat into the fire. No, we'll be satisfied with very little at first; if the Government wants Catholic recruits, they'll have to alter the attestation oath by which men have to swear themselves Protestants; and we on our side will only ask for the repeal of the 11 and 12 of William III."

He seized his hat from the table.

"I must go. Meet me at my lodging this evening, Hugh, and we'll talk at more leisure. This is an historic occasion, my boy; we are about to make one small breach in the walls which have imprisoned us, and in a year or two, please God, we'll be free men."

(ii)

During the next few weeks Hubert's quiet routine was changed into a whirl of activity, as he was swept along in the wake of his vigorous friend. He came in late for meals, and then, scarce able to eat for excitement, would describe to his family how he and Mr Sheldon had waited on the prominent Catholic laymen in town, and how nearly all most heartily had concurred in seizing this unexpected chance of pressing the Government for some relief.

"And so there is to be a general meeting to discuss ways and means, and a card to summon the meeting. And what do you think? Will Sheldon, having drawn up this card, asks me my opinion of it. It read like this: 'You are desired to meet the Roman Catholic gentlemen now in town' – and then it gave the place and time – 'to consult on matters of general consequence to yourself and them'. I said I deemed it very imprudent."

209

"You said that to Mr Sheldon?" his wife exclaimed admiringly.

"Yes; I did," replied Hubert, very solemn. "If it fell into the wrong hands, it might suggest some sort of a plot. You know how the heretics always suspect us of conspiring against them. So Will says to me, Do you draw up another. And here it is."

He pulled a card from his pocket and handed it round. It read:

'Your company is desired on some particular business at the Thatched House tavern in St James'ss Street on Saturday, the 11th instant, at 12 o'clock, and to dine at the half-hour after four if agreeable. April 8th, 1778.'

"Will Sheldon thought it very discreet," said Hubert with assumed carelessness.

"But are you asking nothing for your priests?" his mother asked, when he had told them how it was proposed to appeal only for the abolition of the Act of King William.

"You have forgotten, Mama," replied Hubert, quoting the arguments of his friend, "the clause in that Act whereby an informer is entitled to £100 reward for the conviction of a priest, and the latter is threatened with life imprisonment. Take away the reward and you will deprive the informer of all incentive to prosecute; and by abolishing the penalty of life imprisonment you will remove all danger to the clergy."

She did not remind him that there were other laws against priests. She was uneasy, wanting to share her son's enthusiasm, but distressed by his and Sheldon's refusal to consult the wise old Bishop who had guided his flock through so many perils during nearly forty years.

Hubert had even more stirring news to disclose to his family a few days later.

210

He had been taken by the energetic Sheldon to sound the principal members of the Government and Opposition, and they had found a heartening unanimity among Government supporters on the subject of Catholic relief. There was, it was true, more difference of opinion among their opponents, the Whigs, but even here there was no open hostility; and a most important accession had been gained in Lord Rockingham, a former Prime Minister, who had expressed his entire approval, though he was known to be bitterly anti-Catholic. An Address to the King was to be drawn up, and Lord Weymouth had undertaken to prepare his Majesty for its reception; and Edmund Burke, acclaimed as the greatest orator of the day, had offered to compose one which he thought might be acceptable. It really seemed as though men of all shades of opinion had undergone a change of heart towards an oppressed religious minority.

On the eve of the Thatched House meeting Mr Sheldon gave a small select dinner-party in his lodging, his guests being young men as determined as himself.

"We have had thirty acceptances for tomorrow," Sheldon announced. "Now some of these gentry will be inclined to waste time in talk, the more timorous will raise objections, and others will want us to do nothing without consulting the clergy. But save where doctrine is concerned religion is as much a matter for the laity as for priests, and you all know how timorous our Mr Fisher has shown himself. Therefore I propose that the eight of us here present determine now upon our line of action, and I believe we shall be able to carry the day."

His optimism proved justified. The little group who knew exactly what they wanted easily dominated the meeting, and were appointed the members of a committee who were to prepare the Address to the King, which Address was to be submitted to another general meeting,

211

composed this time if possible of every Catholic gentleman of substance in the country, on April 27th.

Hubert's enthusiasm mounted to fever-pitch in the days that followed. His legal work was neglected while he sat in Sheldon's rooms, opening letters which arrived by every post from over two hundred country Catholics, all of whom were favourable save for five who would have nothing to do with the affair. Meanwhile word came from Lord Weymouth that he had informed the King of the proposed Address, and that they might rely on its being received in a gracious manner; and a day or two before the second general meeting, Sheldon came bursting in with the Address itself.

"Read it! Read it!" he shouted. "And tell me if there was ever a more elegant composition."

But Hubert's admiration for Mr Burke's elegant style was swamped in his distaste for the grovelling servility the Address exuded.

'Our reverence for the Constitution is in no wise diminished by our exclusion from many benefits of it; we have patiently submitted to our restrictions, and thankfully received such relaxation of the rigour of the laws as the mildness of an enlightened age and the benignity of your Majesty's Government have gradually produced; and we submissively wait, without presuming to suggest either time or measure, for such other indulgences as those happy causes cannot fail in their own season to effect.'

"Butter!" chuckled Sheldon, reading over Hubert's shoulder.

'The delicacy of our situation is such that we do not presume to point out the particular means by which we may be allowed to testify our zeal to your Majesty and our wish to serve our country. But we entreat leave faithfully to assure your Majesty that we shall be perfectly ready on every occasion to give such proofs of our fidelity and the purity of our intentions, as your Majesty's wisdom, and the sense of the nation, shall at any time deem expedient.'

"I don't think he need have made us sound so obsequious," objected Hubert, with a flushed face. "Anyone would think we were criminals!"

"Which is precisely how the country at large regards us. Anything like a claim to equality with the heretics would be rejected with indignation. And the important thing is to get George on our side from the start, and being such a little autocrat he loves those who grovel."

Hubert was forced to swallow his distaste, for he found that all older Catholics had grown to accept their enemies' attitude towards them; at the second Thatched House meeting the Address was unanimously accepted, and was signed, in person or by proxy, by each of the two hundred and seven invited. On May 1st, at a public levee at St James's, it was presented by the Earl of Surrey, Lord Petre, and Lord Linton; King George expressed himself as highly gratified by it, and next day it was gazetted.

No public outcry following, the Catholic Committee, who continued to sit by their own consent and now regarded themselves as the mouthpiece of the laity, set about drawing up a Relief Bill, to be treated as a non-contentious measure, since if introduced as a Ministerial Bill there was the risk that it might be opposed on party grounds. Nothing was asked for but the repeal of the 11 and 12 of William III; and Sheldon, having drafted the Bill, carried it to John Dunning who, he had argued all along, would be the best man to introduce it. Though handicapped by an ungainly figure and a provincial accent, Dunning was at this time the acknowledged leader of the English Bar, and in politics he had given ample proof that he would support what he thought most in the

213

interests of equity and justice, even in the teeth of the King and his Ministers.

But Dunning, having read the Bill, asked in surprise:

"Don't you pray for any relief to be granted to your clergy?"

Sheldon repeated the arguments he had used before; adding that he and his colleagues were anxious to show that in temporal matters they were independent of their priests.

"Then," said Dunning coldly, "you must find someone else to introduce your Bill. If you can, I will second it; but that is as far as I will go."

Sheldon was indignant, but refused to be discouraged. That same evening he approached a Nottinghamshire baronet, Sir George Savile, Member for Yorkshire. Hubert was astonished by the choice, for Savile was known to have strong leanings towards Dissent. But it seemed that Sheldon knew what he was about, for Sir George instantly accepted.

(iii)

Sir Stephen Vickery had been abroad on business, and arrived home on May 12th. Next morning when he opened the newspapers which had accumulated during his absence, and read that a fortnight previously King George had received in a most gracious manner an Address presented to him by the Catholic laity of England, he could not believe his eyes. He read the Address itself, reproduced in the *Gazette*; he read the other papers and found them entirely concerned with the American war, without a single comment on the Papists and their impertinence. Surely there must be some mistake, and yet the *Gazette* was the official journal.

At noon he ordered his chair and was carried to White's where he found the members engaged at the card-table as usual or gossiping over their coffee. He listened to their talk. Would the French invade? That was the question of the hour; it was known by this time that they had made a secret treaty with the Colonists, and it was whispered that Spain might join the confederacy. Voltaire was said to be dying; Sheridan's new comedy, *The School for Scandal* had made a great hit last night; there was a proposal to have an annual exhibition of the Royal Academy of Arts at Somerset House.

Not a word about the Catholics; not one single word.

In the famous bow-window of the chocolate-house; he observed an acquaintance, Sir George Savile, sitting by himself, reading the militantly Protestant *Old British Spy,* and went over to talk to him. Stephen was not a man who made friends, but he had always regarded Savile in that light, for both were enormously rich and believed that money could buy anything, and both, for different reasons, detested the Catholics.

"How do, sir?" Savile greeted him. "What a fuss they are making here about Lord Chatham's funeral, his friends wanting to bury him in the Abbey and the City determined to have him in St Paul's. Which has caused Mr Walpole to utter another of his *mots*: 'They want to rob Peter to pay Paul'."

He laughed heartily.

"I have been abroad," said Stephen, "and feel I have returned to Bedlam. First I read in the *Gazette* that the Papists have had the impudence to address the King, and that his Majesty returned a gracious answer; and then I find the town entirely unmoved by so shocking a thing."

"Oh that!" said Savile with a shrug. "Why it is of no great consequence. Or rather, it is mighty convenient."

"I am at a loss to understand you."

215

"Probable invasion by the French, a secret enemy in our midst to be placated, urgent need for recruits – the Government is forced to do something."

"But you are in the Opposition."

Savile fished a hand-bill from his pocket and offered it to his companion. It promised, in the name of the United States of America, a portion of land commensurate with the social status of any Irishman who cared to emigrate to America, with full liberty of conscience.

"A thousand of these have been distributed in Ireland," said Savile, "where I, along with many other English gentlemen, have large estates. It would be most distressing, to say the least, if my tenants were to emigrate *en masse*. Even more distressing if French Papists were to invade us by way of Ireland, and be joined by their Irish and English brethren."

"And so we are to give bloody home-bred Papists liberty to cut our throats, which is what they will do without waiting for an invasion."

Savile lifted a deprecating hand.

"My dear Sir Stephen, you alarm yourself unnecessarily. They are certainly not to have anything like complete toleration, merely a sop to keep them quiet. And political necessity is a hard master. I dislike Papists every bit as much as you do, and yet I may tell you that I have consented to introduce a Catholic Relief Bill tomorrow."

Stephen turned white with anger.

"I thank you for the warning, sir," he snapped. "You will certainly hear me speak against it."

"You will find yourself in a minority, I assure you. Even the King, whose dislike of the Papists you know full well, has been persuaded that in the light of the national emergency this measure is expedient. And wait till you hear the Bill, my dear sir, before you grow alarmed; the relief they ask for is ludicrously slight, yet they are so overwhelmed with gratitude that you would think we had given them full liberty. And even this relief – "

He smiled with one side of his mouth and gently nudged Stephen.

"Well, my dear sir, Bills can be repealed, you know, when they have served their turn. It would be the simplest thing in the world to work up public indignation so that it forces us to repeal this pitiful Relief Bill when the international crisis is past."

The House was not very full when, late the next evening, Savile rose to introduce the Catholic Relief Bill.

There had been hot debates all day on the American situation, the Opposition demanding that all coercion of the Colonists be stopped, and the Government retorting that those wicked savages had leagued with a foreign Power and must be punished. Already Admiral Keppel had been sent to watch the French coasts for signs of invasion. The Members who had not left the House after these impassioned exchanges, listened without much interest to Sir George Savile, of whom the witty Horace Walpole had once written that he had a head as acutely argumentative as if he had been made by a German logician for a model.

"However necessary the penal laws against Roman Catholics originally were," intoned Savile, "whilst the Constitution was yet struggling into reformation, and afterwards confirming itself in that happy settlement, as the causes of persecution have long since ceased to operate, men of humanity cannot avoid lamenting the perpetuating of a line of division by which one part of the people, possessing no share in the common interest, are rendered incapable of forming any part of the common union of defence."

There were sounds of approval from both sides of the House, and Stephen's feeling of nightmare was intensified.

A month ago a mere reference to the Catholics would have provoked hisses.

"Indeed," Savile continued significantly, "the laws seem calculated to compel a considerable body of people to hold an hereditary enmity to the Government, and even to wean them from all affection to their country. Having read a recent loyal Address to his Majesty presented on behalf of certain Roman Catholic lords and gentlemen, I have been induced to beg leave to bring in a Bill for the repeal of the Act of the 11 and 12 of King William III, intituled, 'An Act to prevent the further growth of Popery'."

"Shame!" bawled a voice from one of the back benches.

Savile raised his eyebrows, and other Members smiled broadly. That eccentric young man, Lord George Gordon, humorously referred to by his colleagues as the 'Third Party in the House', could always be relied on to oppose even a non-party measure like the present one.

"My principal end in proposing this Bill," Savile concluded primly, "is to vindicate the honour and assert the principles of the Protestant religion, to which all persecution is adverse. I do not meddle with the vast body of the penal code, but I have selected for repeal that Act which gives the greatest scope to base informers for reward. The late excellent and loyal Address proves the attachment of the Roman Catholics to his Majesty's Government, and I consider it expedient" – he slightly stressed the last word – "that some relief be given them."

He sat down amid general applause, and the ungainly but powerful figure of John Dunning rose to second the motion. He bore testimony to cases he himself had seen in the courts when common informers had prosecuted only for gain, and said roundly that a Statute which had led to such a state of things was a disgrace to a civilised nation, in particular the clause which inflicted life imprisonment on priests.

"Such a law," he went on trenchantly, "in times of so great liberty such as the present, and when so little is to be apprehended from these people, calls loudly for repeal. I beg to remind the House that even then their priests would not have liberty to exercise their functions, as the former laws inflict a year's imprisonment and a heavy fine."

He turned his head and looked directly at Sir Stephen Vickery.

"As for that clause in the Act which gives the Protestant heir the right to seize the estate, it holds out the most powerful temptations for the commission of acts of depravity at the very thought of which our nature recoils with horror. It seems calculated to loosen all the bonds of society, to dissolve all civil, moral, and religious obligations and duties, to poison the sources of domestic felicity, and to annihilate every principle of honour. In a word, it needs only to be mentioned to excite the utmost indignation of this House."

His eloquence received its customary tribute of cheers; and after the Attorney-General and three other Members had spoken in support, the Catholic Relief Bill was ordered to be brought in, and a committee was appointed to consider the same. In speaking against the motion, Sir Stephen Vickery found himself in a minority of two, his fellow dissentient being his neighbour in Welbeck Street, the bizarre eccentric whom, in common with the rest of the town, he had never taken seriously, Lord George Gordon.

(iv)

On the evening of June 3rd, Barbara was sitting at the window of her room in the tall old house in St Clement's Lane, unusually idle.

From this window she could see so many favourite land-marks – the apse of the Sardinian Embassy chapel due north, and to the east of it her dear Lincoln's Inn Fields. She could identify the gables of the Ship tavern, and the chimneys of the Six Cans and Punchbowl where Hubert had been staying when they met and fell in love. Her room, too, enshrined most precious memories; there was the portrait of Blessed Michael Thorne, the work-box, engraved with the Thorne crest and motto, which had been Hubert's mother's, the manuscript book with its proud record of all the sufferings endured by the Thornes for their religion, a picture in wax of Robin as a boy, of Robin who must have been so like her own son.

She was thinking of her son as she sat here now, and wishing she could share whole-heartedly his feeling of triumph. It was indeed extraordinary, almost miraculous, this absence of opposition to the Relief Bill: it had been passed by both Houses without a single division, and only awaited the Royal Assent to become law. The question as to whether King George would sign was casting a faint shadow of anxiety on Hubert's and his friends' jubilation, for George was a despot and unpredictable. But so far the Bill had gone through with astonishing smoothness and expedition; at the beginning of the year any relief for the Catholics had been undreamed of either by themselves or the Government; and now, but five months later, it was almost an accomplished fact.

It was ridiculous of her, reflected Barbara, to fancy that there was something vaguely sinister about this suddenness; old Mr Ashmall, a kindly cynic, had explained to her that, humanly speaking, the Relief Bill was due to a transient political situation, seized on by a group of energetic young laymen to wring from an embarrassed Government a measure of relief.

But apart from her reasonless fears, Barbara could not approve of the Catholic Committee's attitude towards the clergy, and in particular towards Dr Challoner. It was all very well to call him old and timid; the fact remained that during all the years when he had been at the helm of the storm-tossed little ark in which the English Catholics had braved the rocks and quicksands of passive persecution, it had been due to his common sense, self-dedication, and wise prudence that that ark had kept afloat. And now, at a moment so critical as the present, the laity had acted without reference to their Vicar Apostolic; not until the terms of the proposed new attestation oath had been settled between the Ministry and the Catholic Committee had the latter called on Dr Challoner. He had pointed out mildly some alterations which must be made to correct certain errors imperceptible to those unversed in theology, forbearing to say a single word of reproach regarding their cavalier treatment of him, their Bishop.

And cavalier treatment was too mild a term, surely, for the way they had behaved towards Bishop Hay. After the second general meeting at the Thatched House tavern, Michael, who was now in charge of the Catholics in Southwark and who often came to see her, had told her a story which had filled her with shame and indignation.

"It seems," he had said, "that Sir John Dalrymple wrote to Lord Linton, urging him to come to London to represent the Scottish Catholic laity, since his father, the Earl of Traquair, is in France and could not be present. Linton consented on condition that he might bring Bishop Hay; but when the Bishop sought admission to the Thatched House meeting, Mr Sheldon actually caught him by the shoulders and pushed him outside, rudely telling him, 'We want none of your cloth here'."

Hay, went on Michael, had gone to call on Dr Challoner, describing what had taken place and lamenting this outbreak of anticlericalism among the ancient Catholic families who so largely had kept the Faith alive since the Reforrmation. It would lead to the apostasy of many, he had cried; there would be internal dissension which might well prove fatal.

"But Dr Challoner," said Michael, "smiled in that odd secret way he has sometimes, a way which makes you believe the tales of him, that he has the gift of prophecy. And I heard him murmur something I thought, and still think, very strange. 'There will be a new people.' That was what he said."

The bells of St Clement Dane's rang out their pretty chimes of 'Oranges and Lemons', and Barbara, chiding herself for her idleness, rose to fetch some needlework. As she did so, there came through the window the sound of someone running hard down the narrow street. Leaning out, she saw her son, hatless, the queue of his wig bobbing with his haste; he glanced up, caught sight of her, and began waving his arms in wild gesticulation, for all the world like an excited child. Then his feet hammered on the stair, he burst into the room and seized her in his strong young arms, his face radiant.

"We've won, Mama, we've won! The King has given his assent to the Bill; it is law – do you understand? *The Catholic Relief Bill is law!"*

She caught the infection of his frenzied enthusiasm. After more than two centuries of persecution, of the rack and the quartering-knife, fines and confiscations, social ostracism and public contempt or hatred, a religious minority had wrung from the Government a measure of justice. It was pitiful in its inadequacy, but surely it was the thin end of the wedge.

"If only my father could have lived to see this day!" cried Hubert, his eyes full of tears. "The very penalties which most humiliated him have been erased from the Statute

Book; above all, that clause which enabled a villain to seize his estates."

"But not the penalties for saying or hearing Mass," said Barbara with a sigh.

"All in good time, Mama. We have to go step by step, you know; we have to be prudent," said Hubert, the soul of impetuosity and recklessness. "Next year, or perhaps the year after that, we shall press for further relief. And we shall get it, don't fear. Apart from the political expediency, which forced them to give us this modicum of relief, there truly are signs of a more tolerant attitude. Throughout the whole debate, only that silly fanatic, Lord George Gordon, spoke against the Bill; and of course Vickery."

"Vickery," she repeated; and felt as if a cold hand had been laid upon her heart.

# Chapter Four

To young Sir Hubert Thorne and the Catholic Committee the passing of the Relief Bill was a major triumph; to the ordinary citizen of London it was a bit of news tucked away in a corner of the newspapers, to be read with a click of the tongue and some commonplace remark about bloody Papists, and then forgotten in a preoccupation with a topic infinitely more important, the American war.

For throughout that summer of 1778 the shadow of invasion by the Colonists' allies brooded over the town. In July there were alarming reports from the coast; heavy firing had been heard at sea, and so contradictory were the rumours that while some towns rang their bells to celebrate a victory, others were emptied of inhabitants who fled inland from imaginary invaders. The truth, when at last it was known, caused a new buzz of talk – Admiral Keppel had encountered the French fleet off Ushant and would have beaten them had it not been for the cowardice or treachery of Sir Hugh Palliser, one of the Lords of the Admiralty, who had disobeyed Keppel's order to pursue the enemy and had turned a probable victory into stalemate. In October Keppel brought his battered ships to Portsmouth, and was greeted with the news that he, and not Palliser, was to face a trial by court martial.

All through the winter the furious debates in Parliament were reflected in miniature in every club and coffee-house, and the very names of Keppel and Palliser were enough to make gentlemen whip out their swords and the lower sort to brawl in tavern common-rooms. To the average man, Palliser represented the Government who had dragged England into a war she had no hope of winning, and who continually invented new taxes for the payment of their impressed soldiers; while Keppel was the honest, injured public servant who, as a critic of the Government, had been got out of the way by sending him to sea with an ill-equipped fleet, and now was to be made a scapegoat. When, early in February, the acquittal of Keppel became known in London, the town went mad with joy, the mob attacked the houses of the Prime Minister and Palliser, hanged the latter in effigy, and made the nights noisy with squibs, crackers, and drunken singing.

In all this excitement few had time to read a little item of news from Scotland, for Scotland was very far away and completely unimportant. It seemed that the introduction in Parliament of a Bill for the relief of Scottish Catholics, similar to that which had been passed for the benefit of those of England the previous year, had provoked rioting in several towns; some secret Mass-houses had been burnt; several prominent men known to be in favour of the Bill had been threatened with assassination; and a general uprising had been prevented only by the magistrates issuing a proclamation that the proposed Relief Bill had been withdrawn.

While the Government was being bombarded by attacks from the naval and military commanders in the Opposition, and the Whig newspapers were demanding Sir Hugh Palliser's trial, and the fashionable world was all agog with the murder of Miss Ray, Lord Sandwich's mistress, by an infatuated young clergyman, a little group of men were very busy holding meetings at the Old Crown and Rolls tavern at the Holborn end of Chancery Lane. Not one of these men was of any real standing, though they took themselves very seriously. It was the kind of little club which, in that hey-day of the club, was wont to spring into being when men of the same way of thinking got hold of some grievance, and which usually died a natural death.

Its leading spirits were the Rev. Daniel Wilson, a clergyman of the extreme Low Church persuasion; Mr Joshua Bangs, a wealthy coach-maker; and Mr Benjamin Masson, once the keeper of livery-stables on the Kent Road, and now a lay preacher.

Barbara's father had long forsaken the Methodist fold, and now subscribed to the extreme form of Calvinism known as Antinomianism. It was an attractive creed to one of Mr Masson's peculiar mentality; chosen as one of the Elect from all eternity, he could commit no sin, needed no guidance, and was incapable of displeasing his Creator. But its particular appeal to Mr Masson was its watchword of 'No Popery'; its adherents were dedicated to the task of destroying the Beast of Rome, which Beast had seduced the soul of Mr Masson's youngest daughter.

So far Mr Masson had not met with much success in his awful vocation. It was true that during his association with Mr William Payne, known as the Protestant Carpenter, he had secured the conviction of a priest and had had the satisfaction of hearing the victim sentenced to life imprisonment. But four other potential victims had been acquitted on the ruling of Lord Chief Justice Mansfield, who had upheld the plea of the defence that to prove a man to be a priest it was not sufficient to swear that he had acted like one; and Mansfield, known for his bold judgments, had added some very unpleasant remarks about common informers who prosecuted only for gain.

Shortly after this, the Protestant Carpenter, in order to save himself expense, had forged some copies of subpœnas for the trial of five priests and a Catholic schoolmaster; and these spurious documents falling into the hands of the attorneys for the defence, the Protestant Carpenter had decided that the air of London was unhealthy, and had betaken himself and his informing activities elsewhere.

Apart from his mission, this had been a serious blow to Mr Masson, for he had depended on the Protestant Carpenter for his daily bread. But most providentially another patron had appeared, in the guise of Mr Joshua Bangs, a wealthy coach-maker whose residence and place of business was in the vicinity of the newly built Westminster Bridge, not so very far from Mr Masson's old home. Attending one of the trials of the Protestant Carpenter's victims, Mr Bangs had been so impressed by the zeal with which Mr Masson had given his evidence, that he straightway had taken the latter under his wing, and had made over to him one of his coach houses for a chapel.

Here, Sunday by Sunday for nearly ten years past, had Mr Masson held forth to the Elect of Southwark on the iniquities of Rome. He had grown a long white beard which gave him a faint resemblance to John Knox, and in the manner of that worthy he consoled himself and his flock by uttering prophecies concerning the imminent destruction and utter rooting out of the Lord's prime enemies, the Papists. Until, in the spring of 1778, a mine had been exploded under his feet with the passing of the Catholic Relief Bill.

For a while he had felt, as had his unknown connection by marriage, Sir Stephen Vickery, that the world had gone mad. But now, a year later, there was a faint glimmer in the dark; the Elect of Scotland had been roused to action. Letters began to pass between Mr Bangs and other stout

Protestants, and something that called itself 'The Committee of Protestant Interests', whose headquarters was in Edinburgh; and as was the time-honoured habit of Scottish Reformers, this Committee were resolved, it seemed, to come to the aid of their brethren in England.

Oh how consoling it was for the distracted little club who met at the Old Crown and Rolls tavern to read the accounts of what their more vigorous friends were doing in the North! A Catholic Relief Bill? cried the Committee of Protestant Interests. Only over our dead bodies! Riots had been instigated; hand-bills had been scattered. The Committee enclosed one of these circulars for the edification and encouragement of their English brethren. 'Whoever shall find this letter, will take it as warning to meet at Leith Wynd on Wednesday next, in the evening, to pull down that Pillar of Popery, the Massing-house lately erected there. A Protestant. P.S. Please read this carefully, keep it clean, and drop it somewhere else.'

And how successful had been the result of this appeal! The Pillar of Popery had been razed to the ground, and similar hand-bills dropped about the streets of Aberdeen, Peebles, Glasgow, and Perth had caused the savour of many such burnt sacrifices to delight the nostrils of Jehovah. Surely the Protestants of England would not be less forward in so godly a work?

The little group of men who met at the Old Crown and Rolls were galvanised into activity. They gave themselves a name, 'The Protestant Association'; they solemnly agreed that the nation must be diverted from its silly obsession with this American war and made aware of its danger from Papists at home whose wily plots had resulted in a Relief Bill. The Dissenters' meeting-houses began to ring with denunciations and Mr Wesley himself wrote an inflammatory *Defence of the Protestant Association,* in which he declared that 'an open toleration of the Popish religion is inconsistent with the safety of a free people, and every Papist is by principle an enemy to the Constitution of this Country.'

The little club outgrew the confines of the Old Crown and Rolls, and began to meet at Coachmakers' Hall in Long Acre. The members vied with one another in sensational stories and alarming reports. Popish schools and chapels were being opened; Popish books were exposed for public sale. Twenty thousand monks were secreted on the Surrey side of the Thames, announced Mr Masson, ready at a given signal to blow up the banks and bed of the river and drown London. The purple power of Rome was advancing by hasty strides to overspread this once happy nation, warned Mr Wesley. Mr Bangs, who appeared to possess the most detailed inside information, spoke of Jesuits in various disguises gliding about the streets of London, of chains being forged on Roman anvils for the fettering of free Englishmen, of daggers being consecrated for the cutting of Protestant throats, and of nuns practising the *Te Deum* in readiness for the news that England had been led captive to the feet of the Whore of Babylon.

The Rev. Mr Wilson, a more practical man, demanded to know what was to be done. They could not, he said, follow their Scottish friends' example and burn Mass-houses; it was against the law. The legal course was to collect signatures to a petition to Parliament, and if Protestants of all denominations united in this matter, Parliament would be compelled to repeal the Relief Act.

The Associators generally concurred, Mr Bangs being particularly enthusiastic.

"We must prepare the way of the Lord," he cried. "We must implant in every honest breast feelings of alarm, and this we may do by means of wood-cuts and ballads hawked about the streets, and hand-bills scattered everywhere."

"That sort of thing costs money," said a voice.

Some indignation was caused by so sordid a reminder, but Mr Bangs, who was thrifty after the manner of his kind and disliked putting his hand into his own pocket, had a solution to this problem of ways and means.

"In the debates upon the hellish Catholic Relief Bill last year," said he, "there were but two gentlemen who spoke against it. One, as you remember, was the noble lord who has always shown himself the sworn enemy of Rome; the other was a Sir Stephen Vickery. And I am told that this Sir Stephen is a man of very substantial fortune."

(ii)

"I have brought the draft of our Appeal for your approval, sir," said Mr Bangs, bustling into Sir Stephen Vickery's study one morning in late October. "I believe we have most thoroughly prepared the ground, and that it is time for the Protestant Association to emerge into the light of day. Our members have been most forward, especially good Mr Masson – "

"What name?" sharply enquired Stephen, looking up from the *Morning Advertiser* which was full of contradictory reports of the result of a major engagement between General Washington and General Howe.

"Mr Benjamin Masson, a most worthy fellow. He – "

"Does he by any chance own livery-stables in Southwark?" again interrupted Vickery.

Mr Bangs explained that Mr Masson formerly had pursued that trade, but now devoted all his time and energies to the destruction of the Beast of Rome.

"A worthy fellow indeed," murmured Sir Stephen; and a smile, a rather unpleasant smile, lifted the corners of his lips.

"Mr Masson has toiled from morning till night," continued his visitor, "distributing our hand-bills and addressing meetings. And because it has seemed to us that when the time comes to petition Parliament for the repeal of this wicked Relief Bill, we should be able to give the Honourable Members some idea of the growth of Popery, Mr Masson has been drawing up a list of the Massing-houses and schools and other property of the London Papists."

"Most praiseworthy," approved Stephen. "And such a list might prove useful if – er – some little demonstration against these people was found necessary. I look forward to meeting your Mr Masson; I believe I was acquainted with his daughter many years ago."

It appeared to have been a pleasant acquaintanceship, for Sir Stephen, leaning back in his chair, was shaken with silent laughter.

"And now," said he, wiping his eyes with his *mouchoir*, "let me see this Appeal of yours."

There was a long silence while he read through a pamphlet of some sixty pages in the handwriting of the industrious Mr Bangs. It was entitled, *An Appeal from the Protestant Association to the People of Great Britain,* and the greater part of it was concerned with painting a horrific picture of the fate awaiting free Englishmen unless the late Relief Act were repealed. The threat from French Papists, whose invasion was still imminent and who would be sure to be joined by their English brethren, was emphasised; and in the last paragraph the Appeal got down to business.

'Having pointed out the fatal consequences of the late Act of Parliament, to remedy the evil let the Protestants throughout the kingdom associate as one man, and apply to Government for redress. Our Constitution hath marked out the mode of obtaining such redress, and declares that it is the right of subjects to petition. Let petitions be circulated throughout the whole land; let the clergy of the Establishment and all Protestant ministers of every

231

denomination, and all who are zealous for the welfare and safety of the Protestant religion, cordially unite and strenuously exert themselves on this important occasion.'

"H'm," observed Stephen, laying down the sheets at last, "that is very well. But I would suggest a further paragraph. You remember that we are on the eve of a General Election, and I think a little appeal to self-interest may be used to so good a cause."

"Why certainly, sir, if you please," said Mr Bangs, getting out his tablets. It was Sir Stephen Vickery who paid the piper, and therefore had the right to call the tune.

" 'Let petitions against the Popish Bill be sent to Parliament from every city, county, and corporation,' " rapidly dictated Stephen. " 'Let our representatives be instructed by their constituents to support these petitions in the House; and as a General Election is approaching, we have reason to hope that these instructions will be attended to. Should they be neglected, we soon shall have an opportunity in our hands of electing Members more attentive to the voice of the people, and the preservation of the Protestant interest. If such measures be adopted by Protestants with unanimity, and prosecuted with spirit, Government may then with safety relieve us from our fears by repealing the late Act; and have nothing to dread from the resentment of the Papists.' "

"It has been suggested, sir," said Mr Bangs, having inserted this new paragraph, "that our Appeal be published on November 5th, a date when all good Englishmen are reminded of Gunpowder Treason and Plot. Mr Pasham, the printer at Blackfriars, assures us he can have it ready by that date. And we have discussed very frequently the electing of a President. We would be greatly honoured, sir, if you – "

"No, no," modestly interrupted Sir Stephen, "you need a gentleman more in the public eye. I would suggest your applying yourselves to my Lord George Gordon; I am sure you could not find a more suitable or zealous President."

And again that unpleasant smile twitched his lips.

(iii)

Throughout his thirty years of life, Lord George Gordon's main object had been to make a nuisance of himself. This he had achieved in a petty sort of way, but so far had never found anyone willing to take him seriously.

During his school days at Eton he had proved such an embarrassment that his family had bought him an ensign's commission in the Army to save him from being expelled. Military discipline not appealing to young George, he had transferred to the Navy, but his superior officers refusing to listen to his lavishly proffered advice as to how fleets were to be sailed and battles fought, George had decided to devote his talents to politics. His electioneering tactics in his native Inverness-shire, where he gave balls, listened to bards, wore the Highland dress, and toured the countryside with an escort of fifteen young ladies of the beautiful family of Macleod, shipped over from Skye for the purpose, had so alarmed the sitting Member, General Fraser of Lovat, that he had bought from Lord Melbourne the pocket-borough of Ludgershall in Wiltshire, and made a free gift of it to his tiresome young opponent.

That was in 1774; and ever since then George had diverted the House with his wild and irrelevant speeches in the midst of serious debates. Trying he undoubtedly was, but at least he introduced a little comedy into St Stephen's Hall, and had become a sort of tame buffoon, almost a mascot. His lean figure, dressed one day as plain as a Puritan, the next bizarre in velvet coat and red tartan trews, was known everywhere in London, causing intense embarrassment to his noble relations but a welcome diversion to bored hostesses. You could always rely on Lord George to do or say something startling; with his lank hair which he wore loose on his shoulders, his high cheekbones and sallow complexion which gave him a touch of the Oriental, and his large fanatical eyes, he looked his chosen part of the prophet uttering dark warnings which, while they pleasantly thrilled his hearers, had the advantage of never coming true.

So far it had never occurred even to his relations that his moral recklessness, his unbalanced mind, and his savage fanaticism might make him, given the right circumstances, a dangerous man. But it had occurred to Sir Stephen Vickery; and Sir Stephen, having occasion to use a dangerous man, and having no wish to thrust himself forward in any anti-Catholic campaign after the unpleasant remarks directed so pointedly at him by Mr Dunning during the debates on the Relief Bill, had cultivated Lord George's acquaintance ever since the Bill had become law.

All his short life Lord George had dedicated himself to a variety of causes, but in one thing he had remained consistent: his sincere hatred of Popery. Ever since the passing of the Relief Act he had been in a state of frenzy bordering on madness; the debates on the American war and the threat of French invasion had been punctuated by the springing up of that wild figure, and the sound of that loud harsh voice boasting that its owner could put himself at the head of a hundred and twenty thousand men in Scotland who were ready at a word from him to remedy Protestant grievances by the sword. The House laughed at him as usual; but the Protestant Association, its numbers rapidly increasing, were caught in the grip of their President's demagogy and hypnotised by that strident voice, that blazing eye. The enthusiasm he aroused reacted on himself, until he was carried away by a sense of his own

power and lost whatever mental balance he had ever had.
At last someone was taking him seriously.

Authority still refused to do so; to its future cost. He
called on the Prime Minister, pop-eyed Lord North, and
commanded rather than requested that harassed politician
to present the Protestant Association's petition to
Parliament. North, whose majority was falling, his
supporters ratting, brusquely refused; he had trouble
enough on his hands, he said, what with the loss of
Canada, Spain joining the Colonists, the French capture of
Grenada, and Ireland demanding free trade as the price of
remaining neutral.

Lord George betook himself to the King, whom he
found at Kew, bullying his innumerable children,
superintending the erection of yet another Moorish
temple, and lecturing his plain little wife on the diseases of
horned cattle. It was very difficult to talk to his Majesty,
whose habit it was to ask a spate of questions, all ending
with the word 'Hey?', without waiting for an answer.
Moreover, since his attack of insanity (politely referred to
in public as a humour in the chest), his Majesty had been
extremely odd, and there were still unfortunate occasions
when he would turn his back on a distinguished visitor and
solemnly shake hands with the branch of a tree.

But Lord George Gordon, himself mentally unbalanced,
was not to be put off when he approached his Sovereign on
such a mission; and for a full hour he compelled his
Majesty to listen to his reading of the Protestant
Association's literature; it becoming too dark to see, and
King George being very economical over lights, his
Majesty's word of honour was demanded that he would
read the rest himself. Stunned by so much eloquence, his
Majesty meekly promised; which made a good story to be
laughed over in clubs.

But plebeian London was not laughing. Wherever it went it saw on walls and signboards the slogan 'No Popery' scrawled in blue chalk. On its shop counters, from the genteel mercer's to the humble chandler's, there stood conspicuous a collecting-box, cunningly contrived so that when a coin was inserted a pasteboard figure of the Pope fell flat and Lord George Gordon appeared in his place. The door-knockers of houses rat-tatted daily, as men with *The Protestant Association* inscribed on arm-bands, called to collect signatures to a bumper petition. The spouting-clubs where, with the growing fashion of taking outdoor apprentices who were not their master's concern once work was done, lads who fancied themselves as budding orators nightly debated, buzzed with youthful voices demanding vengeance on the Papists. Fiery sermons fanned the growing flame; hack-writers, swift to scent out any current fad, raked up all the old tales of Popish iniquity; astrologers curdled their clients' blood by the Popish assassins they saw lurking in every horoscope.

So thoroughly had public apprehension been aroused that the offices of the Protestant Association in Fetter Lane were besieged by folk begging to be enrolled; and from all parts of the country came copies of the Association's petition, its blank sheets covered with names or with the marks of those who could not write. When a Member, presenting a petition against the new tax on post-horses, trailed it along the floor of the house to exhibit the number of signatures, Lord George Gordon leapt up with a crazy laugh.

"Pooh!" he shouted: "What is all this? With a great deal of pulling, the petition seems to extend, Mr Speaker, from your Chair to the door of the House. In a few days, sir, I shall present you with the petition of the Protestant Association. It will extend, sir, from your Chair to a window in Whitehall that kings should often think of."

No one protested at so treasonable an observation. It was only that mad Lord George Gordon with a bee in his bonnet as usual. Had he not been the Duke of Gordon's brother, undoubtedly he would have been put into Bedlam long ago.

On May 30th, 1780, every London newspaper carried an advertisement with a terrific display of capitals and italics.

'Whereas no Hall in London can contain *forty thousand men.* Resolved that the PROTESTANT ASSOCIATION do meet on Friday next in ST GEORGE'S FIELDS, at ten o'clock in the Morning, to consider of the most prudent and respectful manner of *attending their Petition*, which will be presented *the same day* to the HOUSE OF COMMONS... '

Over their morning chocolate, ladies glance through the newspapers; but they miss this interesting advertisement because they are absorbed in an account of how the 'Young Cub', otherwise Charles Fox, has fought a duel in Hyde Park with Mr Adam, nephew of the architect, and has been slightly wounded. And then there is another instalment of the love-letters of that mad clergyman who murdered poor Miss Ray; and here is advertised an adjustable hoop, hinged at the waist so that never again need one fear the embarrassment of getting stuck in a doorway. Where is St George's Fields, Mama? enquires a hopeful offspring, reading over Mama's shoulder. St George's Fields? My dear child, some low place in Southwark, I believe; you should not even mention such vulgar haunts; and here is Abigail come to take you for your walk in the park.

At White's and the Cocoa Tree, gentlemen ignore the advertisement in their *Lloyd's Journal* or their *Morning Post*, for they are busy reading the account of how Temple Luttrell, brother of the Duchess of Cumberland, has accused Lord North of buying a borough which Luttrell thought he had bought himself. Opposition supporters rejoice, and Government supporters rage, at the number of petitions coming in, and the number of associations being formed throughout the country, demanding peace with the Colonists. And have you heard, sir, that that firebrand Wilkes has harangued the Common Council in the Guildhall against the Government's mismanagement of the war?

In the pit of the Haymarket Theatre (never the same since Garrick's death last year, sir), a Macaroni who has slept too late to look at the papers this morning, listlessly turns the pages of the *London Chronicle* while waiting for one of the fashionable 'grotesque entertainments' to begin. Have you seen this advertisement? he drawls to a friend who is engaged in smoothing his monstrous wig; it might be rather diverting to go to St George's Fields and view the *canaille* at their spouting. And catch some low disease, objects his friend; and by the way, sir, I saw the 'Third Party in the House' at Marylebone Gardens yesterday, dressed (you will scarce credit it, sir) in a tartan petticoat. And on his head a sort of thing like a City flat-cap, with a perfectly monstrous bunch of blue ribbons in it. The creature! Then they begin whispering about the latest amour of the Prince of Wales.

In his armchair at Almack's, Lord Hillsborough, Secretary of State, reads the advertisement, and clashes his snuff-box lid in disgust. Have you seen this impudence? he growls to the Prime Minister, who is walking up and down the room rehearsing a speech with the aid of a pocket-mirror. Don't he know it's against the law for petitions to be signed by more than twenty persons, unless approved by the Grand Jury, or to be presented by more than ten? Oh damn it! petulantly exclaims Lord North. I promised the Cabinet yesterday that I would give orders to the civil magistrates to attend this meeting in St George's Fields and keep the peace, and I have forgotten all about it. But really, what with this frightful new threat of war with the Dutch, and all this agitation for peace with the Colonists... I see Lord George requests the presence of magistrates at this meeting, grunts Lord Hillsborough. Don't he know that those of Westminster and London can't act except within those cities, and that not a single justice of the peace resides in Southwark?

Anyway, says political and fashionable London, it is only Lord George Gordon, that harmless fanatic.

They forgot some forty thousand fanatics, not so harmless.

They even forgot that dreaded, faceless spectre, the lord of misrule, King Mob.

# Chapter Five

(i)

Michael Thorne had read that advertisement; and waking in his attic bedroom in Bandy Legged Alley, Southwark, on Friday, June 2nd, remembered instantly the grim significance of the date. He remembered, too, how on his first meeting with his Vicar Apostolic, Dr Challoner had remarked that, though he did now know why, the mention of St George's Fields had always filled him with a strange foreboding. And now today they were to be the rallying place of Lord George Gordon's Protestant Association.

He got out of bed and went to the window, whence he could see over the crowding rooftops of the Bankside a portion of St George's Fields.

They were the playground of Southwark. Respectable tradesmen and their wives drank the supposedly mineral waters of St George's Spa, apprentices with their spaniels hunted duck on the ponds, highwaymen and other questionable characters divided the swag and planned fresh exploits on the Kent Road, over their gin at the inaptly named Temple of Flora. But for the war the fields would have been built over; with rising prices and labourers impressed into the army, all that remained of these building activities were some crumbling shells of houses, a shelter for runaway apprentices and vagrants.

240

At this early hour the fields were deserted, and even the stark new roads leading to the Obelisk were softened by the mystery of dawn. Over the dewy grass cattle moved peacefully; and as Michael watched he saw a toy figure emerge from the *lactarium*, whither the milk-walkers came to collect the milk and cry it through the streets of London. The ponds round the Dog and Duck tavern were faintly silver, and so quiet was it that he could hear a lark. A morning straight from the hand of God... He set his lips, turned from the window, and prepared to spend the day according to his normal routine.

On weekdays his congregation at Mass consisted only of his landlady, Mrs Murphy, her family, and little Hubert who now lodged with him and attended a tiny Catholic school in the neighbourhood, returning to his parents for weekends. There being no serious likelihood of a raid, the elaborate precautions which Michael observed against intruders at Sunday Mass could be dispensed with; and he had come to love the peace and quiet of his daily offering of the Holy Sacrifice.

But this morning, as he celebrated the feast of the fourth-century martyrs, SS Marcellinus, Peter, and Erasmus, he found himself a prey to distractions, listening all the while for the sounds which would announce a great crowd gathering in St George's Fields.

" 'O God,' " he prayed in the Collect, " 'who dost gladden us by the yearly festival of Thy blessed martyrs; grant, we beseech Thee, that we may not merely rejoice at their reward, but may be inspired by their example.' " Both Epistle and Gospel warned of the sufferings in store for the faithful and promised final deliverance. " 'And you shall be betrayed by your parents and brethren and kinsfolk,' " he read from St Luke; " 'and some of you they will put to death. And you shall be hated by all men for my name's sake. But a hair of your heads shall not perish. In your patience you shall possess your souls… ' "

Patience, endurance. For forty years past those words had been constantly on the lips of Dr Challoner. He had shrunk from the measure of justice offered to the Catholics two years previously, because he had the attitude of a lifetime of being thankful to be let alone and forgotten, needing all his energies for tending his meagre flock, and trusting that God, in His own good time, would rekindle the fire of faith. The laity had complained of him as pusillanimous; but the riots in Scotland last year had justified his fears, and now there was this deliberately incited anti-Popery hysteria threatening to sweep through England also.

If the pathetic little flock, the sixty thousand Catholics in England, were suddenly to find themselves in the front line of battle, how would they behave? Michael wondered uneasily. Would they, like the exorcist and the priest and the bishop whose festival he was celebrating today, face the loss of all they had, even of life itself, with heroic courage? Or would they, who had no memory of active persecution, scatter like terrified sheep? And was their shepherd, a saintly, retiring man of nearly ninety, a leader to inspire them?

He shook such thoughts from him; they verged upon disloyalty to his superior, and in any case it was not his business. His business was to make his thanksgiving, eat his breakfast, recite the Little Hours of the Divine Office, and go out to visit his own small flock, whose home was the workhouse, the gin-cellar, the Marshalsea Prison, or the verminous slum. But though he struggled to keep his attention upon the shadowy figures of the Martyrs who had suffered so long ago, he was alert all the while for the mutter of the coming storm, listening, listening for the footsteps of the enemy.

It was nine o'clock when he closed his Breviary, and here in this back room of a house enclosed within a labyrinth of streets and squalid tenements, he had heard nothing unusual. Then, as he reached for his hat, he remembered certain remarks he had heard his Irish parishioners make during the past few days. If that mad Lord George wanted a fight, begorra he should have one! They'd be at the meeting right enough to bloody the noses of his dirty Protestants. Michael had not paid much attention, but now he was suddenly alarmed. His Irish, chiefly chairmen, porters, and coal-heavers, with seasonal immigrants who came over for the hay harvest and potato lifting, though they were the most devout creatures he had ever met were also the most pugnacious. They were wont to appear at Sunday Mass reeking of strong drink and bearing the scars of the battles they engaged in on Saturday nights. If they started brawling with forty thousand opponents there might be another 'Massacre of St George's Fields'; it was his duty, surely, to be on the spot and restrain them.

He set off in the increasing heat of the morning, picking his way along the filthy alleys, past the high wall of the Anchor Brewery, past the genteel pile of St George's Church, and round the corner of the King's Bench Prison which backed on to the fields. And here he stopped dead, appalled and bewildered.

It was nearly an hour yet before the advertised time of the meeting, yet the huge open space was already filled by a crowd which increased every moment, as groups came hurrying over Westminster, Blackfriars, and London Bridge, from Newington and Lambeth, and along the Kent Road. Michael had expected that if Lord George's summons were answered, it would be a disorderly mob he would find here. Instead, it was something like an army on parade. All were dressed in their best clothes; all either had a blue cockade in their hats or hastened to buy one from enterprising vendors who had set up little booths selling nothing but this Protestant emblem. The fluttering and bobbing of favours, the music of fife and drum, the waving of banners, the undercurrent of hymn-singing, all gave a cheerful holiday air to the gathering, colourful in the bright summer sunshine.

Yet though it carried no weapons, it was an army none the less. As each newcomer arrived he hurried to find his place in one or other of four divisions which formed rings in the quarters of the fields. These rings were three deep, those inside sitting, the next kneeling, and the outer circle standing. Inspecting the one nearest him, Michael saw a red banner floating in the midst, with *No Popery* inscribed in huge black letters.

His heart was sick with dread as he looked upon that gathering, deafened by the bands and the shouted orders and the constant tread of feet. It was like some vast blue flood, he thought, which must overwhelm all obstacles. He tried to calculate the numbers, but it was impossible, for milling round the orderly rings were folk who might be mere idle sightseers, but all of whom, he observed, even to the vendors of gingerbread and oranges, wore the Protestant favour. There might well be forty thousand present; certainly there were more blue-cockaded men in St George's Fields this morning than there were Catholics in the whole ten counties of the London District. Parliament would not be able to resist so formidable a demonstration of public opinion; it would repeal the Relief Bill.

That, at the moment, was the limit of his fear. He thought of persecution as something carried on under colour of the law; of mob violence he knew nothing. He had thought Dr Challoner fanciful when, during the Keppel riots last year, the old man had exclaimed:

"Alas, how soon all this fury may be turned against us!"

Rising above the military music there came from the direction of Westminster Bridge the skirl of bagpipes, incongruous in these London fields. A deep-throated roar of acclamation burst from the multitude, and men drew back to form a lane as a coach was seen driving slowly on to the ground, preceded by pipers in full Highland dress, and surrounded by black-gowned ministers. Peering between the heads in front of him Michael caught a glimpse of a figure, picturesque in a black velvet coat and tight-fitting red trews, descending from the coach and acknowledging the cheers by waving a hat decorated with a huge blue cockade.

The Protestant hero proceeded with his attendants from one detachment to another, standing in the centre of each ring and making an harangue. The crowds became silent as soon as that strident voice began to speak, and Michael was able to catch stray sentences.

" ... I wish so well to the Cause that I am ready to go to the gallows in it...there is no danger that you go into that I will not share... I give you my solemn word that I will be answerable for any molestation which may be offered you in your unanimous petition...the late indulgence shown to Papists is inconsistent with the principles of the Glorious Revolution, endangers the Succession of the House of Hanover, and is sufficient to bring down God's wrath upon our country...remember the Scots carried their point by their firmness; people in my country do not mince matters, and shall the Scots be better than you? ... "

A furious indignation flooded Michael as he listened; that reference to the riots in Scotland was a deliberate incitement to violence, and it was answered by a primitive bellow from the crowd.

Lord George was going in solemn procession now to a blue-draped platform which had been erected under the Obelisk set a few years previously in honour of a Lord

Mayor who had defied Parliament in the matter of publishing its debates. The attendant ministers took it in turn to address the Almighty in extempore prayer, and there was a ripple of movement as hats were swept off. But then the harsh voice was heard again, this time through a speaking-trumpet, and banners were flourished as the moment for action drew near.

"In order to impress the City with our united resolve," bawled Lord George, "we will march six abreast in three divisions, the first to go round by London Bridge, the second to go by Blackfriars, and the third directly over Westminster Bridge. And at half-past two we shall all unite again before the Parliament House."

So then that blue flood divided into streams, flowing towards London under the hot blue sky. At the head of the division which went directly towards Westminster there marched a man grotesquely bowed by the huge roll of parchment he carried on his head, the Protestant Association's petition inscribed with a hundred thousand names. And rumbling along in the midst of the human flood, with bagpipes screaming their inflammatory music before it and the horses decorated with the Protestant favour, could be seen Lord George's coach.

At some time later, Michael found himself alone.

It had sprung forth, that dreadful flood, as if from nowhere, and now it had rolled along its destined course to drown a religious minority already half submerged. Under the scorching sun of noon the fields were as empty as they had been under the dawn; but there was no longer mystery or peace. The grass was trampled and blackened, littered with orange peel and beer bottles, with here and there a blue cockade like an ugly bright weed; the body of a man who had fainted with the heat lay sprawled beneath a tree.

The platform in the centre beneath the Obelisk was like the scaffold of a gallows.

He turned, a dull despair in his heart. He had seen the worst, he believed; tomorrow's papers would inform him that the Catholic Relief Bill had been repealed.

(ii)

Sir Stephen Vickery had driven down to Westminster somewhat earlier than usual this fine June morning. Later in the day there was to be a little drama acted of which he was stage-manager, and he wished to make certain that the scene was set. Going up on to the leads of several of the tall old tenements which overlooked New Palace Yard, he had a word with the men he had placed there, each armed with a blue flag.

It was very amusing to him this morning to watch the solemn procession of the Speaker, to listen to the Chaplain reading prayers, and to see the House getting down to the business of the day. Still more amusing to imagine how all these pompous gentlemen would look before the day was ended. He dined in the small room which one, John Bellamy, had been permitted to open five years previously; and while eating a portion of Bellamy's famous veal pie, he listened to the talk around him. Opposition Members were jubilant; only a month ago they had defeated the Government on Dunning's motion that 'The Influence of the Crown has increased; is increasing, and ought to be diminished', and with the deputation which was ready to wait on the House from the associations throughout England demanding peace with the Colonists, they were confident of bringing down Lord North's Administration. On the other hand, Government Members were rejoicing at the defeat (though a very narrow one) of Sir George Savile's motion demanding a list of the King's pensions.

No one so much as mentioned Lord George Gordon or his well-advertised meeting in St George's Fields.

Stephen pulled his watch from his fob and slipped from the room. It was half-past two. There being no Appeals, the Lords had not sat this morning; but they would be arriving now, and they would find the Protestant Association waiting for them to teach them that it was not to be ignored. He took up a position at one of the windows in the Cloisters, where he could see in comfort; and he beamed with delight at what he saw.

Everywhere he looked there was one thick cobble of heads, each decorated with a blue cockade, intersected here and there by red banners drooping in the windless heat, but flourished now and again to exhibit the large black inscription. *No Popery.* Above the steady murmur of voices and the shuffle of thousands of feet, he caught the sound of coach wheels, and his smile broadened; the Peers were arriving. He glanced at the vantage-points where he had placed his sentinels; yes, they were ready; the blue flags signalled as the first coach forced its way into New Palace Yard, and the play began.

The Archbishop of Canterbury was dragged from the coach, his lawn sleeves ripped off and flung in his face, and a large blue cockade pinned on his breast to a storm of ironic cheers. Lord Mansfield was the next, high on the black-list of the Protestant Association for his acquittal of priests; the glasses of his carriage were smashed, the panels staved in, grimy hands mauled him, raucous voices threatened to tear him limb from limb, and he was in actual danger of being lynched when out from the Peers' entrance rushed the dishevelled Archbishop, somehow managing to drag his lordship within.

The sport grew hotter. Sprucely dressed figures were rolled in the dust; liveried footmen, trying to defend their masters, had their heads broken; elegant figures were transformed into scarecrows. Lord Stormont was held prisoner with his hands bound behind him to watch his new chariot being systematically demolished; a group broke off from the main crowd to pursue the Bishop of Lincoln who, uttering pathetic little shrieks, was trying to reach the safety of the Middlesex Guildhall. Lord Bathurst was being quietly robbed of his money and snuff-box even while he bleated out, "No Popery!" Half a dozen Peers, unrecognisable in their rags, their heads wigless, their persons bespattered with blood and filth, rushed out in a body to the rescue of Lord Bolton who had fallen and was being trampled to death.

Then suddenly the yells of triumph and the savage laughter were engulfed in one spontaneous roar of welcome, as the eccentric figure of Lord George Gordon stepped from his coach and began bowing right and left as he made his way to the door of the House, patronising the formidable monster of his own creation, metaphorically patting it on the head as though it were a pet dog.

The House of Commons had resumed its sitting, and was in its afternoon mood, slightly somnolent, replete with claret and John Bellamy's famous veal pie. It was now debating the Militia Bill, while thinking of its evening engagements at the play, the Pantheon, the masquerade; when gradually it became aware of a most unconscionable din beyond the stained-glass windows. It dawned upon these self-important gentlemen that the neighbourhood of their sacred domain had been invaded by an impertinent rabble; and the baiting of the Prime Minister was postponed while both sides of the House united against the common foe.

'The House being informed,' the Clerk wrote tranquilly in his beautiful copperplate, 'that a large and tumultuous multitude had filled the Lobby and Passages leading to this

House, a motion was made and the question proposed: That the Magistrates of the City and Liberty of Westminster do forthwith attend the House... '

He started and made a large blot, as there was a great dull thud on the floor of the House, and the Protestant Association's petition slowly unrolled itself at the feet of Lord George Gordon.

' ... The Petition of the Protestant Association being introduced,' continued the Clerk, frowning at the blot, 'and the question put: That this House do now resolve itself into a Committee of the Whole House to consider the said Petition: the House divided: The Yeas were directed to go forth... But the Yeas not being able to go forth on account of the tumultuous crowd in the Lobby... And the Serjeant-at-Arms attending this House having informed this House that it was not in his power to clear the Lobby: Mr Speaker directed him to send for the Sheriff and other Magistrates of the County of Middlesex and City of Westminster to attend this House immediately... '

Above a confusion of hysterical cries, accusing the Government of taking no precautions against such an appalling invasion of this hallowed spot, demanding that the Guards be sent for, imploring Members to compose themselves, promising that all was under control, sounded hammering and kicks against the door of the Lobby, punctuated by rough voices chiming in chorus:

"Lord George Gordon! Lord George Gordon!"

As from a seat in the theatre, Vickery watched the strange figure, its lank hair falling over its black velvet coat, its mad eyes glittering, dance up the gallery stairs, fling open the door, and begin a running commentary, egging on the mob in the Lobby below.

"The speaker has just declared that you are here under *pretence* of religion" – (a wolf-howl of rage) – "and Mr Rous has moved that the civil power be sent for; but don't you mind, keep yourselves cool and steady." ("We will, Geordie! But they'd better not provoke us!") "There is Mr Burke, the Member for Bristol, speaking against you. Do you know that the Prime Minister calls you a mob? ... Quiet now, quiet, my brave lads; here is Sir Stephen Vickery has just spoken for you like an angel; but as for Mr Burke, I am sorry for him!"

"Down with traitor Burke! No Popery, boys! Repeal! Repeal!"

"Ay, you have been called a mob, and peace officers have been sent for to disperse you; some have mentioned calling out the military –"

"They called the Colonists bloody savages, but them savages made their armies run!"

"Ay, I hope for their own sakes no one will think of taking such a step. Remember what I told you, that I would not present the petition of a lukewarm people, and was never a man to do things by halves."

"And neither are we, by God!"

"But let me tell you how the matter stands. It has been proposed to take your petition into consideration on Tuesday, but I don't like delays, and see little hope of redress from the decisions of Parliament... Here is Mr Bowen, the Chaplain, wants to address you; will you hear him?"

"We don't want no chaplains! We want repeal!"

"(They will not hear you, sir; you see, it is useless to try to address them.) The House is going to divide on the question whether your petition shall be taken into consideration today or on Tuesday next. There are for taking it now, only myself and six others; but if it is not heard at present it may be lost – "

For several seconds his voice was drowned by a battery of fists upon the door.

" – For tomorrow the House does not meet, Monday is the King's birthday, and on Tuesday the Parliament will be dissolved, so you see how they mean to trick you, my poor lads. But in Scotland they did not wait on the decisions of Parliament, and would you not wish to be in the same state as they are in Scotland?"

All this while the Members below had been buzzing like angry bees. The Speaker must commit a man who so grossly had violated parliamentary procedure; the Mace must be carried out to overawe the rabble; no, no! that precious symbol might never return. The Government had had full warning of that meeting in St George's Fields and its object; why, then, were not the magistrates at hand? The Government was to blame for its cowardly concessions to the Scottish rioters last year; and so on, and so forth. In the midst of such futile recriminations, certain Honourable and Gallant Members clattered up the gallery stairs, and by mingled threats and cajolings endeavoured to bring Lord George to reason.

"My lord," cried General Conway, "I am a soldier, and I shall deem it my duty to protect the freedom of debate in this House with my sword. D'you imagine that I shall allow myself to be insulted with impunity by a rude, unprincipled rabble?"

"You hear what General Conway calls you?" Gordon shrieked to his followers.

"There is only one entry into the House of Commons," thundered Conway, leaning over and addressing the packed Lobby, "and that is a narrow one. Reflect, you dogs, that men of honour may and will defend this pass, and that certainly many lives will be lost before we suffer you to come within the walls of this House."

Colonel Gordon, Lord George's kinsman, was coaxing the madman as though he were a child.

"For God's sake, cousin, don't lead these poor misguided people into danger. Dear cousin, for their own sakes bid them begone."

"My Lord George," barked General Grant, his hand upon his hilt, "do you intend to bring your rascally adherents into this House? If you do, I give you my word that the first man of them that enters, I will plunge my sword not into his but into your body."

The fanatic looked round in a dazed fashion; while the mob below, daunted by the sight of the resolute officers and by their ringing tones of authority, became quieter. Lord George suffered himself to be led back to his place; but after a minute or two, like some *infant terrible* in a tantrum, leapt up and started running towards the gallery once more. He had not taken more than a few steps before Colonel Holroyd seized him, wrenched him round, and snarled:

"My lord, at first I thought you were only mad, and was going to move that you be sent to Bedlam. Now I see there is much more malice than madness in this business. If you go out once more to the mob, I assure you upon the faith of Parliament I will instantly move that you be committed to the Tower."

Gordon swayed a little; he was very pale, as though all the fire had gone out of him. When the Chaplain begged him to come to the dining-room and take some refreshment, he acquiesced meekly; and presently Mr Bowen returned and whispered to the Speaker that Lord George had fallen asleep on a couch.

But though the mob in the Lobby had grown quieter, it showed not the slightest intention of departing, and the Commons were faced with the preposterous fact that they were besieged in their own House. Member after Member addressed the rabble, coaxing, threatening, arguing; insults and a chorus of "Repeal! Repeal!" were the only answers. General Conway and his friends were seriously suggesting opening the doors and cutting their way out with their swords, when the Prime Minister, who had appeared absolutely stunned by the situation, recovered himself and sent for the Guards.

It was nearly nine o'clock, and the exhausted Members listened in acute anxiety as the rattle of hooves and the tramp of disciplined feet announced the coming of the military. All knew it was a desperate measure; nothing was more calculated to arouse the fury of plebeian London. Then faintly through a storm of hissing they heard a voice upraised; and then (oh heaven be thanked!) a ragged cheer. It was the popular Justice Addington who had ridden up at the head of the Guards, and who had promised that they would be sent back to barracks as soon as the multitude dispersed. Sounds from the Lobby informed the Members that this had had its effect and that the crowds were beginning to melt away. A hasty division on the motion to take the Protestant Association's petition into immediate consideration was defeated by a hundred and ninety Noes to only six Yeas; and the Honourable Members, shaken by their ordeal, hurried home through streets which were almost deserted.

But Sir Stephen Vickery was chortling to himself as he drove towards Welbeck Street. The House was sadly misled if it thought that the Protestant Association would go back to its kennel like a whipped dog. Even the maltreatment of its Members had not been sufficient to teach Parliament that Lord George and his followers were in earnest. Very well, then; the curtain must go up on the second Act of the play.

When he got home he went up on to the leads of his house with a spy-glass under his arm; and there he sat himself down, with a flagon of wine beside him, for all the world like a gentleman of leisure prepared to watch some pleasant spectacle.

(iii)

During the course of that day, Michael had received from Dr Challoner an urgent summons to attend a conference at the little house in Red Lion Square. He had found most of the other London priests present, among them a Mr Dillon who had charge of a Mass-centre in Ropemakers' Alley, Moorfields, and who now looked very disturbed.

"Mr Dillon," Dr Challoner said gravely, "having received some threats that his chapel and dwelling-house were to be attacked by the Protestant Association, applied to the Lord Mayor, who told him positively he would protect him. But Mr Dillon's good people not being satisfied with this, came to him and offered to enroll themselves under his leadership and defend their chapel if it were molested."

Some of the other priests murmured that their own people had made similar offers.

"I have asked you to come here," said Dr Challoner, who looked desperately strained but whose manner and voice were firm and authoritative, "in order to tell you that I cannot permit any such thing. It shall not be said that under whatsoever provocation the faithful resorted to violence. We are bidden to resist not evil. Moreover, I myself have been to the Home Secretary, who has pledged his word that if the Protestant Association lifts a finger against our persons or our property, the Guards will be called out to protect us. I must ask you, therefore, to go among your people and induce them to stay quiet."

255

So Michael had come back to Southwark and spent the remainder of the day visiting his pugnacious Irish parishioners, extracting, not without difficulty, the required promise. He was tired and depressed when he arrived home at ten o'clock; the night was stifling and the odours of the Bankside seemed as it were the essence of this awful day.

It was his custom always to say good night to his great-nephew when the boy was in bed; and though he supposed Hubert would be asleep by this hour, he softly opened the door of the little attic room next his own. It was still light enough for him to make out a small figure in a nightgown crouched at the window.

"Oh, sir, is that you?" cried the child, sounding excited. "Do come and look! See how bright the sky is over London."

Michael looked. His lips parted, but he said nothing.

"Oh, look at the sky!" persisted little Hubert. "It's sort of flickering. Is it lightning? Or are there fireworks? Oh, I wish it was tomorrow and I was home! Could we go out and have a look?"

Far below in the alley feet ran past, urgent, purposeful.

"That man's in a hurry! Let's ask him where the fireworks are. Hey you, please – oh, he's gone! Is it the King's birthday? I thought that was Monday. Oh, now there's smoke. That must be bonfires. Oh, *do* let's go and see!"

Michael roused himself from his daze of horror, and put an arm round the child.

"No, Hubert," he said quietly. "They are bad bonfires. You must forget about them and go back to bed."

"I expect Miss Gunner's lit them," remarked Hubert contemptuously. "Silly thing, to think she'll frighten Mr Bear and me."

Michael picked him up, carried him to the bed, and gently drew up the blankets.

"I am going out again, Hubert, but Mrs Murphy and her family are downstairs, so you will be quite safe. And while you are going to sleep, will you say a prayer for – for all those you love?"

A pair of eyes, with the lids drooping drowsily over them, glanced up at him in reproach.

"I said my prayers while you were such a long time coming to kiss me good night, and if it isn't morning, I can't say my morning ones, can I? God's bound to be asleep now, and you can't spect Him to wake up in the middle of the night just 'cause you've 'membered something you forgot to ask Him in your night ones. And anyway, I always ask my Garden Angel to – "

The sleepy voice was swallowed in a yawn, the curly head drooped sideways on the pillow, and little Hubert slept. His great-uncle laid his hand for an instant on that head, murmuring a blessing. Then he walked quickly from the room and from the house, towards that ominous red glare that grew brighter every instant in the neighbourhood of Holborn and Lincoln's Inn Fields.

# Chapter Six

Sir Hubert Thorne had spent the day at the Court of Requests in Westminster Hall, watching a case for his father-in-law who was away in the country, and like the House of Commons had found himself imprisoned by the multitude. When at last he was able to get out of the Hall, he was swept along by the human current which was flowing up Whitehall, and since this was his own way home he made no effort to get out of it.

But as he went, the lamplighter was igniting the cotton wicks floating in fish-oil in the parish lamps, and the shadowy multitude which hemmed him in took on a new and ominous aspect. For it was armed. It grasped spokes of wheels from broken coaches, iron bars, faggot-sticks, coshes made by wrapping old leather aprons round the heads of clubs; and presently there were torches, too, flaring smokily and throwing monstrous shadows. This crowd meant mischief.

And evidently it was under orders. At Charing Cross it divided into two divisions; one, with shouts of "A-hoy for Golden Square!" marched westwards; the other swept him along the Strand. With a vague idea of finding a magistrate, he struggled to get out of the stream, but he was as flotsam on a river in spate. He could but try to keep his feet lest he should fall and be trampled on by the determined mob, who, with their blue cockades and their banners and their primitive weapons, bore him along to Duke Street where they halted before the doors of the Sardinian Embassy chapel.

A helpless spectator, trapped in the midst of this wolf-pack, he saw hands hurling brick-bats and heard the splinter of glass, the crash of iron bars against the door. Above the din a voice was trying to make itself heard, and looking up he saw the nightcapped head of Sir Alexander Wedderburn, Attorney-General, who lived in the adjoining house. Every now and then disconnected sentences were audible, like pathetic little drops of water hissing on a fire?.

" ...diplomatic rights...foreign territory...his Excellency's wife lies gravely ill...be forced to send for the Guards... "

"A spy, lads! A spy!" bawled a voice from the mob; a stone was flung, and the head disappeared abruptly.

The door was down now, and Hubert, fighting and cursing, was swept within, into that chapel where for so many years he had assisted at Mass, at the singing of Vespers and Compline on Sunday afternoons, at Benediction when the shining jewelled monstrance was raised above the bowed heads. He saw that monstrance now; he saw vestments and altar-cloths, images and crucifixes, patens and chalices, some being stuffed into pockets, others passed from one, grimy hand to another to be flung on the bonfire which crackled fiercely in the street outside. He saw *The Taking Down from the Cross*, the great painting by Spagnoletto above the high altar, being hacked and ripped by a knife; he saw men bowed beneath the weight of benches and prie-dieux, staggering out to feed the fire; he heard a howl of rage when the Tabernacle was forced and found empty.

Someone grasped his arm, whether friend or foe he knew not until he found himself in the comparative quiet of a passage, and recognised Count Cordon, the Ambassador.

"I have sent a servant for the fire-engines," gasped his Excellency. "The flames are threatening the Embassy, and we have been forced to drag my wife, sick as she is, to a neighbour's. But I implore you, Sir Hubert, if you can contrive it, get to Somerset House and fetch the Foot Guards."

"The Blessed Sacrament?"

"One of my chaplains rescued It in time, and has carried It to the Ship tavern. Here, sir; slip out this way into Arch Street, and so you may get by Bear Yard into the Strand."

A captain of the Hosts of Israel was Benjamin Masson, an instrument chosen by the Lord from all eternity, as he assisted in this cleansing of the temple, this destruction of heathen gods. He was unconscious of fatigue, of the stifling heat, of bruised hands and aching head; in his nostrils was the odour of burnt sacrifices, on his lips a psalm of exultation.

So he lived his hour; and when the wrecking of the chapel was complete, it was his hand which snatched a burning brand from the bonfire in Duke Street and hurled it through one of the broken windows. The fierce crackle of the flames and the crash of falling timbers prevented him from hearing the disciplined feet that came at the double from the direction of the Strand; he was busy assisting in the breaking up of the fire-engines, when suddenly he found himself with a few of his comrades enclosed within a scarlet hedge, with bayonets threatening him on every side.

He charged blindly; and a white-hot pain ran down his leg. And then he was not a captain of the Hosts of Israel, but just an old man, with singed hair and beard and the blood soaking through his breeches, and tears of agony and bewilderment smearing his blackened face, whimpering as rough hands gripped him and marshalled him off to prison.

(ii)

Alice Thorne was an unimaginative young woman, entirely absorbed in domesticity, especially at present when she was expecting another child. Throughout the last few weeks, when she could not go into a shop without seeing one of the Protestant Association's collecting-boxes on the counter, when inflammatory hand-bills had been thrust through her windows and blue crosses scrawled on her door, Alice, though indignant, had shown no apprehension.

"Nasty low creatures!" she had exclaimed. "Making chalk-marks on my nice clean door, and expecting me to give money to that mad Lord George Gordon."

Even on this dreadful night, when she sat up with her mother-in-law waiting for Hubert to come home, when she had seen that ominous glare across the roof-tops, had heard the echo of shouts and fighting, Alice's anxiety had been only for Hubert. As soon as he came home and she had satisfied herself that though exhausted and dishevelled he was uninjured, she was her competent, practical self. She rang the bell for hot tea; and when there was no answer to the summons, and a visit to the kitchen disclosed the fact that the servants had fled, she made the tea herself, remarking that it was just like modern servants, so unreliable.

Her comment on Hubert's account of the outrage at which he had been an unwilling spectator was that the Government would make that wicked Lord George and his Protestant mob pay for such a crime. Alice's faith in the temporal authorities was as absolute as her trust in God. If one were law-abiding, the Government was bound to protect one; it was true, of course, that in the bad old days governments had persecuted rather than protected Catholics, but all that was changed now; hadn't they just passed the Relief Bill?

Hubert, revived by the hot tea, agreed with her. Apart from anything else, the attack on the Sardinian Embassy chapel, together with that on the Bavarian Embassy in Golden Square, would force the Government to adopt strong measures; they had enough enemies among the foreign Powers without making new ones. And Lord George Gordon's behaviour at Westminster today most certainly would result in his arrest; as for his Protestant Association, it had melted away directly the Guards were fetched, and though it was true that it had committed arson immediately afterwards, again it had dispersed at the coming of the military.

Remarking, with the vindictiveness of certain unimaginative characters, that she looked forward to seeing all these villains hanged, Alice went placidly off to bed, taking with her Dr Cadogan's revolutionary book, *An Essay on the Nursing and Management of Infants*. As soon as the door was shut, Hubert turned to his silent mother.

"There's something very painful I have to tell you, Mama. Grandfather was one of those arrested tonight for the outrage in Duke Street. At least, I am almost certain it was he, though I have seen him but seldom, and he looked so strange – "

"It would be he," she interrupted quietly. "He would be so easily led away by a man like Lord George Gordon, an educated gentleman, a Member of Parliament, and a sworn enemy of the Catholics."

"It must be horrible for you!"

She bent her head so that he should not see her tears.

"It is a thing I have lived with for a long time, my son."

"He was wounded, I think. They have taken him and the other prisoners to the Savoy, fearing lest the Associators should contrive a rescue from the watch-houses."

"I shall try to get an order to see him." She rose with an effort, but as she reached the door she asked, like a child seeking reassurance:

"Hubert, you don't think there will be any more rioting?"

"I'm quite sure there won't be," he said with youthful vigour. "The Government were taken by surprise, though they ought not to have been, but now for their own sakes they must act. Tomorrow you'll hear they have issued a proclamation suppressing this Protestant Association, and that Lord George is under arrest."

She nodded, apparently satisfied. But secretly she was the prey of an old fear, a relic of her childhood. She was afraid that Lord George Gordon's appeal to violence might have roused from their den the vast, mysterious forces of disorder which lay dormant beneath the law-abiding surface of London, and that deep would answer deep.

Saturday passed in comparative calm.

Michael called early on his sister-in-law to reassure himself that she and her family were safe, and gave them his own news. On the previous night he had gone to Dr Challoner's lodging, fearing an attack on the little house in Red Lion Square, and his fears had been increased by seeing men with the blue cockade and the red and black banners parading the neighbourhood, shouting out that they intended to find the Popish Bishop and roast him alive. But it seemed that they had no exact information as to where he lived, and after a while they had straggled off home. Michael had spent the night in Red Lion Square, joining his pleas with those of the two chaplains that Dr Challoner would remove himself to a place of greater security.

"At first he absolutely refused," said Michael, "saying that we were all in the hands of God, and that he would not desert his people in the hour of their need; but this morning we have persuaded him that his presence in London may well bring down further wrath upon us all, and my Lady Stourton has driven him in her chariot to the house of his friend, Mr Mawhood, the army contractor at Finchley."

"I have been all round the town this morning, and it is perfectly quiet," said Hubert, who had recovered his cheerfulness. "And as I expected, the House of Lords has met and has addressed the King, praying that immediate orders be issued for the prosecution of the authors, abbetors and instruments of the outrages, and for full compensation to the Ambassadors."

His mother said nothing, and Michael noticed that the tranquillity he always associated with her had vanished. Only when he was leaving the house did she rouse herself and say:

"I have been trying to persuade my son to ask you if you could find someone to convey little Hubert to Mr Ashmall who is in the country. I think Alice should go also, for she is near her time, but she will not hear of it – no, Hubert, let me finish. Lord George Gordon remains at liberty, and his Association has not been suppressed."

"I entirely agree with your mother, Hubert," said Michael vigorously. "If you will give me leave. I can make arrangements to have your son carried into the country within the next few hours."

Hubert gave in, though privately he thought both his mother and his uncle were worrying themselves unnecessarily. Apart from the burning of the two Embassy chapels, the outrageous conduct of the Protestant Association at Westminster would have been sufficient to make the Government act with firmness. Two incidents that occurred later in the day seemed to justify his optimism. Some of the Protestant Associators attempting to attack the Mass-house in Moorfields were promptly dispersed by the Lord Mayor and his peace officers; and the prisoners taken in Duke Street the previous night were marched to Bow Street by the Guards, evidence was given against them, and they were consigned to Newgate. But Benjamin Masson was not among them; he was lying mortally wounded in the Savoy.

He did not know where he was or how he had come here; he was not even sure of his own identity. Fragments of scenes passed in succession through his fevered mind; now the ghost of an old exultation gashed his cracked lips into a smile, and a voice he did not know was his own croaked out orders to take all the prophets of Baal and slay them, to leave no rag of superstition to cumber the earth. But then he would hear the tread of booted feet, and wince and whimper that the Lord had deserted him, His chosen instrument, in his old age.

"Water," he whined feebly. "Water, for the love of God."

It was miraculously there at his lips. He drank greedily, feeling the blessed coolness on his tongue and brow. Someone was gently supporting his head; someone was speaking.

"Father, it is I, Barbara."

"Barbara. Bloody Papists seduced my little girl's soul. Down with the Papists – "

"Father, try to understand what I am saying. It was not until today that I was able to get an order to visit you, and now they have given it me only because you have but a few hours to live. Father, can you hear me?"

The eyes glittering with fever looked at her, but they held no recognition.

"It is Sunday evening, Father. The riots broke out again today. Your friends went once more to the Mass-house in

Moorfields, and they have destroyed it and several other houses in the neighbourhood. And the Lord Mayor has shut himself up in the Mansion House and will do nothing – "

"Cast down their idols, burn their temples – "

"Father, there will be bloodshed soon. The priest at Moorfields narrowly escaped with his life. My own brother-in-law is a priest; nor he nor one of your own kith and kin is safe. The Government seems paralysed; the Guards cannot act without an order from a magistrate, and all the justices are cowed. Father, listen to me! You were a leader among these misguided people; you must know what other Catholic property they have marked out for destruction. If ever you loved me, if you have any natural feelings, tell me what you know."

He was sinking fast. The restless head turned from side to side, the cracked lips muttered unintelligibly. But even as she despaired, he spoke for the last time, quite clearly, with a ghost of his old savage zeal:

"Where next, boys? A-hoy for Hammersmith! Bloody female Jesuits… "

(iii)

Magdalene had spent that Sunday at Jenny's Whim, the new pleasure-gardens at Chelsea, with Charles, her latest lover, and they had had a violent quarrel.

She knew it was her fault. For months she had been in such a state of misery that she could not control her tongue or her tears. For something she had trampled on for so many years, telling it there was no hope for it, bidding it lie still, fighting it with drugs and drink and a feverish round of pleasure, had risen again in new strength, insisting that it was not too late to make amends. I have made what amends I can, she told it; I have bequeathed the thing dearest to me, the only thing I love, to him from whom I stole it. But the interior voice only cried the louder, It is not enough; there is reparation to be made to God as well as man…

"Some woman, a stranger, brought a note for you, my lady," Hanson told her, yawning discreetly, bored by this mistress who had lost her looks and her admirers. "She wouldn't give her name."

Magdalene snatched the sealed paper; perhaps Charles had repented of all the cruel things he had said today. But the inscription was not in his hand; she flung the note aside unopened, curtly dismissed her maid, locked the door, and sought the deceptive comfort of brandy.

She was awakened from a sleep that was more like a swoon, by strange noises from the street outside. At first she thought it was part of her usual nightmare, for never in this genteel neighbourhood had she heard so vulgar a cacophony. But the din continued, and presently, unable to bear it, she dragged herself out of bed, flung a wrapper round her, and ripped back the curtains from the window, wincing at the bright sunshine. And then she wondered again whether this was not some nightmare.

Welbeck Street was filled with a crowd who seemed to be staging some ghastly victory parade. Some had dressed themselves up in rich garments she recognised as copes and chasubles; one, mock-solemn, swung a thurifer from which there issued a little cloud of incense. In the centre of all a man held aloft a great crucifix; the Figure had been hacked away, and in its place was a dead cat, the bound paws clasping a circle of paper meant to represent the Host. The mob genuflected before it, clasped their hands as though in prayer, gabbled gibberish while they incessantly made the sign of the Cross.

The spectators for whom this demonstration was staged were but two. On the balcony opposite stood the strange figure of Lord George Gordon, clad in a tartan dressing-gown ornamented with a great bunch of blue ribbons; and though she could not see him, Magdalene could hear her husband applauding and encouraging from his own balcony next door to her room.

She turned from the window, sobered, sick with shame. And as she turned she saw lying on the carpet where she had tossed it last night the unopened letter given her by Hanson. Merely to fix her mind on something material so that she might ward off the faintness that threatened her, she picked up the paper, broke the seal, and read:

'This is to tell you that the rioters intend to attack the convent at Hammersmith. If ever you loved someone there, I implore you to do what you can to warn her. She loves you still; she told me she would always do so. Barbara.'

She stood there reading and rereading the brief note; and all the while an image grew inside her mind with startling, poignant clarity. Reverend Mother. Reverend Mother with her crippled hand, and her astringent humour, and her kind, shrewd eyes. Oh how often had she, Magdalene, longed to fly to that maternal tenderness! But always she had told herself that Reverend Mother would turn in loathing from the apostate, the unnatural wretch who had betrayed both her faith and her own family... 'She loves you still; she told me she would always do so.'

"No!" cried Magdalene aloud. "I couldn't. The humiliation of it!"

But then an idea came to the rescue of her pride. She could go to Reverend Mother, not as an outcast but as a heroine, risking the vengeance of the rioters, the loss of all she had. My husband will discover what I have done, of course, she would say calmly, and will turn me from his house; and then she would waive aside their gratitude and drive away alone to face the consequences.

She dressed with feverish haste; she would not call her woman to assist her. After all, whispered the voice of prudence, if you are discreet about this, Stephen need not know. She peeped out of the window; the Protestant Associators had gone, and the street was empty save for a few servants who were sniggering together as they swept up the refuse left by the demonstrators. She went quickly downstairs, meeting no one on the way, and out of the house. From the stand in Cavendish Square she engaged a hackney, on the sides of which were scrawled huge letters:

'GOD BLAST THE POPE.'

She sat forward on the hard seat, her hands clutched tightly, looking through the window at a London in the grip of panic. The hackney crawled along Oxford Street at a foot-pace because of the stream of coaches and chariots all going in the same direction, bearing the fashionable away from a town which had become dangerous overnight. The shops were shut; on nearly every shutter was written in blue chalk, 'No Popery', or 'This is a Protestant house'. The wealthier were barricading their mansions and planting servants with muskets at the windows. Trudging along the sidewalk were families, burdened with household goods, dragging whimpering children; a heavy pall of smoke still hovered over the burnt-out chapel in Golden Square, and the street leading to it was littered with charred fragments and broken glass. Bizarre on the padlocked door of the Pantheon was pasted the notice of the grand concert which was to have been held there this evening.

Hyde Park was one vast camp; the Guards, brought there to protect the fashionable West End, paraded uselessly up

269

and down in their scarlet uniforms, with here and there an officer, whose commission had been bought for him as a boy and who like as not was ignorant of the very words of command, cantering about on a well-groomed horse, and calling out to the fleeing crowds that there was nothing to fear.

And now Magdalene's hackney began to move faster, and she saw green fields take the place of houses, fields which soon became familiar. She began to frame little sentences, to rehearse that scene when at last she would be a heroine of romance, coming to the rescue of the defenceless. But her hands were sticky and her heart thumped with her nervousness when at last she saw a certain high wall in a peaceful village, and over it a roof she knew, a roof under which, in another life surely, she had hoped to live and die.

The bell beside the gate with the judas in it. She must pull the bell. She would not know the portress; old Sister Catherine must be dead long ago. What should she say? ...

"I – I wish to see – to see – "

Supposing Reverend Mother was dead too. She did not know the alias of her successor. Supposing this was all a trick of Barbara's. The hackney coachman was looking down at her curiously from his box; she had told him to wait, but had that been wise? Supposing he knew that this was a convent. Supposing he belonged to the Protestant Association; he had that horrible slogan chalked on his coach... The portress, a stranger, was speaking, but Magdalene paid no heed. Through the open gate she saw two figures coming down the path from the convent, one supporting the other who leaned heavily upon a cane. Then Magdalene was running towards that crippled figure, tripping over her skirts, forgetting all her fine speeches.

"Reverend Mother! I – you won't remember me, perhaps – I only came to warn you – the rioters – they intend to attack the convent – "

"They have been, my dear child, and gone," said the tranquil voice she had not heard for more than twenty years.

Magdalene blinked as though she had been struck.

"Gone?"

"They came last night. I told them that Queen Elizabeth had been educated here. I hope God will forgive me for the lie, but at any rate it satisfied them. Fortunately they were very ignorant, poor souls."

"I see," Magdalene whispered from the depths of her humiliation. "I'm sorry I troubled you. I mean – "

A crippled hand took hers and held it firmly.

"Of course you are sorry, my dear child. But as for the rioters, they may return. We are taking what precautions we can. We have buried the Blessed Sacrament in the garden, and Livermore (you remember our good old gardener) is watching over It. And I have arranged for one of us always to be standing guard at the turret window to warn him if she sees the rioters coming from London again. But we are so few now that I wonder, my dear child, if you would like to help us? It so happens that this next period of watching has not been assigned to any of the Sisters."

A voice like a child's answered humbly:

"Yes, please."

"But it was the period of watching you had reserved for yourself, Reverend Mother," exclaimed the nun who was supporting the crippled woman. "And you had been looking forward to – "

"I was going to watch for rioters," interrupted Reverend Mother, following with a compassionately tender glance

271

the figure stumbling in haste towards the convent, "but there is someone for whom I have been watching for a long, long time. And I saw her afar off, thank God. I had to find something with which I could welcome my prodigal daughter, and I don't think we have any fatted calves."

(iv)

Through the streets of London the blue flood rolled on its destructive course, shouting out its slogans, flourishing its banners, taking revenge on the magistrates who had committed the prisoners on Saturday, and on the witnesses against them, by attacking their houses and looting their shops. And during that Monday night the blue flood began to be joined by tributaries trickling in from all directions.

The mob was up.

Like rats creeping out from a sewer, the scent of plunder called them forth, a jungle telegraph wakened them in their lairs. "No Popery!" they shouted; but 'No Government' they meant. No Government to commit them, on the most questionable evidence, in its 'justice-shops' for stealing a yard of cloth, to fling them into Newgate, to offer them the alternatives of starvation or the gallows, to impress them when it wanted soldiers, to forget them and their miseries in times of peace.

The progeny of gin-sodden parents, dropsical, undersized, some wilfully maimed in childhood to attract sympathy when they begged. The precarious survivors of smallpox and jail-fever; runaway servants and 'prentices, deserters from the Army, hog-tenders from Whitechapel, labourers from the brick-kilns which smoked in a chain round London, escaped blacks who were bought and sold in coffee-houses, Jewish pedlars and coiners from Houndsditch, the laystall-keepers of Tothill Fields.

Blackened stokers from the glass-houses, smiths' hammermen and nightsoil carriers, the cinder-sifters of Tottenham Court, the rag-picker and the keeper of a tripe-shop, whose home and place of business was a wretched stall. Little boys with the faces of cunning old men from the cloth-weaving sheds in the Tower Hamlets, coppersmiths with green-stained skin, deaf brass-workers and palsied glaziers, hump-backed tailors, women prizefighters with broken noses from the ring at Grosvenor Gate, body-snatchers stinking of their awful trade, Tyburn's nursery, the shoeblack, and the chimney-boy.

The mob was up!

From slaving sixteen hours a day over charcoal furnaces and molten lead; from forging iron and sawing timber with bare hands; from cutting endless pairs of shoes from offal-leather at the princely wage of six shillings a week; from small crowded rooms from which the air must be excluded lest it made the precious silk you were weaving lose weight, with the iron bar of the loom pressing against your belly till you were black and blue. From frogging buttonholes till your eyes were blind with it; from toiling all night at the washtub in fine gentlemen's houses till the rheumatics crippled your hands; from twisting gut till your fingers were raw with it; from forcing your way up chimneys till your lungs were eaten away.

From the sponging-houses of Fleet Market and Shoe Lane; from the stews of Southwark; from the purlieus of the Clink and the Marshalsea and the Houses of Correction; from the ancient sanctuaries of Alsatia and the Mint, whose ruffianly denizens still kept the constables in dread. From the brothels of Blackfriars, from the rookeries of Smithfield, from the shambles in Clare Market, from the river hinterland of Lambeth and Rotherhithe, from the labyrinthine courts and alleys round Drury Lane. From penny lodging-houses, the breeding-ground of typhus, where you haggled with a fellow lodger over paying a halfpenny for half a bed; from cellars where you stifled in summer and froze in winter, with the rain and snow coming through the crazy flap in the street; from the gin-shop where you could still get dead-drunk for twopence, and forget your misery on verminous straw provided free.

From all those jungles where the desperate lurked with as much security as wild beasts in the deserts of Africa, human beasts came to the banquet provided for them by Lord George Gordon.

Wretches with their hand against every man, seeing their betters whip out their swords on the slightest provocation, taught from earliest childhood that nobody wanted them, nobody cared whether they lived or died, abandoned, like as not, in infancy, or turned out of doors when they could scarcely walk, grown wild and fierce as stray dogs. Vagrants escaped from the poor-cart on their way to the county border, the deformed who lived on the exhibition of their hideousness, highwaymen and footpads with their gangs, half-animal creatures branded on face and hand with the R for rogue and vagabond, the P for perjurer, the SL for seditious libeller. Shoved out of the road by running-footmen, flicked with the whip of haughty coachmen, referred to always as rabble and scum; but united making governments tremble and kings whisper fearfully the dreaded word 'mob'.

So they rose on that sweltering June night in 1780; and for nearly a week thereafter Lord George Gordon and his Protestant Association were swept along upon a tide of absolute anarchy and London was at the mercy of her underworld.

# Chapter Seven

It was not until late on Tuesday evening that Sir Stephen Vickery learnt that his wife had disappeared.

Monday he had spent in the company of Lord George Gordon at the City mansion of Alderman Bull, a leading Protestant Associator, reviewing the success of their campaign so far. It was really excellent. The Mass-houses in Wapping, East Smithfield, and Southwark had been entirely demolished, the spiritless Catholics making no attempt to defend them; the swift vengeance which had overtaken those magistrates who had committed the prisoners on Saturday was causing other justices to refuse to read the Riot Act without which the troops could not fire. And to impress upon the Government that unless its demands were granted the Protestant Association would stop at nothing, the Prime Minister's mansion at Hyde Park had been assaulted, Sir George Savile's furniture dragged out and burnt in the street, and Lord Sandwich had been set upon in his chariot, and rescued with the utmost difficulty by a troop of Light Horse, who had beaten off the mob with the flat of their swords.

On Tuesday Sir Stephen amused himself by attending the debates in the House of Commons. The Members were in a state of uproar, and the sight of 'St George Gordon', as the witty Horace Walpole had christened him, sitting in his usual place with the colours of sedition in his hat was not calculated to calm them. Neither was the news, brought late in the day, that the rioters had seized the arms and ammunition from the Artillery Ground and were marching to burn down Newgate. The Commons, having passed a resolution that all available troops be called out, hastily adjourned.

In the West End the theatres were open as usual, but Stephen noticed that most of the fashionable who were flocking thither had deemed it prudent to don blue ribands in spite of the cordon of troops drawn across the Strand for the protection of Society. Stephen had promised himself a different form of entertainment, and was going up on to the leads of his house again to count the number of fires eastwards, when his wife's maid came sidling up to him.

"My lady, sir, has not been seen or heard of since yesterday forenoon. I would not trouble you before, for I thought maybe – "

She left the sentence unfinished, and smirked. Her look said plainly, 'I thought maybe she had an assignation.'

"But when I was ordering her room this morning, sir," went on Hanson, "I found something on the floor I thought it my duty to give you."

She slid a creased paper into his hand, obviously expecting a reward.

He smoothed out the crumpled note and read it; she could not make out his expression, for he stood in shadow. He gave her no vail, said nothing at all, and walked straight up the stairs and into his wife's bedchamber. And all the while a name repeated itself over and over again in his mind, mocking him:

'Barbara.'

This woman whom he had always hated because somehow or other she had made the great, the powerful,

276

the rich Sir Stephen Vickery feel inferior, this woman whose spirit ought to have been broken when he had turned her out of her home, this woman had sneaked into his house during his absence, and with brazen impudence had appealed to his wife to aid the Catholics whom he had chosen to persecute.

And Magdalene, leaping at the chance of playing the heroine once more, undoubtedly had gone to the Hammersmith convent to warn the nuns. And would have found it burnt down. He laughed to himself with savage glee... But wait. Masson, Barbara's own father, had been assigned the command of that job and he remembered now that someone had told him Masson was dead. If she had found the convent demolished, Magdalene would have come creeping home; she had not come home; then the likelihood was that there had been no attack on the convent. And that she whom he had baited and cowed for so many years, she over whom his power was absolute, she over whose head he had held the threat to repudiate their marriage, had deserted him to return to her religion and to share the hazards of a parcel of silly women crouching in their convent. Oh, it would make a fine tit-bit of gossip to be laughed over at the tea-table and the club!

In his smouldering fury he was pacing about the room, and as he passed the toilet-table he noticed the jewel-case on it. Ah, my penitent sinner, my new St Mary Magdalen, he thought savagely, I'll wager you did not go empty handed; I'll wager that in your play-acting you remembered to take your valuables. The case was locked, but with his pocket-knife he forced it open. The glittering rings hung on their hooks, the bracelets nestled in their velvet beds. But surely she must have taken her diamond tiara. Plunging his hand into the casket, he groped; his fingers came in contact with a bulky packet. Wrenching it out, scattering the jewels, he read the inscription:

'Not to be opened until after my Death.'

He laughed aloud. A death-letter! How typical of Magdalene! What an emotional orgy she must have indulged in, denouncing him on paper, imagining him reading it after her death, she who had never had the spirit to stand up to him in life. Shaking with laughter, he broke the seal; but the letter was not to him, and before he had come to the end he had ceased to laugh.

For the writer informed her nephew, Sir Hubert Thorne, that she had made a will, properly drawn up and witnessed and given into the custody of James Gaffrey, solicitor of Barnard's Inn, leaving her nephew her only possession, rightfully his, the house and estate called Old Park.

(ii)

Hubert was fighting his way across Blackfriars' Bridge in the direction of London.

He tried not to think of the past few hours, of the onset of his wife's labour-pains, of the impossibility of getting assistance, of the refusal of the hackney coachmen to drive her to a hospital, even though he had offered them ten guineas, because he was a known Catholic. He had been on the point of despair when a neighbour, about to flee into the country with his family, had found a place for Alice in his overloaded vehicle, offering to convey her to the lying-in hospital in Great Surrey Street over Blackfriars' Bridge. But then Alice, the sensible, level-headed Alice, suddenly had become hysterical, and must have her husband with her on the journey. Torn though he was between his mother and his wife, he could not but give in to Alice in such an hour, and had accompanied her to the hospital which, like all public buildings in London, now had a posse of troops to guard it. She was safe; at least he must force himself to believe that she was safe, for he needed all

278

his wits and his courage for the task that remained, to get back to his mother, alone in the house in St Clement's Lane.

Half an hour previously he and Alice and their charitable neighbours had been swept over the bridge in a stream of refugees, on foot and in every sort of conveyance, who were stampeding towards the country. But now he was going in the opposite direction he had to struggle against the human current, now gaining a few paces, now borne back, bludgeoning his way with grim determination, careless of the knocks he gave or received.

The river below him looked like blood from the reflection of the flames which lit the town in all directions, so that it seemed as if all London was on fire. When he reached the toll-house at the north end, his feet sank into heaps of coins as thick as shingle on a beach; the mob had broken open the toll-house and were stuffing the halfpennies into sacks. He ploughed and buffeted forward; he was in Fleet Street; he was nearly home.

But then the nightmare deepened. Great rolling clouds of smoke poured down on him, obscuring every landmark. From every alley and court fresh trickles of panic-stricken folk impeded him, dragging bits of furniture or carrying bundles of stuff snatched from their burning homes; and mingling with them, ruffians who staggered under the goods they had looted. The heat of the weather, the flames shooting skywards, the buildings which were a glowing mass, made every street an inferno; but what was worst of all was to see the soldiers standing about like idle spectators while the mob coolly plundered, and a desperado mounted on a brewer's horse decorated with fetters from a Newgate now in ashes, extorted money from the stampeding crowds.

Amid the screams and the shouts and the crackle of the flames, Hubert caught fragments of talk which were exactly like those a man hears in nightmare. Rumours, each more frightful than the last, ran from lip to lip; every prison in London was down, and the most desperate criminals were loose, among them the murderer who had butchered an entire family. And Bedlam, too; the lunatics were released. Worst of all, the mob had freed the lions from the Tower…

He had lost all sense of direction now; he was deafened and blinded, and what remained of his reason told him plainly that his quest was hopeless. Yet something stronger than despair drove him forward; and suddenly he was aware that though driven out of his course he was not so far from his home. He was in Holborn. He recognised it still, though it was like a child's picture of Hell. In the glare of the flames, which ate their way through the defective bricks of newly built houses as if they had been cardboard, he saw familiar things and fixed his mind upon them. He would not look at the figures which ran to and fro like lost souls, crying for shelter, beating their fists against barricaded doors, screaming out the names of loved ones, piteously begging for aid, gibbering with terror.

No; this was Holborn. Another effort and he would reach Great Turnstile; the short-cut across Lincoln's Inn Fields and he would be in St Clement's Lane…if it still existed…

He was fighting his way past Barnard's Inn when his nightmare attained its climax of horror. Next door to the Inn was a large distillery, owned by a known Catholic, a Mr Langdale. The mob was solid here; there was an interval when he was entangled in a determined wedge of ruffians engaged in beating down the doors. Then there was a crash, followed by a yell of triumph, which drowned all other sounds; and as he fought free again he saw a stream of raw alcohol come pouring into the street, catching fire as it came, gliding like blazing serpents in every direction.

(iii)

"You go forward at your own risk, sir!" roared a white-faced officer, as Stephen, alighting from his coach at Little Turnstile, pushed through the cordon of troops towards Holborn.

Stephen laughed and gave him an ironical salute. He felt invulnerable, a god among these panic-stricken crowds, these futile soldiers. He was Sir Stephen Vickery, who so largely had financed the Protestant Association, who had stage-managed its demonstrations, and who now, with a large blue cockade in his hat, was going to its offices in Fetter Lane to discover whether his orders regarding the destruction of the Hammersmith convent had been carried out, and if they had not been, to send a contingent there forthwith.

He whooped with glee as he noticed that the Ship tavern was on fire, and that a fellow was parading before it with a banner proclaiming, 'Here the bloody Popish Bishop used to preach'. He was not a man of any great physical courage, but his lust for vengeance made him almost careless of the cascading bricks, the toppling chimney-stacks, the crashing timbers, and the flames that licked the street. The stifling heat was less to him than the fire of malice within his own breast, and as for the crowds they were either helpless human flotsam or his own henchmen. He had but to snap his fingers and call out a Protestant slogan, and a hundred would come running, ready to obey his commands.

And presently it seemed to him that his high spirits were infectious. The lamentations and the cries of terror were drowned in sounds of revelry, a savage revelry congenial to his mood. Holborn had become a monstrous open-air tavern; everywhere he looked he saw hands holding tankards, jugs, buckets, all kinds of household utensils and every one of them brimming over. Somewhere an unearthly conduit spouted drink in such profusion that rivulets curled along the paving-stones, ran in little streams along the gutters, gushed out of doors. And like thirsty animals at a pool at evening, men, women, and children were flinging themselves on their knees to lap at the raw spirits, or scooping them up by the pailful, fighting to get at this free liquor. Some lay prostrate, blind drunk, kicked aside by heedless feet; others, gasping and vomiting, lurched stupidly around with their hair and clothes on fire; yet others still lugged out casks from the burning distillery and piled them into one more bonfire, dancing and hallooing round it until they collapsed into the flames.

But they were all as shadows to Stephen; for across the width of the street he had seen Sir Hubert Thorne.

It was but a glimpse through the mêlée, but he knew him. From his coach or his chariot or his chair, and sometimes in the courts of law, he had caught other glimpses of this young man who now struggled furiously westwards, the dispossessed heir who bore so striking a resemblance to Stephen's dead enemy, Robin Thorne. The young man to whom Magdalene had left Old Park in a will properly drawn up and witnessed and in the custody of Stephen's own lawyer.

The malice of a lifetime narrowed to a point; the demon of revenge which possessed him demanded one thing only: murder. He yelled at the top of his voice:

"Stop that man! He's a known Papist! *Stop that man!*"

His voice was tossed away on the roar of the flames and the tipsy hallooing. He plunged across the street, flooded now with a great stream of spiritous liquor, dragging along with it broken furniture and staved-in casks and the dead body of a child and anonymous litter, dancing with blue flames.

"A hatful of guineas to anyone who will stop that man! My good friends of the blue cockade, you all know me; Vickery's the name – Sir Stephen Vickery!"

But he was a god no longer; the crowds were not obedient henchmen trained to do the will of the man who paid them; they were just a mob maddened by drink. Broken teeth snarled at him; bodies cannoned into him, shoved him helplessly to and fro. A fellow with a great cask on his shoulders lurched and staggered; Stephen shrank aside to avoid him, and his foot slipped. He clutched the air, screaming, his bowels moving with his terror; and then he was down.

He was flat on his face, drowning in the human flood, his mouth on fire from the stream of alcohol into which he had fallen, his body trampled by indifferent feet. Trampled and trampled, until they squelched when they trod in their panic or their drunkenness upon the bloody, broken, shapeless something which once had been a man.

(iv)

Hubert dragged himself doggedly westwards, unconscious of anything except his goal. And when he came stumbling weakly into St Clement's Lane at last, and saw his home still miraculously standing and a figure at the door with arms outstretched to him, for a little while he was a child again, weeping with his head in his mother's lap.

# Chapter Eight

It was wonderful to Michael to find the garden in Lincoln's Inn Fields looking just the same as he came into it one afternoon in August. Portions of the iron palisade had been torn up by the mob for use as weapons, but otherwise it had escaped unscathed. There were the children playing, and the dogs romping, and the folk reading newspapers which were full of the coming General Election. And on her old bench by the fountain, busy with a pile of needlework, was the lady he had come to find.

He had not seen Barbara since the riots, for he had been too busy to come into London, but Hubert had paid him a brief visit to assure himself of his uncle's safety and to give him the news. It had not been until the Thursday morning of that awful week that the Government had acted, and then it had been an attack on the Bank which had roused the authorities, or rather the King. George was at his best in moments of peril, and at a Council meeting that morning had declared that though all the magistrates of London appeared to have lost their courage, he, the Chief Magistrate, had not. When a mob was engaged in a felony, the formality of reading the Riot Act was not required; and a Royal Proclamation had been issued forthwith empowering the military to repress the riots by force.

"I shall never forget that day as long as I live," a sobered Hubert had told his uncle. "The mob had grown used to seeing the soldiers standing idly by, and their officers knocking up the pieces of those who would have fired. I was in Fleet Street about six o'clock in the evening, going to see my wife, when I saw the mob coming down the street. They took no notice of a detachment of Horse Guards stationed at Temple Bar, until suddenly there came a volley, and about twenty of the rioters fell dead. There was a howl of rage from their comrades, and a mad rush forward, and then... Well, I saw the Guards returning to their barracks an hour later, their bayonets dripping blood."

Next day London had awakened to find itself under martial law, and for days and nights thereafter the streets had resembled a battlefield, with bodies lying everywhere, the gutters running red, the sound of heavy platoon firing coming from all directions, the soldiers billeted in the Royal Exchange and encamped in St Paul's Churchyard, and hourly arrests being made. After a last desperate stand at Blackfriars Bridge, a party of the rioters had flung themselves into the river. As Michael had walked along Fleet Street this afternoon, some six weeks later, crowds were still gaping at the ruins, and many of the shops were still shut.

Barbara greeted him warmly; but he saw at once that she looked very tired, and that there was a small white wing in the hair which showed under her cap. She said at once:

"I shall not ask you to tell me anything about your experiences during that week. I don't think any of us who lived through it would willingly speak of what we saw and heard, though we were the fortunate ones."

"We were indeed! You are very busy today."

"Garments for the homeless for Mr Fisher's committee. How is he, Michael?"

"In spirit, as he ever was, devoting all his failing strength to consoling and succouring his poor people. But in the conferences he gives us now he dwells much on the subject of death and the necessity of being prepared for it; and I do not think his own will be long delayed."

She raised her head sharply, as a distant uproar came from the direction of Holborn.

"It is another execution," she said painfully. "They are hanging two cripples in Bloomsbury Square for the assault on my Lord Mansfield's house in June."

Her hands were unsteady as she rethreaded her needle.

"The mob has always been a sort of ogre to me," she went on, "ever since my father's stables were burnt when I was a young child; and when I grew older and asked my parents why, they just shook their heads at me and said something about it being only the nasty mob at its tricks. I came to think of the mob as a Thing, anonymous and motiveless. If they'd told me it was Bill Smith the scavenger or Jim Jones the chimney-sweep who had burnt my father's stables, I wouldn't have been so frightened; men like that get rough and lawless when they've been in a gin-cellar, but at least they're still individuals. But the mob seemed inhuman."

"It is a thing created by a weak and corrupt Government," said Michael. "The sort of Government which during the late riots were criminally inert in the early stages, which indeed did not act at all until the Bank was threatened, and now make examples of the least guilty. It's true that Lord George Gordon was captured on his flight to Scotland and is now in the Tower awaiting trial, but they say he will certainly get off through the influence of his great connections."

She was hardly listening; she had laid down her needle-work and was following a line of thought of her own.

"For the first time in my life the mob has ceased to be a Thing, and has resolved itself into human beings, pitiful, misguided human beings. I was in Holborn when a boy of fourteen was being taken to Bow Street to be hanged there for the attack on Sir John Fielding's house; he was weeping in the cart – oh, how he was weeping! And then there were the women executed on Tower Hill, and the black and the half a dozen youths on portable gallows carried about the town so that the victims might suffer near the scene of their crime. But the ringleaders, the really guilty, who were educated and knew what they were doing and persuaded simple men like my late father that such violence was lawful and godly, they took care to keep in the background once they had organised the first outrages and inflamed the common people. It makes me furious!"

"I hear that no one knows what has become of Vickery."

"No," said Barbara in an even tone, taking up her work again. "Being in his way a public figure, he can't have been among the three hundred and eighty either killed outright by the Guards or who died of their wounds. But of course there must be hundreds still buried under the ruins. The last anyone saw of him was at Little Turnstile, it seems; an officer saw him going down Holborn with a blue cockade in his hat and warned him that he went on at his own risk. For many years now I've tried not to think of Vickery; I put him in my prayers among 'all those who have wronged me or whom I have wronged by ill-will or misunderstanding', and I hope God will understand that I'm not big enough to mention him by name."

"I wondered," Michael said slowly, "as I came through the streets today, whether you could bring yourself to sit here in this favourite garden of yours now, and see how many familiar landmarks have disappeared, particularly the Ship tavern."

She did not answer for a moment, and he saw an odd little smile on her lips as she worked at her sewing.

"Do you remember, Michael," she said presently, "how when you were a child you used to talk about ''tachment'? Hubert told me. Well, God has made it very plain to me all through my life that I must learn to detach myself both from persons and things, because always they have been taken away from me. There was my own home, and my parents; and then there were Hubert and Old Park; and now the Ship, where I was received into the Church, and the Sardinian Embassy chapel. I know that is being rebuilt, but it won't be the same. It's true my son's home was miraculously spared and this dear garden is just the same; but I would be very stupid, you know, if I hadn't learnt non-attachment by this time."

"I think what I thought the first time I met you," he said, regarding her with affection, "that you are a very fortunate lady."

There was a long silence, broken only by the soft cool sound of the fountain. There was something he had to say to her, and he did not in the least know what her reaction would be. For a while he sat cogitating, drawing a meaningless pattern on the gravel with his toe, reminding her of that day when Hubert had done the same thing with his riding-whip before asking her to marry him. Her husband seemed very near to her lately.

"Barbara," he said at last abruptly, "yesterday I went to see Magdalene at the convent. She sent for me. I take it that you have not seen her or heard from her?"

She smiled wryly.

"No. I knew she was there, for Reverend Mother wrote me. But I have hesitated to visit her or to write. People

288

don't change all of a sudden, especially in middle age, whatever tremendous ordeals they go through, and Magdalene never liked me. Is she – is she well?"

He did not answer the question. He put his hand on hers and said very gently:

"I wanted to tell you this before mentioning it to your son. It seems that several years ago, Magdalene made a will leaving Old Park to her nephew; but now she wishes to make a deed of gift of the estate immediately, renouncing all claim."

Barbara said nothing, but he felt her hand stiffen beneath his.

"Since the Act of William III under which she was able to seize it remains repealed," went on Michael, "Hubert can accept. I know that he has lived all his life away from Old Park, but he is the rightful heir and surely he cannot refuse it, even though he chooses to live in London most of the time. And who knows but one day it may become a centre of Catholic life again, as it was for so many centuries."

Still she said nothing, and she did not look at him.

"But I wondered whether you could bear to return there, Barbara. You told me once it had become a place inside your mind. And from what Magdalene tells me, Vickery changed it almost out of recognition. Yet even though my own memories of it are so dim, I do remember some strange quality it had. Generations of my family altered it and pulled it about, but still it had a quality of remaining – just Old Park."

She disengaged her hand and fumbled for her handkerchief, and then he saw that she was weeping.

"I am so very sorry," muttered Barbara. "It's foolish of me. But to go back to Old Park! To be near Hubert; to show his grandson the 'cathedral trees' (surely Vickery won't have cut those down!); to hear the rooks again and feel the sea mist – "

Then she laughed through her tears, and in that laugh was a trace of her old schoolgirlish giggle.

"And here have I been talking in such a superior way about non-attachment!" exclaimed Barbara, wiping her eyes.

"That is why you can go back without pain," he said quietly. "This is your reward."

They sat silent again, watching a sparrow taking a dust-bath, perhaps a descendant of those sparrows with which Barbara had shared her frugal lunch when she had been turned out of her parents' house.

"And in accepting that reward," he said after a while, "you will be performing a great act of charity. To Magdalene. People don't change when they are middle-aged, Barbara, as you so rightly said; at least their personalities don't change. Magdalene wanting to make reparation will do it in the grand, romantic manner which is native to her. But sincerely she wants to make reparation; that is the important thing."

Barbara turned to him impulsively.

"Oh, how petty you make me feel! I remember how I kept talking about myself and my own concerns the first time we met here when you had come over from Douai, and your real concern must have been for your sister. Tell me, Michael, what is she doing at the convent?"

He answered thoughtfully:

"I am not quite sure. I asked Reverend Mother, who was evasive, and said something about how much time it must have needed for the Prodigal Son to adjust himself after he came home. And I asked Magdalene herself; at least I probed, I hope gently. She smiled in rather a strange way, and all she said was, 'I am making myself useful about the house'."

(ii)

There was a thick fog when Michael left St Thomas's Hospital very early one January morning nearly six months later, but he decided to take the short-cut across St George's Fields as usual, for he knew every inch of them by now.

He had just administered the Last Sacraments to a dying Irish labourer, one more victim of the riots. Southwark had suffered worst of all. The tenement in which he had said Mass had been demolished, he himself with his landlady and her family escaping by the roof, whence they had been forced to slide down a wooden pipe while the mob were beating down the doors. The King's Bench Prison had been completely destroyed, and the very last attack, repelled by the military with great loss of life, had been on the Marshalsea. All through the autumn and winter he had scarcely had time to eat or sleep, being continually at the bedside of the sick, the injured, and those who had lost their reason as a result of their ordeal. And there were the swarms of homeless too; some belated compensation was being made by the Government to the thousands who had lost their all, but it was of little use yet to the families whose tenements were heaps of rubble, and who were still encamping on all the open spaces around London.

Yet exhausted though he was, he was happy and proud. When he had come to London from Douai he had missed acutely for a long while the peaceful scholarly life to which he was accustomed, and it had seemed to him that he was of little use here; despite all his efforts he had not been able to overcome a feeling of discouragement engendered by the apparent hopelessness of keeping alive a faith which so nearly had died out in England. But then had come violent

291

persecution; and miraculously, instead of stamping out the last embers of that faith, it had revived the spirit of the scattered, downtrodden Catholics, and even had bred a new tolerance in their Protestant neighbours.

Several times he had been stopped in the street by those who guessed who he was, and who previously had called down curses on him or who had studiously ignored him. It was a crying shame, they told him now, this attack on helpless folk whose only crime was their religion. And what most astonished them, and himself, too, was the way his people had behaved when attacked. They had obeyed their Vicar Apostolic and had made no retaliation. Had they done so, London might well have been reduced to ashes.

"Who would ever have thought that those Irishers, who are always spoiling for a fight, would have stayed peaceable under such provocation?" was the question the average Londoner was still asking.

But as Michael trudged through the marshy fields this morning, he was thinking of one victim of the Gordon Riots who had 'stayed peaceable' all his long life, and whose Requiem he had attended yesterday in the newly rebuilt chapel of the Sardinian Embassy. There was no doubt in the minds of those who had known him that this outbreak of persecution and the consequent sufferings of his people had hastened Dr Challoner's death.

Michael had heard the story of his end from Mr Bolton. On January 10th the aged Bishop had sat down to dinner with his chaplains, appearing his usual self. Just as he finished eating, his right hand had fallen suddenly from the table; and seeing that something was amiss, Mr Bolton had risen to go to him. As he did so, the old man's head had jerked down on his shoulder. With his left hand he had fumbled in his pocket and brought out a paper containing a list of alms given him for the poor, at the same time murmuring, "Charity". It was his last spoken word.

Just after midnight on Friday, the 18th, without any pain or struggle, that tranquil spirit had gone to its reward. Michael, who was present at the reading of the will, had felt that not one of the literary labours he had undertaken so unremittingly for the needs of his poor flock had been more typical of Richard Challoner or had contained a greater lesson. The entire estate of the Vicar Apostolic amounted to two hundred and fifty pounds, which he left to the poor; for his faithful old landlady, her servants, and the nuns at Hammersmith in whose convent he had been consecrated bishop forty years previously, there had been pathetic little personal mementoes; and he had concluded by lamenting that his narrow circumstances had not permitted him to leave a legacy to 'Alma', the beloved English College at Douai, or a guinea to each of his London priests as his predecessors had done.

They had carried his body to the Berkshire house of his great friend, Mr Briant Barrett, and there in the private chapel a Requiem Mass had been celebrated in the presence of the coffin with its plain metal crucifix, before it had been buried in the village churchyard with Protestant rites according to law. All his life so self-effacing, he was regarded now by his people as a saint, and the word 'Venerable', properly applied only to those Servants of God the process of whose beatification has been formally introduced, prefixed his name in every private conversation and even in his mortuary bills.

Michael started violently, as he almost cannoned into a small figure which loomed up suddenly out of the fog.

"Morning, sir," said a cheerful voice.

"Hubert! What in the world are you doing in the fields so early?"

293

The child did not answer for a moment, but fell into step beside his great-uncle, his hands thrust into his pockets, and his curly head downbent as though deep in thought. Then he said abruptly:

"I had a strodinary dream last night, 'bout these fields, and I came to see if it was really a dream, 'cause it didn't seem like one."

"Was it a bad dream, about Miss Gunner?"

"'Bout who, sir?" the child enquired politely.

"Miss Gunner – you know, and Mr Bear."

"I don't know any Miss Gunners or Mr Bears," Hubert said with some impatience. "I'm telling you 'bout this dream."

He paused in his walk and peered about him, as though searching for something strange in these familiar fields.

"Well, I s'pose it must've been a dream, after all. I dreamed I was playin' in these fields, when suddenly I came on a great big church. It was a hugeous church; it was bigger than – than" – he struggled to find a comparison – "than St Paul's. And it was all white, and it had a tremenjus tower with bells in it. And as I went inside, the bells began to ring because it was the Elation – "

"The Elevation. Do you mean it was a Catholic church?"

"*Course* it was a Cath'lic church," replied Hubert, deeply shocked. "You don't s'pose sir, I'd go into a her'tic church, do you? Well, it was absolutely *packed* with people, and it was High Mass, like they say at the 'Bassy chapels where Mama used to take me before she had this baby, but now she's too busy, and Gran'ma used to take me too, only she's gone down to Old Park, and I'm going there for Christmas, and I'm going to help bring in the You'll log, only I can't make out who the 'You' is who owns the log…and now I've forgot what I was going to say."

"You were telling me about this dream."

"Oh yes. Well, after the bells stopped ringing ('cause I wouldn't talk during the Ele-what-d-you-call-it)," said Hubert righteously, "I whispered to someone beside me, 'Isn't it awfully dang'rous to ring the bells and let everyone know Mass is being said?' "

"Yes, I should think it would be," observed Michael gravely.

"That's what I said. But d'you know what? They laughed at me (quietly, of course, 'cause otherwise it wouldn't have been rev'rent), and they said, 'Well, what else d'you suppose people would expect in a Cath'lic 'thedral?' And then I woke up."

They walked a few steps in silence.

"That was a very strange dream, Hubert," the priest said slowly after a while.

"P'raps I'm a prophet," Hubert suggested complacently. "P'raps I can see into the future, like the Ven'able Dr Challoner. *He* was a prophet, wasn't he? D'you think they'll call me Ven'able when I die?"

"I should think it extremely unlikely," said Michael. "People who wonder whether they will be called Venerable usually aren't."

"Oh," said Hubert, losing interest. "Well, I'm afraid I can't stay talkin' here or I shall be late for school. Goodbye, sir."

"Goodbye, Hubert. God bless you," said Michael, and stood looking after the sturdy little figure until the mist swallowed it.

And even then he stayed where he was, thinking of that morning when St George's Fields, so desolate and empty now, had been filled with Lord George Gordon's Protestant army, flaunting their 'No Popery' banners, fluttering their blue ribands, singing their truculent hymns, rank upon rank of them united by a common hate. He had thought of it as a huge blue flood risen as it were from the slime, flowing into London to sweep away the pitiful little modicum of justice afforded by the Catholic Relief Bill. Instead, it had nearly drowned London itself.

But it had not accomplished its object. It had not quenched that little live ember in the ashes, the ember which glowed brighter now. Parliament had refused to repeal the Relief Bill; and some of the younger and more energetic among both priests and laity already were talking of their determination to press for a far greater liberty of conscience than had been granted in 1778.

He walked on; and now he was not thinking of the crack-brained fanatic whose great connections had secured his acquittal in his trial for high treason, nor of the mob violence he had called forth. He was thinking of his dead brother Hubert and of a few others like him who, without the glamour of active persecution, had endured, had held on, had accepted social ostracism and calumny and continual frustration in their daily lives, the unknown heroes who had kept the ember alight, even as the blood of the martyrs before them had fed the mystical body of the Faith.

And he thought also of that strange prophecy of Dr Challoner's, made in the midst of wholesale apostasies, that there would be a 'new people'. People like Barbara, perhaps, born outside the Faith, finding their way to it by many different roads, brave enough to turn their backs on home and kindred and all familiar things to follow the voice of conscience.

Just before he left the fields and turned into the squalid alleys of the Bankside, Michael paused again and looked back.

A little wind had risen, soft but persistent, driving the fog before it, piling it into a phantom building from which branched shapes which might be buttresses, and a wavering finger which had the semblance of a tower.

Almost he could persuade himself that he heard the threefold stroke of the bell he had heard every day of his life at Douai, proclaiming to the sick and the dying and the prisoner that once more God had come to dwell with man under the homely veil of bread.

He smiled at himself; and yet as he walked on through the dirty lanes towards the wretched tenement where Mass must still be said behind locked doors, a strange conviction remained in his mind that one day, long after he and perhaps even little Hubert were dead, there where the latest onslaught against the Faith had been inaugurated, there on desolate St George's Fields, a great church would rise, filled with a new people.

# JANE LANE

## A CALL OF TRUMPETS

Civil war rages in England, rendering it a minefield of corruption and conflict. Town and country are besieged. Through the complex interlocking of England's turmoil with that of a king, Jane Lane brings to life some amazing characters in the court of Charles I. This is the story of Charles' adored wife, whose indiscretions prove disastrous, and of the King's nephew, Rupert, a rash, arrogant soldier whose actions lead to tragedy and his uncle's final downfall.

## CONIES IN THE HAY

1586 was the year of an unbearably hot summer when treachery came to the fore. In this scintillating drama of betrayals, Jane Lane sketches the master of espionage, Francis Walsingham, in the bright, lurid colours of the deceit for which he was renowned. Anthony Babington and his fellow conspirators are also brought to life in this vivid, tense novel, which tells of how they were duped by Walsingham into betraying the ill-fated Mary, Queen of Scots, only to be hounded to their own awful destruction.

# JANE LANE

## HIS FIGHT IS OURS

*His Fight Is Ours* follows the traumatic trials of MacIain, a Highland Chieftain of the clan Donald, as he leads his people in the second Jacobite rising on behalf of James Stuart, the Old Pretender. The battle to restore the King to his rightful throne is portrayed here in this absorbing historical escapade, which highlights all the beauty and romance of Highland life. Jane Lane presents a dazzling, picaresque story of the problems facing MacIain as leader of a proud, ancient race, and his struggles against injustice and the violent infamy of oppression.

## A SUMMER STORM

Conflict and destiny abound as King Richard II, a chivalrous, romantic and idealist monarch, courts his beloved Anne of Bohemia. In the background, the swirling rage of the Peasants' Revolt of 1381 threatens to topple London as the tides of farmers, labourers and charismatic rebel hearts flood the city. This tense, powerful historical romance leads the reader from bubbling discord to doomed love all at the turn of a page.

# Jane Lane

## Thunder on St Paul's Day

London is gripped by mass hysteria as Titus Oates uncovers the Popish Plot, and a gentle English family gets caught up in the terrors of trial and accusation when Oates points the finger of blame. The villainous Oates adds fuel to the fire of an angry mob with his sham plot, leaving innocents to face a bullying judge and an intimidated jury. Only one small boy may save the family in this moving tale of courage pitted against treachery.

## A Wind Through the Heather

*A Wind Through the Heather* is a poignant, tragic story based on the Highland Clearances where thousands of farmers were driven from their homes by tyrannical and greedy landowners. Introducing the Macleods, Jane Lane recreates the shameful past suffered by an innocent family who lived to cross the Atlantic and find a new home. This wistful, historical novel focuses on the atrocities so many bravely faced and reveals how adversities were overcome.

2102530R00163

Printed in Great Britain
by Amazon.co.uk, Ltd.,
Marston Gate.